I0642331

Forgotten Loyalties

Also by Michael J. McCann

The Ghost Man
Blood Passage
Marcie's Murder
The Fregoli Delusion
The Rainy Day Killer
Sorrow Lake
Burn Country
Persistent Guilt
No Sadness of Farewell
A Death in Winter
In These Disconsolate Woods
The Long Road Into Darkness
Project Changeling
Twilight Road
The Disappearances

Michael J. McCann

© 2024  The Plaid Raccoon Press

Forgotten Loyalties

A March and Walker Crime Novel

Forgotten Loyalties is a work of fiction. Names, characters, institutions, places and events are either the product of the author's imagination or are used fictitiously. Any resemblance to actual persons, living or dead, events, or locales is entirely coincidental.

FORGOTTEN LOYALTIES
Copyright © 2024 by Michael J. McCann

The Plaid Raccoon Press supports copyright, which protects creativity and the right of authors to profit from the fruits of their considerable labour. Thank you for buying an authorized edition of this book and for complying with copyright laws by not reproducing any part of this book, paperback and/or e-book, without permission from the publisher.

This novel is entirely the product of the author's imagination, hard work, and creativity. No artificial intelligence applications or similar tools were used to write this story, nor will they ever be. Organically grown fiction is always the best!

ISBN: 978-1-927884-30-0 (paperback)
         978-1-927884-31-7 (e-book)

Cover image: Mysticartdesign/Pixabay
Interior images: Michael J. McCann
Author photo: Michael J. McCann

Visit the author's website at www.mjmccann.com

This novel is respectfully dedicated to the memories of OPP Provincial Constable Grzegorz (Greg) Pierzchala and OPP Sergeant Eric Mueller.

Requiescat in pace.

Chapter 1

Ontario Provincial Police Constable Terence Maynard never saw it coming.

At 10:23 AM on Monday, May 1, he was patrolling King's Highway 7 westbound, between Carleton Place and Perth, when a vehicle passed him in the eastbound lane in a big-assed hurry.

Maynard's radar lit him up at 124 kilometres an hour in an 80-kilometre zone, so he moved over onto the shoulder of the road, hit his roof lights, and pulled a U-turn in pursuit.

The vehicle was a white Volkswagen Jetta. Having worked traffic for more than twenty years, Maynard knew that white cars actually drew more speeding tickets than red ones, for whatever reason. On top of that, Jettas were one of the top targets, even more so than other cars you might think of as speeders, such as Lexuses, Beamers, and Audis.

Maynard didn't really care. They were all grist for the mill, as far as he was concerned. Pull them over, write them up, and move on with your day.

This one must be in a big rush to get home, he thought, approaching close enough that the driver couldn't help but see his flashing roof rack in his rear-view mirror. He gave his siren a quick tap, just to emphasize the point.

The Jetta's brake lights fluttered briefly, and its speed dropped a little, but the pursuit continued for another half-kilometre before acceptance of the inevitable seemed to sink in and the driver slowed down. Instead of pulling over onto the shoulder, however, the car turned right onto a side road, which happened to be West Shore Drive, Drummond Township.

The Jetta rolled on for about fifty metres before coming to a stop, just across from the entrance to a long driveway leading up to an old brick house. The house was set back maybe thirty metres from the road, with trees and lilac bushes around it. The car's lights flickered in front of him as the driver shifted into park.

After informing dispatch that he was leaving his vehicle, Maynard grabbed his hat and slid out. Approaching the Jetta, he stooped a bit for a quick visual but couldn't see anyone inside the car other than the person behind the wheel.

The driver's window slid down.

"Licence and registration. Insurance."

"This is fucking ridiculous, man. I'm just trying to get home."

"Yes, sir." Given the surly attitude, Maynard decided to write him up instead of letting him off with a warning.

"I'm just going to open this," the driver said, pointing at the centre console.

Maynard watched him raise the lid and retrieve a blue plastic pouch, from which he passed over his vehicle registration and his insurance slip.

"Just a sec." The man lifted a haunch to remove a fat wallet from the back pocket of his jeans. He fished around in it and tweezered out his driver's licence.

Maynard compared the photo on the licence to the man in front of him and nodded. "Please turn off your vehicle and remain here."

Maynard went back to his cruiser and ran the licence plate, which confirmed the information on the registration form—the Jetta was registered to an Earl Avery Black, DOB 03/04/63, with an address on Radford Road, Ramsay Township, a gravel strip just below Almonte.

This information jibed with Black's driver's licence. A quick check revealed that Earl Avery Black had no wants or warrants against him, that he'd received three previous tickets for traffic violations in the past two years, and that he'd paid all his fines.

Bitching about it the whole time, no doubt.

Maynard wrote up number four for him and walked it back to the Jetta.

"Try to stay within the speed limit next time, sir." He passed the ticket in through the open window.

"Yep." Black tossed it on the passenger seat, his contempt for the law and its unfair limits on his personal freedom obvious in his sour expression and stiff body language.

Maynard returned to his cruiser and, tossing aside his hat, took out his notebook. Since Black was probably the type to complain about his treatment, Maynard decided to make notes on the stop right away, rather than put it off until later. He'd learned through long experience that it was always a good idea to get it down on paper while the details were still fresh in his mind.

Black turned into the driveway, backed out, and drove away.

Maynard half-listened to the radio as he wrote, following the exchanges between the dispatcher and various units patrolling in the area. Everything sounded routine. As a law enforcement lifer, he found the voices comforting: a normal part of his everyday world.

As he continued to write, he became aware of a vehicle coming down the driveway from the house. It sounded like a pickup truck of some sort, one of the bigger ones. Its tires popped gravel as it approached.

He looked over his shoulder in time to see the truck stop at the end of the driveway. It was large and black, the kind that farmers liked to have around for the heavy work.

The driver got out and walked across the road toward him.

Maynard lowered his window, notebook still in his lap, to see what the guy wanted.

The man stopped an arm's-length away from the open window, raised a gun, and shot Maynard twice in the head.

Chapter 2

Ontario Provincial Police Detective Constable Kevin Walker sat in an uncomfortable chair at the back of the chapel in the R.W. Morrow and Sons Funeral Home in Brockville as the service crawled its way toward its inevitable, if everlastingly distant, termination.

The front row on either side held a few people, and a handful of other attendees were scattered about, mostly positioned at the ends of the rows in order to facilitate a quick getaway.

The minister was a middle-aged woman Kevin hadn't met before, brought in by the funeral home to conduct the service for a pre-arranged stipend. Usually they met with the surviving spouse beforehand, picking up a few of the high points of the deceased's life and work experiences and whatever other crap they thought might fit into the allotted time in which to praise the departed loved one. Perhaps she had met with the widow; it sounded like the sort of desperately optimistic crap she might have mined from the poor woman's crushed dreams of marital bliss.

Kevin was not normally a bitter or cynical person—quite the opposite, in fact—but the stuff the woman was uttering was such patent bullshit, from start to finish, that he had to bite his lip to keep his mouth shut.

The corpse in the coffin at the front, its lid open to facilitate viewing, should one wish to take a last look, belonged to the former and now demised John William Walker, a.k.a. Johnny Walker, son of the late Grant Walker and June Smith, life-long resident of Brockville and retired foreman at the local detergent factory.

Kevin's father.

Last Friday morning Kevin was sitting in his workstation at the Lanark County OPP detachment office in Perth when his cellphone buzzed. He didn't recognize the number but answered the call, as he always did.

"Detective Constable Walker."

"Your wife gave me this number," a woman's voice said tentatively. "I hope I'm not disturbing you while you're doing something important."

"No, it's fine. Who's this?"

"Carla."

Kevin drew a blank. "Sorry, who?"

"It's Carla. Carla Walker. Your step-mom."

Kevin found himself at a loss for words. He'd never met his father's second wife and had never spoken to her. Their only contact for the last sixteen years, from the time that she and Johnny had married, was a Christmas card that arrived faithfully every year, obviously without her husband's knowledge or consent, optimistically signed "Love Carla and Johnny" in shaky, nervous penmanship.

It was always a very nice card, cheerful and in keeping with the spirit of the season, and Kevin had made a practice of admiring it for thirty seconds or so before throwing it into the garbage, followed by old coffee grounds, spoiled salad greens, or cat litter from Boo Boo's box.

"I'm sorry to bother you like this," Carla plunged on, "and I'm sorry to be the one to tell you, but your father passed away on Wednesday. The funeral's on Monday. I hope you can be there."

"I'm sorry for your loss," Kevin said.

"Thanks. It was his liver. It's been a couple of years coming, but you'll want to know, he went peacefully. Drugged to the gills with enough painkillers to knock out a horse. Here at the house. In his own bed."

She sobbed, startling him.

"I see."

"Can you?"

"Can I see?"

"No, can you come? To the funeral?"

Kevin sighed. "He wouldn't want me to, Carla."

"Well, yeah, he did say that to me once, but he probably didn't mean it."

"Trust me. He meant it."

"Well, I don't think it's right. You should feel like you're welcome, never mind what happened in the past. You're his only kid, after all."

"I'd rather not."

"As a favour to me? A few of his old work buddies said they'd be there, but I don't know them and I can only imagine. I don't have anyone on my side. Just a couple of friends I used to work with. It'd be like I actually had some kind of a family after all these years. Now that he's gone, I mean. At least some family left."

He'd listened to her sob for a while longer before relenting.

"I'll be there."

When the service finally ended and the coffin was taken out the side door to the hearse for transportation to the cemetery,

Kevin slipped through the front entrance and stopped at the edge of the parking lot, taking out his sunglasses from his inside jacket pocket.

"You're Kevin, aren't you?"

An elderly man peered up at him, his wife's hand resting lightly on his forearm. The resemblance to Johnny was unmistakeable.

They shook hands. "My god, I haven't seen you since you were a boy, Kevin. Look at you."

"How are you doing, Uncle David?"

"Not bad, not bad. Minding my Ps and Qs."

"Are you still in Thunder Bay?"

"Oh, yeah." He glanced at his wife. "I'm retired now. We're glad to be able to travel a bit, now that the pandemic thing is over."

Kevin had forgotten what his uncle had done for a living, if he'd ever known it at all, so he just smiled and nodded. David Walker had somehow managed to escape the hell of alcoholism into which his older brother had fallen, and he'd lived a normal life with a normal family. Or at least that had always been Kevin's impression.

His wife gave a subtle little tug, and David sighed. "I guess we'd better get moving if we're going to follow them to the cemetery. Otherwise, I'll get lost."

Kevin shook his hand again, nodded at his aunt, whose name was on the tip of his tongue, and watched them shuffle across the parking lot to their vehicle, a large, expensive-looking RV parked at the back. Well, at least someone in the Walker family had a bit of money to spend, it would seem.

A few of Johnny's former coworkers, whom he knew, approached him to pass on their condolences. They were mostly old men now, retired themselves and busily engaged in drinking themselves to death after the example of their late buddy, but he bore them no malice and shook their hands one by one.

He was about to leave when another man approached. He

was by himself, wearing a dark suit and sunglasses, and his hair was combed back in a silver pompadour that Kevin recognized instantly.

"Uncle Emmett," he said, shaking hands with his late mother's oldest brother. "It was very nice of you to come."

Emmett patted him on the shoulder. "Couldn't let you go through this by yourself, could I? Anyway, I wanted to look in that damned coffin and make sure the son of a bitch is actually dead."

"He's dead."

"Yes, he is. How are you doing these days, son? I hear you're making quite a name for yourself as a detective. Your mom would be so proud."

For the first time, Kevin felt a wave of emotion. "Thanks."

"Although I remember she wanted you to become an English teacher, like she was."

Kevin's vision blurred for a moment. Embarrassed, he rubbed his eye with a finger.

The last time he'd seen Emmett Stevens had been at his mother Estelle's funeral. Seventeen and feeling awkward because of his size and shyness, he'd stood around in the living room, getting in everyone's way. Finally, Aunt Amelia, who'd made all the arrangements for the reception, took him in hand.

She sat him down in one of the chairs set up in the Walker living room, between Uncle Emmett and herself, and engaged him in mindless conversation while his father quietly got drunk in his La-Z-Boy in the corner and ignored everyone.

Emmett had introduced him to his mother's older sister, Aunt Diana, and her husband, Uncle Donald Winston. He'd never met either of them before. Somehow he remembered his manners and stood up to shake hands. They settled into chairs and chatted to him about hockey and school and what he wanted to do after he graduated.

When he admitted that he'd already decided to become a police officer, there was quiet laughter among the Stevenses, but not the malicious kind. They smiled at each other and at their nephew, knowing what Estelle would have said to her beloved only son.

"Oh, Kevin. You know I'm afraid of guns."

He promised to try to visit them in Port Hope some time, but they all knew it was something everyone said on these occasions, well-meaning and sincere, but never to be followed up on.

One funeral filled with emotion for a beloved lost parent, and the other void of any feeling whatsoever, other than impatience for it to be over so that he could get back to work.

He forced himself to walk alongside the hearse to where Carla stood, looking lost. She was older than he thought she would be, with dyed reddish-brown hair, a knee-length black dress covered with lint, and worn-out black shoes. Her face was puffy and dotted with liver spots.

"Thanks so much for coming," she said through her tears.

He refrained from embracing her, since they were strangers and he was determined to keep his distance from her grief, but he patted her arm and said, "It'll be all right."

He was amazed that anyone would have cared enough about Johnny Walker to be reduced to tears by his death.

"Will you come around to the house? We've got lots of food. I'll never eat it all."

"No, but thank you."

"I'm really so sorry about everything."

"Don't worry about it, Carla. It is what it is."

"I know. You're a good man. Johnny made a mistake. He made a lot of mistakes in his life, yeah, but with you . . ."

"Never mind. It's okay."

She was about to say something else, but his cellphone buzzed. He took it out and looked at the caller ID.

"I'm sorry, I have to take this."

"Work?"

"Yeah. Nice meeting you, Carla. Sorry it had to be under these circumstances."

"The privilege was all mine, Kevin. All mine."

He strode off to find a private spot to answer the call. "Walker."

"Sorry to interrupt," said Detective Sergeant Sonja Freeling, "but you better get your ass up here ASAP."

"Oh?"

"Officer down, Kevin. Move it."

Chapter 3

The motor pool-issue grey Crown Victoria rolled through the inner perimeter barrier and bounced into the entrance of the field where a command centre was in the early stages of being set up.

Ontario Provincial Police Detective Inspector Ellie March shut off the engine, got out, and looked around. On the road about thirty metres in front of her, a large white OPP van belonging to Identification Services sat with its back doors open. Someone garbed in white protective outerwear leaned inside, stocking up a case with extra supplies. Another fifty metres or so beyond that, other white-clad figures swarmed around the police cruiser and the mouth of the driveway across from it, while still others moved up and down between the road and the house, heads down, eyes roving.

It was a sunny May Day morning, mild, with a slight breeze,

but Ellie wasn't interested in the weather.

"According to Dr. Phong," Detective Sergeant Sonja Freeling said, her boots hissing in the grass, "he was shot about forty minutes ago. His last contact with dispatch was eight minutes before that. The nine-one-one call was at ten fifty. The guy who phoned it in is over there with Skelton. He was driving by on his way to the marina and saw something was wrong when he passed the cruiser."

"Thanks," Ellie said. Sonja was upset. Ellie could hear it in her voice. But they all were. A fellow officer had been shot and killed in the line of duty.

An unspeakable outrage.

"She's behind the house right now with the other victim," Sonja continued, referring to Dr. Phong, the coroner. "Female, mid-fifties. Shot once in the back and twice in the head."

They both turned around as an OPP SUV rolled into the field and parked next to Ellie's Crown Vic. Staff Sergeant Gary Dunn got out on the driver's side and his passenger, Inspector Colleen Galvin, eased out on the other side.

"Can't shake hands," Colleen said, holding up her right arm. She wore a fibreglass cast on her wrist.

Ellie grimaced. "What happened?"

"Stupid. Fell off the ladder cleaning out the eavestrough. Broke my wrist." She looked at Sonja. "It's Maynard?"

Sonja nodded.

Colleen turned to Ellie. "Mal's ordered Inspector Kennedy to assume command of the scene. He should be here shortly."

"Fine." Ellie understood. The murder of a law enforcement officer inevitably triggered a major response, particularly with the killer still at large. The regional commander, Chief Superintendent Jordan Malcolmsen, would be pulling out all the stops.

Normally a sergeant would control a crime scene as incident commander, but given the fact that it was a case that would receive intense scrutiny as it moved forward, internally as well as externally in the media and the public eye, Malcolmsen had tapped a commissioned officer for the job.

"Is Kennedy—" Sonja began.

"He's fine," Dunn snapped.

Ellie raised an eyebrow. Tall and stocky, in his mid-forties, with pale blue eyes and thinning reddish hair, Dunn was the detachment's operations manager. An experienced police officer with superior administrative skills, he was being groomed by Colleen as a future detachment commander. He was normally even-tempered and affable, but not this morning.

Their attention was drawn to the sound of voices raised in argument. Ellie left the field and started up the road toward the cruiser. As she passed the forensics van, Serge Landry, the tire tread and footprint specialist, looked up at her while snapping the clasps on his supply case. He held out a pair of blue booties. His face was grim and his eyes were dark.

Identification Sergeant Dave Martin, commander of the forensics unit, stood toe-to-toe with Kevin Walker. Arms akimbo, he glared up at Kevin.

"No! I said no. Not now."

"What's up?" Ellie asked, putting on her booties.

Martin turned on her. "I've got Padgett standing over there all set up and ready to go. See? Right there. Would you people please clear the hell out so we can get our work done?"

Ellie glanced at the civilian technician loitering nearby with an elaborate-looking contraption that resembled the camera array on top of a Google car.

"Have you cleared the cruiser?"

"Yes, we've cleared the cruiser, and yes, Phong looked at him in situ, but if you don't mind, I want to have the three-D images shot before Bigfoot here starts fucking around."

Kevin stirred his size thirteens in irritation.

"Well," Ellie said calmly, "I wouldn't mind having a look myself right now. Give us two or three minutes, Dave, and then it's all yours."

Martin opened his mouth and closed it again. Ellie was an inspector, after all. What she asked for, she got. He waved an arm. "Be my guest."

The window was down. Maynard would have lowered it to talk to the assailant. The body was slumped over to the right. She could see an entry wound just below the cheekbone, and another in the temple. Spatter covered the steering wheel and instrument cluster, but there was very little on the passenger side, and no holes in the door or window.

The shots were not through-and-through. The bullets were still inside the victim's head.

She stepped back to allow Kevin to take a look. He studied the scene for a moment, then moved to his left and tried to look in over the side mirror at the footwell under the steering wheel. Then he took out his cellphone, reached inside, desperately trying not to touch anything, and took several pictures of the floor around the victim's feet.

He stepped back and took a look at the photos, then held the phone out for Ellie to see.

"His notebook," she said.

"Open. It must have been on his lap. He was sitting here taking notes."

"Caught off guard."

"Yeah."

Ellie walked back to Martin. "What about the other one?"

"You can go up and take a look," he said, with much less vehemence than before. "Just stay off the driveway because we're still processing it. The lawn on either side has been searched already."

Ellie nodded.

They started walking toward the house, which was set back quite a way from the road. The trees on either side were mature: maples, a butternut tree, and a very tall quaking aspen. They threw distended shadows diagonally across the lawn, the crown of the butternut on the left painting a blur on the edge of the driveway.

On the right, the aspen's leaves shook as the wind stirred, making a sound like faint applause.

"He's upset," Kevin said, referring to Martin.

Ellie said nothing, her eyes on the house ahead of them. They were climbing a slight incline, enough so that if you shifted your car into neutral and someone gave you a push, you could gently roll down to the road.

The house was an old three-storey brick structure with white trim that had seen better days. The limestone foundation was showing a bit of damage; the trim had needed repainting five years ago; and one of the shutters on the attic window had come loose and was hanging by its lower hinge.

A small white car, some kind of hatchback, was parked at the side of the house.

Ellie stopped. Kevin had squatted at the edge of the driveway and was taking photos of something.

"Interesting," he said.

Chapter 4

It was a typical rural driveway. At one time it had been surfaced with gravel, probably back when the house still looked smart and in good repair, but over the years the passage of time had caused most of the gravel to disappear, leaving behind shallow potholes and a narrow strip of green down the middle.

Kevin had been looking at the numbered plastic evidence markers left behind by Martin's team, and when he came to a patch of dirt large enough to see for himself what they had observed and documented, he stopped for a closer look.

"A dually," he said, snapping another shot and pointing. "Looks like it went up and back down again."

Ellie bent down to look over his shoulder. A dually was a type of large pickup truck with dual rear wheels, often used for towing heavy trailers. "Not pulling a load."

"No. Here's a passenger car." He pointed again and, looking

up at the white hatchback, nodded to himself. "That one, I'd say. Came in yesterday or last night. The dually's tires went over its tread marks here, see," he gestured with his hand, "and then over its own tracks here on the way back down."

Ellie grunted. "Fresh."

"This morning. Clean and crisp."

A scenes-of-crime officer stood on the front verandah, hood pushed back, doing something with her digital camera. Kevin led the way around the side of the house, one stride for every two that Ellie took.

Another team was busy back here with the second victim, who'd been discovered by one of the responding officers while making a quick circuit of the house to see if anyone was home.

At the rear was a wood-frame back-summer kitchen, its white paint patchy and grey, its screen door wide open. Evidence markers led from the stoop outward into the backyard to a point where blue- and white-clad figures gathered around the second victim.

"We're still waiting on the warrant for the house," Identification Constable Jayne Witten said, watching as Dr. Phong withdrew her liver probe to check the temperature of the body, "but we saw her wallet on the kitchen counter with her cards pulled out and scattered around. The picture on the driver's licence matches."

The victim was a woman in her late fifties. She wore flat black canvas shoes, jeans, and a yellow cardigan sweater stained with blood. She'd been shot once in the back and twice in the head.

"Running away," Kevin said, looking again at the open back door.

"I would say so," Dr. Phong agreed, putting away her liver probe and standing up. "The bullet in the back stopped her from running, but was likely non-fatal. The two in the head took care of that."

"Like Maynard," Kevin said.

"Yes, and very recent also. But I can't say right now which victim was first and which was second."

"Who was she?"

"Dorothy Kerr," Witten said. "This was her residence."

Kevin turned around to see Ellie walking away. He followed her around the house and across the lawn diagonally, away from the driveway and toward the road where Sonja and Colleen stood, waiting for her.

"I want everyone back at the detachment office now," Ellie said. "Skelton, Hope, all of the crime unit. ASAP. We need to get started right away."

Chapter 5

Kevin had to push and shove his way into the meeting room, using his size to jostle through the doorway toward a spot along the wall. Everyone seemed to be talking at once—uniformed officers, civilians, detectives, and administrative staff. Even McGregor, the office manager, was here trying to make himself heard.

Ellie stood at the end of the table, about two metres from Kevin, and while he could see her mouth moving, he couldn't hear what she was saying.

He watched her expression grow dark.

Here it comes, he thought.

She climbed up onto the table, knocking aside someone's notebook in the process.

"HEY! QUIET! *QUIET!*"

The room instantly fell silent.

"This meeting is for crime unit personnel only! Everyone else, out! Now!"

People stirred, but no one left. It was impossible, since the doorway was clogged and others were gathered outside in the hallway, trying to see in.

"I understand everyone's upset," Ellie went on, lowering her voice a notch. "But we need to get down to work immediately. Please check with your sergeants to stay updated. I know you want to help, and I'm sure there are a hundred different things you'll be able to do when the time comes, but right now you all need to return to your desks and let us get to work. Now!"

"Hey, hey, hey," a voice boomed out in the hallway, "what the hell's going on here?"

It was the drug team sergeant, Miles Gibbons, who'd emerged from his office. "Back to work! Move it! Come on, let's go."

Everyone slowly shuffled off. Gibbons stuck his head in and looked up at Ellie, who was still standing on the table with her hands on her hips. He shook his head and disappeared.

"Shut the damned door." Ellie climbed down and sat in her chair, her face red.

Detective Constable Heather Hope looked at Kevin and bugged her eyes out, jaw slack.

As the remaining people found places around the table, Ellie leaned forward and looked at each of them in turn.

"Everyone's upset. I understand. Emotions are running high, and emotions can lead to mistakes. Mistakes lead to acquittals. If you knew Constable Maynard personally, you have my sincere condolences. However, you *will* depersonalize this matter right now, immediately. Is that understood?"

A murmur rippled around the table, and several heads nodded.

"Sonja, we haven't had a chance to confirm assignments, and I apologize, but here's how we're going to work. Alaric, you're primary. You'll also flex between teams and reach out to your intelligence contacts for whatever you can get."

Detective Constable Alaric Quinn nodded, running a hand through his beard.

"We're going to borrow Detective Constable Jahara from RST again to be our warrant writer," Ellie continued, "and Constable Byrnes, you're our file co-ordinator. All set?"

A young redhead nodded. "Absolutely, ma'am."

"Don't call me that. Alaric will work closely with you. Everyone, you'll all be expected to get your reports to Kate promptly for entry into the system. Time will be a factor, and I don't want Alaric wasting time chasing after you. If you need help, Kate, ask for it."

"Will do."

"Ballistics will confirm it, but we'll proceed on the assumption that the two murders are related and were committed by the same person as part of a single incident. So, we'll follow two investigative tracks. One, Constable Maynard was the primary target and Dorothy Kerr was either a secondary target or collateral damage, a witness to the Maynard shooting."

She looked at Detective Constable Skelton. "Doug, you and Bob will work this track. Look into Maynard's jacket, complaints filed against him, reports he might have submitted that caused this kind of trouble for someone."

The veteran on the team, Skelton had put in more than a decade in the crime unit. Detective Constable Bob Pierce, recently transferred in from regional support, kept his head down, writing in his notebook.

"Second," Ellie went on, "we'll investigate the possibility that Dorothy Kerr was the primary target and Constable Maynard was either a secondary target or collateral damage, a witness who was preventing the assailant from leaving without being seen."

She looked at Kevin. "You and Heather will be responsible for this track. Who was Dorothy Kerr? Why would someone kill her? See what's there."

Kevin glanced at Heather. She'd gone to her locker before

the meeting and changed out of her T-shirt, which had featured a tuxedo cat riding a chicken, into a navy polo shirt and blue tweed jacket.

"A quick reminder. The media scrutiny's going to be incredibly intense. The regional commander has ordered Kerry McGuinness to take the communications lead, so all public statements will either come from him or Constable Townsend. If at any time someone asks you a question, you will either say 'No comment' or 'Please contact Mr. McGuinness with your questions.' Is that understood?"

"Civilian," Skelton muttered.

"Yes, he is. Is it understood?"

A murmur passed around the table, and once again heads nodded, including Skelton's.

"Get to work."

As people left the room, Kevin saw that Ellie was beckoning to him. He maneuvered against the current to reach her and, when the room was otherwise empty, she stood up.

"I understand you just lost your father. My condolences."

"Thanks."

She looked up at him, a neutral expression on her face. "Will you be taking bereavement leave?"

"I had a couple of hours off this morning for the funeral. That should do it."

Chapter 6

A small group of journalists with cameras and microphones had gathered outside the building, and Ellie had to pass them in order to get to her car.

"All statements will be coming from RHQ," she said, holding up a hand without stopping. "Please direct all your questions to Mr. Kerry McGuinness."

"What, in Smiths Falls?" someone asked.

She got into her car and started the engine. Cameras continued to shoot her behind the wheel as she put on her sunglasses and shifted into drive. Only with reluctance did they ease back enough to permit her to leave without running over someone's foot.

As she drove, she turned over in her mind what she knew about Grayson Kennedy, who was taking command of the crime scene. He was from Manitoba. She remembered the name of the town—Justice—because it seemed like a good place for a law enforcement professional to be from. After graduating from high school, he went directly into the RCMP and spent more than a decade (thirteen years?) patrolling the back roads and highways of Saskatchewan and Manitoba.

He married young and had two daughters. Ellie remembered hearing someone tell her that when his oldest was nine and his youngest was seven, Gray attended the scene of a severe traffic accident as a responding officer only to discover that one of the victims was his wife.

The drinking apparently started at that point.

Ellie's thoughts moved to Terry Maynard.

She couldn't recall ever having met him, so there was no sense of personal loss. Just a simmering anger, leaking into her clenched jaw and narrowed eyes.

There were well over four thousand uniformed OPP constables on duty across the province, and what happened to Maynard could conceivably happen to any one of them at any time. It was dangerous work, involving a level of risk that had to be dealt with by all officers in order for them to perform their duties at an acceptable level of effectiveness. You couldn't go to work afraid that something bad would happen to you. You had to go to work feeling confident that your training, equipment, and fellow members would see you through.

Otherwise, how could you possibly expect to be an effective cop? To serve the public as you'd sworn to do?

> *I solemnly affirm that I will be loyal to His*
> *Majesty the King and to Canada, and that I*
> *will uphold the Constitution of Canada and*
> *that I will, to the best of my ability, preserve*
> *the peace . . .*

Of course, when she'd taken the oath many years ago, she'd declared her loyalty to Her Majesty Queen Elizabeth II. As long as she'd been alive, Elizabeth had been queen. It felt so strange not to have her there, on the throne of the United Kingdom.

She approached a line of traffic on the highway up ahead and came to a stop just before the Drummond Centre crossroads. A roadblock had been set up, and because Highway 7 was a fairly busy two-lane thoroughfare running all the way from Toronto and Peterborough up to Ottawa, the delay was not sitting well with the motorists ahead of her.

At the head of the line, two uniformed officers in body armour were speaking to drivers before directing them to follow a detour to the left on the intersecting concession road. There was also a turning lane that allowed traffic to leave the highway on the right, to travel east below Mississippi Lake. Two more officers were filtering traffic in that lane.

Ellie plugged in her dashboard emergency light and, edging over onto the gravel shoulder, eased up alongside the waiting vehicles to the intersection. She waited until a car was waved around the corner from the turning lane before rolling across the road. She parked, got out, and walked up to the sergeant standing with several constables at the barriers.

"Anything unusual?"

"Not so far, Ellie." Sergeant Ed Turner worked out of the Carleton Place satellite office, and he and Ellie knew each other slightly. "Typical Monday morning traffic. Everybody's pissed at us for slowing them down and making them detour."

"Too bad."

They stood next to a cruiser that was parked in the far lane, forming part of the roadblock. A constable sat behind the wheel, monitoring a computer screen and relaying information to the four constables screening traffic detouring left and right.

Several cars had been directed to make their turn onto the concession road and to pull over, where other constables were conducting what amounted to traffic stops.

Ellie looked at the cameras mounted on top of the cruiser, facing forward and backward to catch traffic approaching from either direction.

The cameras were part of an ALPR system installed in the vehicle, an automated licence plate reader. It scanned each plate and ran it against a hotlist downloaded into a mobile workstation tablet attached to a dashboard docking station.

The hotlist consisted of a watch list of licence plates connected to expired stickers, stolen or suspended plates, stolen vehicles, and unlicensed or suspended drivers, among other alerts currently entered into the databases of the Ministry of Transportation of Ontario and the Canadian Police Information Centre system referred to as CPIC. The list was downloaded into the ALPR each time the cruiser was being readied to hit the road.

"We're not total bastards," Turner said. "We're just issuing warnings on the expireds, but we've gotten a couple of suspendeds we're ticketing. They got a stolen Mustang from Ottawa up at the other end."

Ellie nodded. Turner was referring to a similar setup at the north end of the outer perimeter.

The ALPR had the capability of storing the image of each plate it read, along with date, time, and location information. Not unexpectedly, the Information and Privacy Commissioner of Ontario had issued strong recommendations on the retention and use of "non-hit" information. If a licence plate didn't ring the bell, IPCO expected that the data collected would either be purged right away, to protect the privacy rights of the individual, or stored only "briefly."

The regional commander, after consultation with in-house counsel and the commissioner, had ordered that "briefly" in this particular situation would mean that all plate information would be stored for the duration of the investigation, whether hits or non-hits. The reasoning behind the decision being that a plate not on the hotlist might turn up to be connected to a person later identified as a suspect.

Ellie drove through the barrier and continued on to the intersection of West Shore Drive, where she checked in at the inner perimeter and bounced into the field that was now the site of a full-blown command post. With some difficulty, she found a spot to park and got out.

A large OPP truck with "Eastern Region Mobile Support Unit" emblazoned on the side had arrived, along with more SUVs and OPP pickup trucks and cruisers. She made her way to a canopy in the middle of the field and held out her hand to Inspector Grayson Kennedy.

"We've met before," she said, "but it was quite a few years ago."

"Orillia," Kennedy replied. "I remember."

"Can you give me a situation report, Gray?"

"Sure. ERT and TRU are deployed, conducting searches for physical evidence along the highway inside the perimeter and also down West Shore to McCullough's Landing and the lakeshore. Door-to-door canvassing is under way, and a shelter-in-place order's in effect for the area. There are only two other residences on this road before you reach the Landing, and neither had anything to offer. We're going through the hamlet now as we speak."

He rolled his eyes. "As luck would have it, the campground opened today for the summer season, so we're covering that too. Plus, the Marine Unit is patrolling the lake in the unlikely event they escaped via water. We've also got drones in the air."

"Good job." Ellie had stood a pace or two closer to him than she normally would when talking to someone, and she'd smelled neither alcohol nor breath mints. Just stale coffee. She took a step back, on the pretext of checking the road.

"The bodies have been transported?"

He nodded. "Coroner's gone. Ident's still here, of course. Going to be a while for them. Not to mention all the crap they'll have to process from the road searches later. No gun yet, though. We wouldn't be that lucky."

"How are people doing, Gray?"

He understood what she was asking. "All right, considering.

A few flare-ups and anger spikes, but by and large they're staying professional and under control."

"They know what's at stake."

"We all do."

She met his gaze and nodded. His pale blue eyes were clear; his handshake had been firm; and his voice, although rough and gravelly from years of cigarettes and alcohol, was steady.

"Keep me posted. You have my number."

"I do. We've got this."

Ellie nodded and left him there to get on with it.

Chapter 7

The offices of the Perth *Sentinel* were located on the second floor of a tenement building on Gore Street, above a bookstore and a shop that sold wool, patterns, and knitting supplies. A weekly freebie that usually ran about sixteen pages, the paper covered local stories and ran regular columns about birds, gardening, and town politics.

Alaric Quinn had prepared a brief biographical sketch on Dorothy Kerr for Kevin and Heather to begin with, and they'd decided, after seeing that she'd worked for the *Sentinel*, to start there.

The publisher and editor, Patrick Dillon, was an early-thirties journalism graduate from Oakville. Five years ago, he bought the *Sentinel* out of receivership and moved to Perth to fulfill his dream of becoming the next great Canadian newspaperman. He was a tall, skinny kid with John Lennon glasses and tawny hair that was thick and wavy.

He solemnly shook hands with Kevin and Heather.

"Condolences," Kevin said.

"Thanks. Please, come into my office."

They followed him into an adjoining room with high ceilings and large, arched windows. The furniture and fittings were all vintage, made of walnut, oak, and brass—that is, what you could see of them. Books were piled everywhere, alongside stacks of newspapers, old magazines, and numerous collectibles and oddities.

Patrick cleared off a visitor's chair and gestured to Heather, who settled into it with a brief smile of thanks. He shooed a sleeping cat from the other chair so that Kevin could sit down.

"I hope you're not allergic to cat fur," Patrick said, dropping into the chair behind his desk. "We have three of them."

"Not a problem," Kevin said. "We need to ask you a few questions about Ms. Kerr."

He rubbed his forehead. "I can't believe what happened. Poor Dorothy. When Larry told me what he'd heard on the scanner, I went nuts. This is small-town Canada for chrissakes, not Toronto or Vancouver."

"Larry?"

"Wilson. Larry Wilson, my other staff reporter. He's in Smiths Falls right now. Your Inspector March blew him off and sent him on a wild goose chase for an official handout from RHQ in the City of Lost Employment. What's the point of that? I want to know what actually *happened*."

"When was the last time you had any contact with Dorothy?"

"Contact? Um, let's see. Friday, I think. She came in to talk to me about a thing she's working on. Corruption in the local scrap metal trade. We talked for, oh, I don't know, half an hour? Then she went off to get some lunch."

"Anything problematic with the story? Anything she was upset or worried about?"

Patrick shrugged. "The manager of the company's a gnarly son of a bitch. She'd tried to interview him once and it didn't go well, so she was going to try again this week. She was hoping to talk to one of the owners. Family business. But I don't think it was that kind of story." He bit his lip. "You know, something that would get her killed."

Heather glanced down at her notebook. "Was she full time or part time?"

"She was a staffer when the paper went under. After I bought it I read through her stuff and convinced her to freelance for me, then brought her back on full time. Her work's really great. She lives alone and doesn't have any relatives left here." He blinked. "Lived, I mean."

Heather nodded. "What kind of person was she, Patrick?"

"Oh, she was a hard-assed old sweetie." He tried to smile. "She reminded me of my Aunt Laura, my mom's older sister. When I made a goof of some kind, she'd give me that look, but when I 'done good' it was like the sun coming out from behind a cloud and shining all over me."

Heather jotted something down.

"She was born in Halifax," Patrick said, "but I didn't hold it against her. Actually, her family was from right here in Drummond-North Elmsley."

"Is that right?"

"Yeah. Her house, on West Shore Drive, was where her father was born and raised. It went back four generations, I think."

"Oh? How do you know? Did you run a background check on her?"

Patrick chuckled. "No, no. This all came straight from the horse's mouth." The chuckle trailed off into a long sigh. "One night we were up pretty late putting a tough issue to bed, and afterward we had a couple of toots. She sat right there where you're sitting, Detective Hope. She was a gin-and-tonic person. I'm mostly a beer guy, myself. Anyway, we got a little oiled and she opened up about herself. First and only time."

A large, fluffy orange cat strolled into the office, went directly over to Heather, and jumped up into her lap. Heather barely had time to lift up her notebook to accommodate her new friend.

"Her dad, Robert Kerr, was a mechanical engineer," Patrick continued. "He worked for a steamship company in Halifax, which is how Dorothy came to be born there. When she was eleven, uh, in '78, I guess, Robert was severely injured in a boiler explosion. While he was recovering, he found out his mother had died back here and left everything to him, including the house and property. After his convalescence, he decided to move home."

"On disability?"

Patrick nodded. "Dorothy's mom decided to stay where she was. Dorothy said she was probably seeing someone else already. Anyway, they divorced. Once they came back, Dorothy looked after Robert, who was never able to work again. Dorothy went to high school here in town."

Heather stroked the cat absent-mindedly while she listened.

Kevin was taking his own notes. He knew her memory was excellent, and that nothing was being missed.

"She had a part-time job at the marina during the summer, renting out paddleboats and cleaning the washrooms. Her dad had taught her how to sail, you see, when she was a kid back east. They had their own boat, just a little dinghy, I guess, but they brought it back with them and kept it at McCullough's Landing, down at the end of the road. What she earned helped pay for the fees, so Robert could still say he owned a boat. She took him out, once or twice, and after he passed away she kept on with it herself."

The cat jumped down and stalked away. Kevin watched Heather glance at the cat fur on her lap and decide to leave it.

"Did she have any relationships?" Kevin asked. "Boyfriend, girlfriend?"

"Not that I'm aware of. She was what our grandparents would have called a spinster. A loner, really. She liked to quilt.

She belonged to a group. They met once a month at someone's home. I don't know who. They'll be upset."

"Where were you this morning?"

"Here. Uh, I got here about eight. I'm a morning person. Kip gets in a few minutes before nine. He's marketing and sales. Larry went straight from home to the detachment. Jane, our copy editor-slash-proofreader, was a few minutes after nine."

"Are they all still here?"

"Yeah. Although nobody's getting very much done this morning."

Chapter 8

"Come on in," Jane Stewart said, staring at her computer monitor. "Sit down. I'll be just a moment."

Heather took a visitor's chair on the right, while Kevin closed the door behind him and dropped into the chair on the left.

It was a much different office than Patrick's. The same size, with the same high ceilings and arched windows, but minimally furnished and completely free of clutter. Other than the desk and several filing cabinets, the only other item in the office was a large maple table with two chairs in the centre of the room. A newspaper lay open on the table with four books stacked next to it: *The Chicago Manual of Style*; *Fowler's Modern English Usage*; *The Globe and Mail Style Book*; and *The Concise Oxford Dictionary*.

"I'm editing the obit," Stewart said, her eyes still on the screen. "Almost done."

A steno pad and a ballpoint pen waited by her left hand, and after a moment she jotted down a few notes, clicked the mouse, and gave the two detectives her attention.

"Sorry. What did you want to ask me?"

Kevin glanced at Heather, who pushed out her lips. He raised his eyebrows.

"Just a few basic questions," she said. "First, where's your cat?"

Stewart frowned. "They don't come in here. They know I don't like them."

"Okay. How long have you worked here?"

"Patrick hired me during the pandemic. We had an interview on Skype and then he e-mailed me a contract. I worked from home until COVID was under control and we started coming back to work."

"Is it a good gig?"

"It's fine. It pays enough to be an acceptable second income. My husband's a teacher."

"Oh? What does he teach?"

"High school geography."

Heather looked at a picture of two children on her desk. "Yours?"

"Yes." Her response was short and clipped. She obviously wasn't interested in get-to-know-you talk.

"How well did you know Dorothy Kerr?"

She thought for a moment, framing her answer. "I knew her more as a reporter than as a co-worker. She was always in and out of the office, and it's difficult to become acquainted with someone on that basis. As a reporter, she was fine. A much better writer than Wilson, and almost as good as Patrick, for someone coming into the field without the background. In journalism, I mean."

"Dorothy didn't have a degree?"

"No, she was an amateur when she started. Before the paper was sold."

"She was working on a story about a local scrap metal company. Know anything about that?"

Stewart shook her head. "Nothing. I learn about the stories when I read the copy; never before."

"When was the last time you saw her?"

"Last Friday morning. She came in to see Patrick."

"Did you talk to her?"

"No, she was in and out. As usual."

"How did you get along with her? Any differences of opinion or what have you?"

Stewart glanced at her monitor, clearly more interested in getting back to work than in talking about Dorothy Kerr.

"No, no differences of opinion. I don't really care what they write about, just that they write reasonably well so I don't have to spend all day rewriting their copy."

"Okay. But I mean personally. Did you like her? Dislike her?"

Stewart sighed. "These people are not my friends or my enemies, all right? I have no opinion about her or Patrick or the others one way or the other."

"You're indifferent to them."

"Completely."

"So much for your empathy superpower," Kevin murmured as they walked down a short hallway to the office of Kip Benson, the marketing and sales guy.

"Hey, I have to work with the material I'm given, all right? This guy's yours."

"Okay." Kevin stuck his head into the doorway in time to see a liquor bottle disappearing into a bottom drawer.

"Mr. Benson? Detective Constable Walker, OPP, and Detective Constable Hope. Could we have a moment of your time?"

Benson shot to his feet. His short-sleeved white shirt was

untucked on one side. He poked it back into place and waved them in.

"Sure, sure! Come on in. Here to talk about Dorothy, are you? Terrible, terrible thing. I don't know what this world's coming to, I really don't."

They shook hands and sat down.

"Can I get you anything? Tea or coffee? Something cold? I think there's tonic water in the fridge."

"Nothing, thanks. We only have a few questions. When was the last time you saw Dorothy?"

"Friday. Friday morning. Yeah. I was coming in with coffee, I get my own down the street, and she was just leaving. I said, 'You look very nice this morning,' and she said, 'Thank you, Kip.' Then she went down the stairs and out the door. That was it. That was the last time I saw her. The last time I'll ever see her, I guess."

Heather had her notebook out on her lap, and she'd written something down in large block capitals. She tipped it slightly toward him.

Looks like Bruce Campbell.

Kevin bit his lip. In fact, Kip Benson did bear more than a passing resemblance to the famous star of the *Evil Dead* franchise, *Burn Notice*, and other films and programs. Kevin could see it in the lantern jaw, the dark, flashing eyes, and the curly black hair.

Heather wrote below it:

Chuck Finley.

Kevin looked away. "How did she get along with everyone else in the office?"

"Oh fine, fine. Everybody liked her. She was a tough old girl sometimes, but she could make you smile just the same."

"You got along with her okay?"

"Oh, yeah. You bet."

"What about Jane Stewart?"

"She's all right, I guess. She wants her space, and I got no problem with that."

"No, I mean did Jane Stewart get along with Dorothy, or was there a problem there?"

"Oh! Oh, I see. Nah. Nothing at all. It's a pretty good place to work, all in all. Everybody gets along. No cat fights or backstabbing. Even the real cats get along."

"What do you know about the stories Dorothy was working on?"

"Nothing, man. Nada. She was Pat's go-to guy for the local political stuff, and she did some investigative stories, but I mean, look where we are. It ain't exactly Toronto, man."

He paused. "Other than the hockey guy, Burnham, and the taxidermy thing." He shuddered. "That was over the top. Otherwise, though, pretty quiet."

Kevin stood up. "Thanks for your time. Sorry for your loss."

"Yeah, yeah. Thanks. Listen, do something for me."

Kevin glanced at Heather, who was putting her notebook away in her bag.

"What's that, Mr. Benson?"

"Catch the son of a bitch, and don't be gentle about it. All right?"

Chapter 9

Doug Skelton pulled his dark-green Range Rover over to the side of the road and shifted into park. Bob Pierce stirred in the passenger seat, staring through the windshield at the trailer set back only a dozen metres or so from the edge of the road.

"Should be here by now," Skelton said, glancing in his rear-view mirror.

Pierce said nothing. He unholstered his weapon, checked the load, and shoved it back in again.

A few moments later, an OPP cruiser pulled up behind them. Skelton shut off his engine and got out, Pierce following on the other side. The two uniformed constables lowered their windows.

"Vehicle's parked beside the trailer," Skelton said. "No sign of any activity outside."

"How do you want to do this?" asked the constable behind

the wheel, whose name was Laroque.

"Well, we haven't got Tactical here, have we? So I guess I'll just go up and knock on his door."

"You're the boss." Laroque and his partner, Behringer, got out and followed the two detectives up to the entrance to the lot on which the trailer sat.

Its white siding was grey with accumulated road dust, and its blue trim had faded from years of exposure to the afternoon sun. There was a small, two-step porch made of unpainted boards in front of the door, and the windows facing the road were all screened and curtained.

Skelton loosened his firearm in its holster but didn't draw it. Behringer motioned Laroque to skirt around the side of the trailer to cover the back.

The trailer's resident, Earl Avery Black, was 53 years old, white, and employed in Perth as a forklift driver in a local factory. He lived in the trailer with his wife, Brenda.

Black had no wants or warrants against him, but Skelton had requested backup because Pierce had made some noise about it. Black had been issued a number of speeding tickets over the past several years, including the one handed out this morning by Constable Terry Maynard, so he was a repeat offender as far as traffic violations were concerned.

However, since there had been no specific instructions about summoning Tactical when approaching a potential suspect in this case, Skelton hadn't bothered. He didn't like having them around when he was questioning someone and considering whether or not to place them under arrest. In his opinion, they overreacted and dominated the situation, whereas Skelton much preferred good, old-fashioned police technique. Look the man in the eye, ask him questions, and watch how he responds.

Skelton stepped up on the porch and pounded on the screen door.

"Earl Black! Police! Open the door and step outside!"

The screen door opened out, so Skelton moved back off the

porch and to his left, out of direct line of fire from the door. Behringer had taken up a position to the right, close to the trailer but not touching it, his weapon drawn and held at the low ready position. Pierce was a pace behind Skelton, on his left, his gun also out.

"Earl Black!" Skelton shouted again. "OPP! Open the door and come outside!"

A moment later the inner door opened and the screen door rattled. "What the hell's going on? Who is it?"

"OPP!" Skelton held up his badge. "Step outside and close the door behind you."

"OPP? What the hell? Again?" A stocky, dishevelled man in a white A-shirt and black track pants came out, scratching his head. "I was just about to go to bed. What the hell's going on?"

"Earl Black?"

"Yeah, yeah, yeah. What the fuck do you want?"

"Show us your hands, Mr. Black."

"My hands?" He held out his hands.

Behringer holstered his weapon and frisked him for weapons. He shook his head at Skelton and stepped back.

"Please come down off the porch, Mr. Black. Who else is inside the trailer?"

"My wife. What's this all about?"

"Anyone else?"

"Yeah, the entire fucking cast of *Star Wars*, man. No, there's nobody else."

"You were issued a speeding ticket this morning on Highway 7 by OPP Constable Maynard, is that correct?"

"Yeah, sure." Black rolled his eyes. "All I was trying to do was get home and go to bed. I'm on midnights right now and I fucking hate it."

"Do you own a firearm, Mr. Black?"

"What? Yeah, sure."

"Handgun?"

"A hunting rifle and a bird gun. Why? Who gives a fuck?"

"Where are they right now?"

"In the trailer. Listen, either you tell me what the fuck you want or I'm going back inside and going to bed. This is fucking ridiculous."

Behringer stepped forward, invading Black's personal space. "A little less lip, asshole."

"Or what?" Black's eyes flared. "You gonna shoot me, numbnuts?"

"Did you shoot Constable Maynard?" Skelton demanded.

"What? Who? What the fuck. Get off my property right now."

Behringer crowded him closer.

Black's hand shot out and struck Behringer on the shoulder. "Back off, fuckhead."

Behringer reacted instantly, grabbing Black's wrist, twisting his arm behind his back and slew-footing him to the ground. He rolled him onto his stomach and quickly zip-tied his wrists behind his back.

The screen door banged open and a woman emerged with a shotgun in her hands. The barrel was pointing down but her eyes were angry and her mouth was twisted.

"You let him go, right now!"

Constable Laroque emerged from the far side of the trailer, his gun levelled at her. "Drop your weapon! Drop it!"

Pierce took a step forward. As her eyes moved to him, he put away his gun and held both hands out. "Put the gun down, slowly and carefully. Then get on your knees and put your hands on top of your head."

She stared at him and began to sob.

"Please, ma'am," Pierce said.

Very carefully, she bent at the knees and placed the shotgun on the porch.

"Now, down on your knees. Hands on top of your head."

Still staring at him, tears running down her face, she complied.

Laroque holstered his weapon and rushed forward. He shoved the shotgun off the porch with his boot and secured her hands behind her back. "*Sacrament*," he muttered.

Pierce took a long breath, his first in what seemed like forever.

Behringer hauled Black to his feet and hustled him off to the cruiser.

"You're going to pay, you fucking bastard," he whispered in his prisoner's ear.

Chapter 10

As Earl Avery Black and his wife Lana, née Olverson, were being processed and prepped for interrogation, Kevin and Heather sat down in the meeting room with Ellie and Alaric.

"We've got a few minutes," Ellie said. "I want you to bring me up to speed on Kerr."

"We're still doing background on her," Kevin said. "She was a reporter at the *Sentinel*, the local weekly paper, so we talked to the publisher and her co-workers. We've got a bit clearer picture of who she was, and maybe a lead or two to follow."

He looked at Heather.

"She was working on a story about a local scrap metal dealer that may have been a little wonky," Heather said. "Alaric's doing a workup on them. The manager is apparently a prick, so we thought we'd look him up and have a little talk."

"No living relatives," Kevin said. "She belonged to a quilting club or group or whatever they're called. We'll interview them to see if something turns up."

"The house on West Shore has been in the family for several generations," Heather said. "Her father was born and raised there."

"What about a will?"

"We'll ask Kate if one's been logged in yet."

The door opened and Sonja stuck her head in. "We're about to begin."

"Thanks." Ellie looked at Heather. "Talk to the scrap metal dealer. See if there was animosity there."

Ellie watched them leave. She was afraid it might be the wrong track to follow, that Kerr had not been the primary target after all, but they were currently in a no-stones-unturned phase, and every lead had to be run down.

Including the one she was about to observe.

Doug Skelton had just begun the interrogation of Earl Black, and they were still in the early stages. Cautions and warnings on one side; curses and defiance on the other.

Ellie sat down in the empty chair directly in front of the monitor between Sonja and Bob Pierce. "No subtlety, I take it."

Sonja shook her head. "He's going to go after him full-bore."

Ellie said nothing, her skepticism rising again. She preferred Kevin's approach, which was an adaptation of the Reid technique in which a baseline of truthfulness was established through preliminary, non-threatening questions before turning on the heat and exerting pressure to obtain either a confession or incriminatory statements. It suited Kevin's personality, and was closer to how she herself had conducted interrogations as an up-and-coming detective.

"You've got quite a record," Skelton was saying. "Looks like you have zero respect for the law. Isn't that right?"

"Speeding tickets. Big shit."

"Where's the gun you used to shoot Constable Maynard?"

"I didn't shoot anybody. I already said that a hundred times."

"When we search your house, where are we going to find it? Or is it in your car? Or did you throw it in the ditch after killing him?"

"You're nuts, man. My guns are in the trailer, like I said before. I haven't used them in a couple months."

Skelton had been on his feet, hovering over Black, but now he sat down. "I went through the registration records. Rifle, shotgun—no, two shotguns. What do you need all the firepower for, Earl?"

"Target shooting. And me and my buddies go hunting. In season. With licences."

"Where's your handgun, Earl?"

"No handgun, pal."

"When it matches the gun used to kill the constable, your ass is grass. Why don't you tell us about it now, Earl, and save yourself a lot of grief later."

Earl folded his arms stubbornly.

"Did it piss you off, getting another ticket?"

"Fucking right it did."

"So you shot him while he was standing there," Skelton lied, "while he was giving it to you."

"No! I didn't have a gun in the car with me, I tell you. I gave him my licence, and the registration and insurance. Like he asked me to. Like always, for chrissakes. Then I took the ticket and drove away. That's it."

Skelton walked him through it several more times, but Ellie could see that Black was consistently sticking to his story and didn't look like he was going to budge.

"We'll hold him on the assault charge," she said to Sonja, "and see if a handgun turns up in the searches."

Sonja stood up. "Time to question the wife."

Chapter 11

Kevin and Heather bumped into Alaric in the corridor.

"Got the stuff on Drummond Scrap we're looking for?" Heather asked.

"Sure. Let's retire to the study, shall we?" Alaric led the way to the comm room, which he shared with a civilian data entry assistant named Simon O'Connor. In his mid-thirties, Simon wore his long, frizzy black hair pulled back in a ponytail to accommodate his headset. He caught their arrival in his peripheral vision and gave them a quick wave over his shoulder.

Alaric pulled up chairs for them and, scratching his beard, settled his bulk down at his workstation. His set-up included two open laptops and two different workstations with multiple monitors. On one of them Kevin saw the log-in screen for CPIC, and on the other their internal OPP intranet.

Also on his desk were three of the little wire figures with

big plastic hands and feet that were sold in the dollar store as cellphone holders. One of them held an iPhone and the other two sported the latest Samsung Galaxies.

"You're wired for sound," Heather observed.

"You bet. Now, you're looking for info on Drummond Metal and Salvage. Let's see what I've got." He brought one of the laptops to life and bent over it, clicking and typing. "Here's my report. I've uploaded it to the case file, but I'll give you the *Coles Notes* version now."

"Family owned," Heather said, edging forward.

"No peeking. Yeah, second-generation business started by Gordon White, now deceased, at its current location on Churchill Road, Drummond Township. Current owners are Frederick and Peter White, a.k.a. Fred and Pete, his two sons. Fred spends most of his time in Florida while the younger one, Pete, lives in Drummond Centre and runs everything. As scrap metal dealers they specialize in non-ferrous recycling, and they don't take end-of-life cars or hazardous materials. They're big into aluminum, nickel, copper, lead, tin, and zinc."

"Copper," Heather murmured.

"Yeah. We've looked at them a couple of times for receiving stolen wire but so far, no luck. If they're into it, they're super careful."

He used one of the laptops to access the external Internet. "Here's their website."

Heather looked at him. "They have a website?"

"Yeah. Actually, it's a good one. On the home page, as you can see, they post their prices for the various commodities they buy. In Canadian dollars, per pound. The industry seems to prefer Imperial to metric, or maybe I'm wrong, but there it is."

Kevin leaned in for a look. According to the list, which bore today's date, they were paying seventy-five cents a pound for aluminum siding, fifty-five cents a pound for stainless steel, twenty-four cents a pound for lead batteries, and a whopping four dollars and fifty cents a pound for bare copper. The list included other items they accepted, such as electronic components and cables, with the notation: "Price TBD."

Alaric switched to the "About Us" page. "They've got a brief history here of the company, starting with the late father, Gordie. Then bios on the two brothers."

"Gordie looks like a dumpster diver," Heather said.

"Hardscrabble business to be starting up from scratch," Alaric observed, "especially back before recycling became popular and profitable."

"And regulated," Kevin said.

"Just so. According to this, the older brother Frederick quit high school to help out his father when their volume started to grow. He reorganized the yard, built up their fleet of heavy equipment, and expanded the staff. They're at sixteen employees right now."

"The other one's got a degree," Heather said, looking at the screen.

"Yeah. A business degree from Western University. Then he spent four years working for Suncor in Calgary before coming back home. Looks like he took over, and Fred and his family did the Florida thing."

"So, okay." Heather leaned back. "Anything else on them?"

Alaric switched to the desktop computer connected to the OPP intranet. He entered his password and navigated to a logon screen. He signed in and clicked and typed until he had the page he was looking for.

"They're required to submit monthly transaction logs. What they buy and who they buy it from, and what they sell and who they sell it to. I skimmed through the last six months and then generated some reports for you. You can read through them at your leisure, but you'll see these guys are really making it happen. They have regular customers they buy from, mostly home renovators, demolition companies, and scavengers bringing in old stoves and fridges and other home appliances like that. Plus the companies they sell to, like aluminum producers. Did you know that more than 30 per cent of aluminum produced in the world is from recycled material?"

"I didn't know that," Heather said.

"What I'm trying to say is that we're too short-staffed to analyze all the logs we receive every month from every business in our jurisdiction, so I can't answer your question right now. But we can talk to Ellie about requesting that a case file be opened on these guys if you think it's warranted."

"We'll see," Heather said. "Anything at all worth mentioning?"

"There's a connection to the so-called Freedom Convoy a couple of years ago."

"Oh?"

The protest had started out as a demonstration supporting truckers who were upset about vaccination requirements at the Canada-United States border. It quickly devolved into an illegal occupation of downtown Ottawa and a blockade of Parliament Hill, as dozens of trucks filled the streets and hundreds of supporters camped out in the snow, creating chaos in the nation's capital.

"What kind of a connection?"

"There were a number of people using social media to document the businesses whose trucks were down there. They took pictures and posted them online." He opened a file and scrolled down past numerous photographs of bobtail tractors to a shot of a black pick-up truck with "Drummond Scrap Metal" and the company logo emblazoned on the passenger door. A second photo, from the back of the truck, revealed a number of stickers plastered on the rear window, including the inevitable "F*CK TRUDEAU" and the less common "Trudeau: Rat Goof!!" along with an inscription written in white soap: "It is for Freedom that Christ Set us Free! Galatians 5:1."

Heather scowled. "Yeah, I'll bet Saint Paul was all geared up about COVID shots at the Macedonian border when he came out with that one."

"Do you know who was there from Drummond?" Kevin asked.

"Their manager at the time, Gary Pedersen. According to Pete White, he took the truck without permission and was fired."

"It's a story, anyway."

Heather turned away. "Makes me wonder what story Dorothy Kerr was chasing."

"It'll take several days to process her house and go through her computer files," Alaric warned.

"Let's go find out for ourselves then," Kevin said. "Right from the horse's mouth."

Chapter 12

As they drove out of town on their way to Churchill Road, Kevin glanced over at Heather. "How are you holding up?"

It had been a long, trying day for her. She'd removed her jacket and tossed it on the back seat, and her navy polo shirt was wrinkled and showing perspiration stains at the armpits. She stared straight ahead through the windshield, her eyes hidden behind her sunglasses.

"Thank god for pharmaceuticals," she said.

"Hell of a day."

"Yeah."

There was something in her tone that bothered him. "Did you know Maynard well?"

"Yeah. He was an asshole."

"I didn't know that."

"You haven't been around here long enough."

They drove in silence for a while. Finally she looked at him over the top of her glasses. "Stop wracking your brain. It's making a grinding noise that's getting on my nerves."

"Sorry."

"I take meds for chronic depression, all right? No big deal. It was a joke, Kev. Like it's helping me cope with all this shit right now."

He looked over at her. "I'm sorry. I didn't know."

"Well, that's the general idea, Kev. Medicate and soldier on." She finally glanced over at him. "But enough about me. Condolences to you on the loss of your father."

"Thanks."

"Were you close?"

"Very, very far apart. His idea, which I came to agree with."

"I'm sorry to hear that."

"Don't be. It wasn't a problem."

They arrived at the entrance of Drummond Metal and Scrap. A man in a safety vest and white hard hat was in the process of closing the gates. Kevin edged up, and when the guy came around to the driver's side, he lowered the window.

"Sorry," the man said, "we're closed. Open tomorrow at seven thirty."

Kevin badged him. "We're looking for the manager. Is he still here?"

"Mr. Prescott. Sure. Straight ahead. Brick bungalow on the right."

"Thanks." Kevin raised his window and rolled ahead, watching in his rear-view mirror as the gates closed behind them.

As junkyards went, it seemed pretty tidy and organized. On the left was a scale of the type used to weigh vehicles before and after unloading their materials. Beyond that was a tread tractor with a tall crane and a grapple on it, like an eagle's talons. It was working at a pile of metal, scooping it up and dropping it into a contraption that Kevin guessed might be a baler. Another rig had a big magnet on it, and it seemed to be separating ferrous scrap from non-ferrous.

He stopped at the brick bungalow just as a man was coming out the door, cramming a white hard hat on his head. He was stout and middle-aged, wearing the same safety coveralls that everyone else in sight was wearing. He stopped as Kevin and Heather got out of the car.

"Sorry, folks, we're closed for the day. Gate shouldn't still be open."

Heather waggled her badge, which was fastened to a lanyard around her neck. "OPP. We're looking for Peter White."

"I'm Harry Prescott. Pete's around here somewhere, I'm just not sure where. Can I help you?"

"You're the manager, aren't you?"

"Yeah, that's right. What's this about?"

"We're investigating the shooting death of Dorothy Kerr. We understand she was out here talking to you folks not long ago. What was that all about?"

Prescott held up a hand. "Whoa, hold on now, missy. I don't know anything about anyone getting shot, and second of all, that woman talked to Pete, not to me."

"For one thing," Heather bristled, "you call me *detective*, not missy. And second, you might want to find Mr. White for us, like, right now, before I start looking around here for things to talk about with my friends in regulatory places."

Prescott unclipped a push-to-talk communicator from his belt. "Pete. Can you come to the office?"

The comm crackled. "Can it wait? We're in the middle of something."

"No, it can't wait. OPP."

Silence for a moment. "I'll be right there."

Prescott clipped the comm back on his belt, gave Heather a look, turned on his heel, and went back into the office.

"What a sweetheart," Heather said. "If he likes cats and sushi, we might have the start of a wonderful relationship."

It took White only a minute or so to walk through the yard to the office. Kevin noted his confident stride and his greetings to employees as he passed. He was mid-thirties and tall. His dark hair stuck out from underneath his grimy white hard hat. His beard split in a grin as he reached them, holding out a hand.

"Pete White. How can I help you folks today?"

They showed their identification and shook hands with him. "We're investigating the shooting death of Dorothy Kerr," Heather said. "We understand she talked to you not long ago about a story she was working on."

"Yeah, yeah." Pete tipped his hat back. "I heard what happened on the radio. That's terrible."

"What kind of questions was she asking you?"

"The predictable kind. She obviously thought we were buying copper under the table, you know, stuff people steal from work sites and rip out of walls. That's the big thing these days. Copper's a hot commodity, and the thieves have to sell it somewhere, right? She figured it must be to us."

"Interview got kind of heated, did it? She got under your skin?"

"Well, nobody likes to be accused of being crooked, but I did my best to change her mind. I took her around and showed her where we receive and process our copper, how the transactions work, all the information captured in real time and transmitted to our computer in the office and automatically added to the database. Seller's ID, date and time stamp, the works. I showed her a typical monthly report, with all the entries for purchases and for sales to our copper buyers. They always balance. Right to the pound. Then I showed her a security cam setup that monitors the area."

He took out a pair of work gloves and twisted them in his hand. "Like I say, copper's the thing these days. We buy and sell a lot of it. Our current price is four dollars and fifty cents a pound, and our mark-up when we sell it brings us a nice profit. Really nice. We don't need to buy stuff under the table and put everything at risk. It doesn't make sense."

"How did she take all this? Was she buying any of it?"

"I don't know. She would have been a good poker player. But so am I. When I was at school, I paid the rent on my apartment in London with my Saturday night winnings. I could tell she didn't have anything specific on us, just a general tip that *some* company in the area was receiving stolen copper. Could be the guys in Smiths Falls, right? Who knows?"

"Did you tell her that?"

Pete shook his head. "That's not how it works. What they do is their business and not mine. I just went out of my way to explain that we're successful enough that we don't have to take those kinds of risk. I can give you the same tour I gave her, if you like."

"Maybe later." Heather looked around. "Where's your dog?"

He frowned. "At home. Why?"

"Doesn't every place like this have a junkyard dog? You know, Cannibal the Rottenweiler or whatever?"

Pete snorted. "Patsy's a golden retriever, and she stays at home. I don't particularly like dogs that bite, so our security is strictly high-tech."

"You've said a couple of times that business is good," Kevin said. "How good?"

"You've got access to all those numbers through our monthly reports," he said. "Let me put it to you this way. This isn't your grandfather's scrap metal world. Every year, eleven million metric tonnes are recovered and recycled in Canada, and the industry generates more than ten billion dollars annually. Believe me, we're getting a nice piece of the pie, but we work our asses off around here to earn it."

"How many times did she come around to see you?" Heather asked.

"Twice. The first time she talked to me, as I was telling you. The second time, it was Harry. I wasn't here that day. He basically threw her out after five minutes. That was it."

"What did Harry say to you about it afterward?"

Pete laughed. "I can't repeat a lot of it. My mother expects me to go to church every Sunday, and if I let that kind of language cross my lips I'd have a lot of explaining to do. But I can paraphrase. He's not very good around women, as you probably noticed, and he said a lot of pretty raw stuff about her that had nothing to do with the story she was working on. As far as *that* was concerned, he thought she was barking up the wrong tree and trying to stir up sewage and cause trouble where there was none to begin with. That sort of thing."

Heather nodded. "Had this kind of trouble with Harry before, have you?"

"Not really. Not this kind, anyway. A few customer complaints about his, ah, interpersonal skills. But since we moved him into the office we don't get a lot of that these days. Besides, most of the guys who come in here, the home renovators and contractors, have a pretty thick crust. They can dish it out a lot better than he does. So it's not really a big deal."

"You're saying you don't get a lot of female customers?"

"I'm saying he generally doesn't have any contact with our female customers."

Kevin caught Heather's eye and raised a brow. She shrugged.

"Thanks for your time, Mr. White," he said.

Chapter 13

Two victims.

Two homes.

Two teams gathering forensic evidence, such as it was, while building a picture of private lives cut short by murder. Intrusive? Yes. Productive? Maybe. Avoidable? No.

Pierce was attending the search of 2117 Concession Street, Apartment 9, the home of Provincial Constable Terence Maynard. It was a two-bedroom condo on the fourth floor of a six-storey building located at the northeast corner of town. The place was managed by a numbered company which Alaric (through perseverance and creative research) was able to connect to a company called Bridgewater Realty, headquartered in Vaughan, Ontario.

Pierce watched Identification Constable Cole Sullivan and two SOCOs process the apartment. The kitchen was a galley-type affair with nearly new appliances, plenty of cupboard space, and an island that separated it from the dining area-living room combination. The shelves were well stocked and the refrigerator held a decent assortment of produce, dairy products, and beverages, including beer. In the freezer were several packages of chicken legs, ground beef, and steak. Pierce concluded that Maynard did his own cooking. Might even have enjoyed it.

A widescreen television dominated the living room, with a stand below it for the cable box and a DVD player. Browsing through a nearby shelf, Pierce saw that Maynard's taste in entertainment tipped toward action movies, vintage war films, westerns, and slasher-type horror. There were a few pornographic titles mixed in, but not so you'd notice them unless you were looking closely. On the walls were framed posters for *Gone in Sixty Seconds* and *The Fast and The Furious*, and next to the sliding balcony door a bookshelf filled with plastic model cars.

In the bedroom, Pierce looked at a neatly made double bed, a dresser, and a closet with T-shirts, jeans, and extra uniform wear all carefully arranged on hangers. On the wall was a photograph of a young woman smiling self-consciously at the camera. It looked as though it had been taken in a studio in the early 1970s; maybe at the Sears store, back when they used to have a small photography section next to the children's clothing department. Pierce guessed that this was Maynard's mother, Roberta.

Pierce saw her in another framed photo on the bedside stand. She was much older, her hair white and her face lined with years of care, and she was posing with another woman in her thirties who was obviously her daughter. This would be Maynard's sister, Pierce guessed. He couldn't remember her name right off the top of his head.

Pierce caught his reflection in the dresser mirror. His hair would need to be trimmed very soon. A couple of horizontal lines showed on his forehead. He was only thirty-seven, but he figured the camera at this point would probably add at least five years, maybe eight. He tugged at the lapels on his jacket, fitting it better across his shoulders. Looked good. It was a lightweight wool suit, blue, with a good drape, that he liked to wear in spring. It was breathable and wrinkle resistant. A good working suit that complemented his dark hair and medium complexion.

He left the room and entered the other bedroom, which Maynard had converted into a study. There was a small desk-and-chair set with an outdated computer, monitor, and printer, along with a three-drawer filing cabinet next to it. Ident would be going through Maynard's e-mail, his social media interactions, and saved documents for any sign of trouble that might lead to a suspect. The metal cabinet offered files of household bills he'd paid for with cheques before switching to online billing; personal copies of letters and memos from his years of service with the OPP; pay stubs; and a drawer full of receipts from various companies he'd bought things from over the years.

The rest of the room was given over to a worktable, two plastic supply cabinets on wheels, and a large shelving unit filled with plastic car models. Another such model was partially assembled on the worktable, as though Maynard had been working on it before his death.

"Man," Cole Sullivan said, coming up beside him, "he was definitely an enthusiast."

"Model cars?"

Sullivan laughed at the confusion in Pierce's voice. "Yeah, no shit. My brother was big into it when we were kids. Take a look at this one, for example." He pointed a gloved finger at a blue Pontiac Trans Am with white and chrome trim. "You could pay a couple hundred for it on eBay, plus the shipping. Revell was my brother's favourite brand."

"Wow." Pierce frowned at shelf after shelf of model cars displayed with the original boxes in which the kits had been sold. He thought of all the hours Maynard would have put into assembling and painting all these models, dozens of them, and it surprised him that someone would spend their time this way. Between work and family, Pierce himself didn't have a lot of time for a hobby.

Sullivan scanned the shelves. "There were four main companies back then: Revell, AMC, MPC, and Monogram. They churned out thousands of one-to-twenty-five scale model kits. This one, AMC, ran from the late forties to the late seventies." He pointed at a 1968 Torino model pace car. "Three hundred, easy. They often timed their new models to releases of new cars by the automobile manufacturers, who sometimes chipped in a lot of cash to make sure they were getting the details correct, because they were a great promotional tool. Now? Serious nostalgia stuff."

Pierce nodded, moving away.

"You share a bedroom with somebody for eight years," Sullivan said, "and you pick up a lot of stuff whether you want to or not. Joey talked and I listened, I guess."

Sullivan turned around. He was alone in the room.

A second victim. Another home. Another team from the forensics unit, this one led by Identification Constable Jayne Witten, with Heather Hope attending as the crime scene detective overseeing the evidence collection process.

She'd waved Kevin home before jumping in her car to follow Witten and the big white van, knowing that he had a family to get back to, while she had an empty apartment waiting for her and a take-out pizza she'd have to remember to pick up when this was finally done.

They were particularly interested to know whether the person who'd killed Dorothy Kerr—while assuming, of course, ballistics pending, that she and Maynard had been killed in the same action—had entered the house at any point. For this reason, Witten's team of SOCOs was investing a lot of their time collecting latent prints from every conceivable surface that this person might have touched: doorknobs; door frames; the edges of doors; kitchen chairs; kitchen countertops; the kitchen table;

window ledges; window sashes—the list went on and on. It was going to take a while. Heather bit her lip, trying to remember which pizzerias in town stayed open after midnight.

Heather wandered from room to room on the main floor, taking it all in. There were two more floors upstairs, and an unfinished cellar below. Witten had dispatched extra SOCOs to cover these other levels, but the main action was thought to have taken place here, between the side entrance leading through the mud room into the kitchen, and through the door next to the antique wood stove into the back summer kitchen and beyond, outside, where she'd been chased down and shot dead.

What did Heather know about Dorothy so far? Fifty-six years old, she'd never married, preferring to live alone. A journalist, she'd been intelligent, focused, and reliable. She belonged to a quilting group. She'd been born in Halifax but her father, Robert Kerr, had been born and raised in this house, which had been owned by several previous generations of Kerrs.

Yes, a will had been bagged and tagged. It would be examined and analyzed later, Witten said.

Witten had given her a quick tour before heading off to the kitchen. There was a front entrance that was never used, complete with a beautiful antique hall rack, umbrella stands filled with carved walking sticks, and a change table with an antique china bowl. To the right was a large room Witten explained was the front room. It would have been used by the family for personal time, hence the baby grand piano, antique gramophone and extensive collection of 78s, and large rockers and wingback chairs for sitting and reading, or knitting, or other quiet means of passing the time.

Across the hall was another large room that was more formally furnished. The parlour, Witten said. For receiving visitors and entertaining guests. The antiques were just as breathtakingly valuable in here, and Witten remarked that she could only guess at what the stuff would all go for at auction.

A short hallway, running alongside the staircase leading up

to the second floor, led past the front room to the kitchen. Here they would be spending most of their time, and Witten observed that they'd already lifted latents from the door that were different than the various prints found elsewhere in the room.

Heather left her to it, and drifted back through the hallway into the front room.

Then across the hall into the parlour.

There was no sign of Dorothy Kerr in either of these rooms. They were filled with objects her father had grown up with, and his father before that—Kerr family heirlooms. Assets representing a substantial cash value, yeah, but things that had held meaning for other people long dead and buried, but perhaps not so much for Dorothy.

It was doubtful that she'd ever played the piano, for example. The keyboard cover was closed and filmed with dust. The gramophone was the same. Upstairs, Heather knew, having made a brief trip to the second floor for a quick look around, was an entertainment room equipped with a flatscreen TV, a set-top box connected to the satellite dish on the roof, and other items new enough that Dorothy would have bought them herself, for her own use. But down here, she'd obviously had no place among the artifacts of her family's past.

It must have been like living in a museum. How strange was that? Heather could only imagine. When her parents retired, they'd sold their factory and farmhouse in Keene and had taken only a few extra things with them to Bermuda, selling everything else in an auction that Heather had chosen not to attend. She'd kept her childhood dresser, the kitchen table and pressback chairs, and a few dishes that she liked, but allowed everything else from the Hope family home to disappear into the truck beds and trunks of strangers to be hauled off only God knew where.

It was the way it should be, as far as she was concerned. Life was short enough as it was, and couldn't be tied up and preserved in inanimate objects.

Other than comic books, of course. They were the sole

exception to her rule.

Was there a stash of comic books salted away somewhere in this house? A scrap of Dorothy's own childhood, ever available to relive with pleasure in the quiet hours?

Somehow Heather doubted it very much.

Chapter 14

It was a forty-minute drive for Ellie from the Perth detachment office to her cottage home on Sparrow Lake, so she spent the time on the hands-free updating Commissioner Dart on the day's progress. The sun had just dropped below the treeline, but orange coals still flickered through the gaps in the branches. She glanced at her dashboard clock and saw that it was ten minutes before nine o'clock in the evening.

It had been a long day, and she was tired.

After refreshing Dart's memory on their dual-track investigation, she admitted they were still uncertain as to which victim was the intended target and which was collateral damage.

"At the moment we're leaning toward Maynard," she said. "Our interrogation of the driver he stopped just before his death, Earl Black, was inconclusive, but he assaulted one of the arresting officers and we'll hold him on that while we execute the search warrants."

"Which will be when?"

"They'll probably get started a little before midnight," she said, glancing at the clock again, "and it'll run past dawn, I expect."

"The reason I'm asking is, I want to know if we can announce an arrest tomorrow."

"The press conference's at eleven o'clock, correct?"

"Correct."

Ellie paused to decide what she wanted to say. She hated being hurried, and taking shortcuts to fit an investigative process into someone else's timelines went against the grain. She understood the pressure Dart was facing, however, and knew he was asking her to make a decision on Black as a suspect before eleven o'clock tomorrow morning. After a moment's thought, she chose a middle ground.

"We can't hurry these things too much. If we find a handgun, we'll rush it to ballistics. At the same time, we'll fast track the shoe treads and all the rest of it as much as we possibly can, but we may find it's all inconclusive. If you want my advice, the best you're probably going to be able to say is that a person of interest was arrested on other charges, but the investigation continues."

There was silence on the line for a moment. "I suppose you're right. We have to manage everyone's expectations at this point. The public's, the union's, the media's. Mine."

"Yes, sir. We're working around the clock, but unless we're extremely lucky, it's going to take a bit of time to get it right."

"Let me know by ten tomorrow, will you, Ellie?"

"Yes, sir."

"Let's catch the bastard, shall we?"

"Yes, sir."

Chapter 15

It was after sunset when Kevin finally got home. The stars in the sky overhead faded out as he drove into town, washed away by the street lamps and car headlights around him. When he turned into his driveway and shut off the engine, he felt the weight of fatigue on his shoulders. An awful, stressful day.

He got out and leaned against the car for a moment, looking around. Their duplex occupied the last lot on Cockburn Street before a strip of the Last Duel Park edging the Tay River, and it was far enough from the traffic on Gore Street to be quiet.

Almost as quiet as their little bungalow in Sparrow Lake had been.

Lights were on behind the curtains on both sides of the duplex. A shadow moved across the living room window closest to the driveway. With a little jolt of electricity, he recognized Janie's silhouette, coming in from the kitchen to sit down in her favourite spot on the couch.

On the other side of the duplex he could see no movement, but he knew Barb, Janie's mother, was likely watching TV. She might be knitting something for one of the kids. He and Janie had bought both sides and offered the other half to Barb, whose agreement with the condominium she was renting in Brockville had come up for renewal. At half the rent she'd been paying before, and with her family right next door to her, it was a good arrangement all around.

Thankfully, she was Kevin's third-biggest fan, so he felt comfortable with her there. Caitlyn, of course, being his biggest fan by far. Followed closely by Janie.

Went he went inside, he was surprised to find the kids were all still up, waiting for him. It was a stampede. Josh was closest, so he wrapped his arms around Kevin's thighs and held on for dear life. Brendan was next, tall enough now to encircle his neck in a death grip. Then it was Caitlyn, a willowy sixteen-year-old, slipping her arms around his waist from behind him and squeezing tightly.

"Let him breathe," Janie said from the couch.

"It's okay," Kevin said. "I'm okay."

"We were worried," Brendan said.

"Come in with your mom, and we'll talk about it for a minute. Then it's time for bed, monkeys."

Caitlyn sat down on one side of her mom on the couch, and Brendan the other side. Josh refused to let go, so Kevin hiked the boy's feet up on top of his shoes and walked him into the living room the way he would have when he was smaller. At six, Josh was already showing that he was going to have Kevin's physique—he was an inch over four feet and weighed fifty-seven pounds, both above the average for his age.

"Josh, for godsakes let your father sit down," Janie said.

Kevin made it to his recliner. Josh reluctantly released him and sat down on the floor, his back against the edge of the coffee table. Kevin collapsed, shot out the foot rest, and put his head back.

"Have you eaten? There's lasagne."

"Nanna made it," Caitlyn said. "It's really good."

"I'm fine, Janie. I had a sandwich earlier. Don't ask me what it was or when I had it. I'm not hungry."

"Were you there when the officer was shot?" Brendan squeezed his hands between his knees. It was obviously his chief concern.

Right away Kevin knew he should have called home at some point to reassure everyone that he was all right. What an idiot. What had he been thinking? Of course they would have been sick with worry that he'd somehow been caught up in it. Maybe hurt; maybe even shot, like Maynard. This sort of thing very seldom happened—Mark Allore being the last colleague who'd been shot on duty, thankfully non-fatally, several years ago—and here Kevin had been in full detective mode all day. It hadn't occurred to him to think about what his family was going through, listening to the news on the radio.

"No, I was down in Brockville when it happened. Constable Maynard was shot this morning in Drummond, near Mississippi Lake."

Caitlyn nodded. "You were at Grandpa's funeral."

"Yeah. We can talk about that later."

"Did the constable have a family?" she asked.

"He was divorced. I think his wife lives in Bowmanville. They didn't have any kids."

"Why did they shoot him?" Josh wanted to know. "Were they having a fight?"

"We don't know yet, Josh. It doesn't look like it, though. Constable Maynard was sitting in his car at the time."

"Maybe it was someone who just hates cops," Brendan muttered.

"I guess this is something we've never really talked about before as a family. Cait, you and I have gone over it a few times, but it hasn't really come up yet with you boys."

"Are you proud of Kevin?" Janie asked. "Proud he's a cop?"

"Damned right," Brendan muttered again.

"Language. So am I. Being married to a cop is hard. Every day when your father goes out the door, I'm not sure if the next time I see him it'll be in a hospital emergency room. Been there; done that; got the T-shirt. Not fun at all."

Brendan frowned at her. "But you don't show it. You always seem okay. Don't you care what happens to him?"

"Of course I do," Janie flared. "What do you think I am, some kind of cement head or something? Jesus, Brendan."

"Your mother's learned to compartmentalize it," Kevin said. "That's the key. For all of us. It's what I had to learn to do when I first started out at a policeman. You see horrible things on the job and people say nasty stuff, but you learn after a while to take it and put it into a little box and store it in the back of your head out of the way. Concentrate on the things in front of you that you can control. The other stuff, that you can't control, leave it in the little box until all the bad feelings have faded, and when the time is right, you can take it out, deal with it, and throw it away."

"We can talk about it later, Bren." Caitlyn leaned on her mother's arm to look at him. "It's easy when you know what to do."

Kevin noticed a tear rolling down Josh's cheek. He held out his arms. "Come here, big guy."

Josh crawled into his lap. Kevin gave him a hug. "I should have explained to you a long time ago what my job is like. Constable Maynard was a traffic cop. He dealt with the public every day. He was what we call a front-line officer. I used to do that job too, Josh, but I don't any more. I'm a detective now. That means I go into a situation after the bad stuff has already happened, and it's my job to figure out who did it. There's not as much risk. I'm almost never in any kind of danger at all. Pretty boring, for the most part."

Josh sniffled. Kevin caught Caitlyn's eye. She was staring

at him, listening to every word, and he understood she knew he was over-simplifying things for Josh's sake. It was the truth, but maybe not the complete truth. But she gave him a tiny nod to encourage him.

"Please don't worry, Josh. Brendan. We love each other, and that's what'll get us through hard times like this. Okay?"

"What happens when you find the guy?" Brendan asked. "Will he try to shoot you then?"

"I sure as heck hope not. Anyway, I'll be surrounded by guys wearing uniforms and body armour, so he'd have to get through them to get to me, and that'll never happen."

"Time for bed," Janie said, standing up. "Come on, Josh. Let's give Kevin a little alone time."

Kevin squeezed his son again. "I'm fine, pal. No problems."

He watched them file out of the room. Caitlyn stopped at his chair and leaned down to kiss his forehead. "I love you," she murmured.

"I love you too, Cait."

Chapter 16

Ellie ate a light supper, macaroni casserole and potato salad from the back of the fridge, and then decided she needed some air.

She poured a glass of Jack Daniels, neat, and took it out onto the back deck. She leaned on the railing, staring out into the night.

Clouds passed rapidly overhead, dark smudges, and then the moon emerged to throw faint silver light across the view in front of her. The boughs of the evergreen trees around her hissed and bobbed, and sparks flickered on the surface of the lake as waves dipped and rose, disturbed by the wind.

She drank half the glass in one swallow and left it on the railing to walk down to the water's edge. It took a few extra steps in the gloom until she found the pail she'd started keeping there for times like this.

When she'd brought it home from the store a month or so ago, it had held dog biscuits. Reggie made short work of them, and she'd tossed the empty pail into the recycling bin.

A day or two later she was out on the deck, smoking a cigarette and watching Dean Othman, the next-door neighbours' boy, skipping stones off the end of their dock. He had a pile of stones next to his foot, and he methodically chose the flattest one, bounced it in his hand once or twice, then flung it out over the surface of the water. After a while, Ellie found herself counting the skips. It was almost mesmerizing. Typically, Dean didn't show whether he was enjoying himself or not, but he kept at it until the stones were all gone, so Ellie guessed that he must have gotten something good out of the whole thing.

He went back inside, and by the time Ellie had finished her cigarette and dropped it into the tomato juice can she kept out there as an ashtray, an idea had occurred to her. She fetched the biscuit bucket out of the recycling bin and took it up the slope to the gravel lane passing her cottage. She filled it with stones that were smaller than a hardball but larger than a golf ball. Round, not flat. Then she carried it down past the cottage to the water's edge. She picked out a stone experimentally and threw it as hard and as far as she could.

You throw like a girl, she told herself.

That'll change.

A few days after that she came home early after having attended a particularly upsetting hit-and-run on County Road 34 just past Calabogie. A teenage boy had been walking along the wrong side of the highway when he was hit by a passing car. His shirt became caught up in the undercarriage, and he was dragged for almost a kilometre before the shirt tore away and the boy rolled onto the shoulder. While she was at the scene, a woman was stopped at the perimeter. It turned out to be the boy's mother. He was supposed to be coming to his grandmother's house for a visit, but the person giving him a ride forgot, and he'd apparently decided to walk.

It turned out he was the same age as Dean.

It was likely to become a ritual—the whisky, the pail of stones, and a few tears of frustration as she emptied the bucket, throw after throw.

Now, in the dark, it was her anger at the senseless, animalistic murders of Terry Maynard and Dorothy Kerr that gave strength to her arm as she picked out a stone and fired it into the darkness. The moon had momentarily been occluded by a cloud, so she didn't see its flight, only heard the distance splash.

Grunt.

Splash.

Dammit.

Splash.

Twice in the head. Never saw it coming.

Splash.

Splash.

Stone after stone, flung into the darkness in defiance of the senselessness of human existence.

Chapter 17

Kevin discovered that he was hungry after all, so he nuked a plate of Barb's lasagne and ate at the kitchen table while Janie sat with Josh in his bedroom, consoling him in between bedtime stories.

Caitlyn was right; the lasagne was really good.

When he was done eating, he put the dishes in the dishwasher, grabbed a six-pack from the back of the fridge, and went outside. Navigating by the light of the moon, he walked down their backyard to a large boulder at the edge of their property. It was close enough to the river that he could hear the water moving in the darkness, although he couldn't see it. He could also smell it, a fresh, fishy odour that he'd come to find pleasant and calming.

Right now, though, his thoughts were jumbled. The trip to Drummond Scrap Metal had triggered an association and an unwelcome memory of his father in one of his typically arrogant moments.

When Kevin was a boy, there was an old man who used to drive around town looking for cast-off appliances, eavestroughing, and other scrap metal that he could salvage and sell for a few bucks. Back then, it wasn't the booming megabusiness that it seemed to be now for Drummond and other upscale metal recyclers. It was poor people, mostly out-of-work men in their fifties with an alcohol problem and an old pickup truck, selling junk to coarse good old boys behind barbed-wire fences looking for something for nothing.

The people next door to the Walkers had moved out, and they'd left an old stove and refrigerator behind on the front lawn. The next day, the old man happened to show up. He got out of his truck and looked the appliances over. He knocked on the door of the house, but there was no one there. The place was empty.

Kevin was in the driveway, bouncing a tennis ball against the wall and catching it with his baseball glove. His father was sitting in their enclosed front porch, sipping from a mickey. Johnny saw the old man look uncertainly over at their house and, heaving himself out of his lawn chair, went out for a little fun.

"Folks next door move out, did they?" the old man asked.

"Maybe they did," Johnny said, "and maybe they didn't."

"Was wondering, because the curtains are gone and I can't see nobody inside."

"I think they all died from some disease. Polio or smallpox or something."

Kevin held the ball in his glove, mortified. He wanted to run away somewhere, maybe down to the tracks just to get away from his father's nastiness, but he couldn't move. He was frozen in place.

The old man frowned. He pulled out a large red handkerchief from the back pocket of his coveralls. Pushing up the bill of his baseball cap, he mopped the sweat from his face and stuffed the handkerchief away again.

"They say anything about the fridge and stove?"

Johnny took a quick hit from his mickey. "They gave them to me. Said I could sell them for ten bucks each. Want them or not?"

The old man's frown deepened. "Are you serious?"

"Need them for your kitchen? Maybe they work. You don't look like you could afford it, though. Tell you what I'm gonna do." He consulted his pint, swallowed, and snorted. "You can have the two of them for fifteen. Does your shack have electricity?"

The old man pulled his cap down over his eyes and nodded. "You have a real nice day, now."

He got into his truck and drove away.

Johnny turned around, a little unsteadily, and looked at Kevin. "That's how you take care of the riff-raff, kid. Don't ever forget it."

Kevin emptied his can of beer and opened another one. He took a sip and set it down beside him on the rock. After a moment, he heard footsteps approaching from behind. As Janie reached the rock, he picked up the can and moved over to make room for her.

"How's the scenery out here?"

"Dunno. I can't see it."

"Are you sure you're okay?"

"Yeah. Rough day."

She looked at the beer. "You really need that?"

He handed the can to her and watched her empty it thirstily. He seldom drank, in large part because of Johnny's alcoholism.

"You can have the rest," he said.

She tossed the can on the grass and held the rest of the six-pack on her lap.

"I'm sorry I didn't call," he said. "It was completely brainless of me."

"You were at work. A lot of heavy shit going down. Don't worry about it."

"I should have thought."

"Forget it, champ. How was the funeral?"

"Quiet. Total bullshit, but that's what Carla wanted to hear, so. Needed to hear, I guess."

"What's she like?"

"Sad. Nice. God knows how she put up with him all those years."

"See anybody you know?"

"A couple of uncles. Johnny's crew, what's left of them." He shook his head. "My mom's brother came. Emmett. Said he wanted to look in the coffin to make sure the son of a bitch was really dead."

Janie snorted.

"At the end of the day, I guess that's why I was there, too."

"Now can you move on, Kev? Just forget about him and move on?"

"Yeah. That's the plan."

"Can I tell you something?"

A little shock of electricity went through him. He thought he recognized that tone. "What?"

"Christ, Kev, you don't have to sound like you're being lined up in front of a frigging firing squad."

"Sorry."

"Jeez. Now maybe I won't bother."

"I said I was sorry."

She sighed. "Okay. You remember, no, you probably don't, but anyway, about six weeks ago you got all athletic on me and your condom came off. Remember?"

He didn't, but—

"Caitlyn hopes it's a girl. How about you?"

The darkness inside him lifted away as though it had never been there, and he realized he was grinning. He reached out and found her wrist. She entwined her fingers in his. He squeezed.

"A girl," he said, "would be absolutely wonderful. Completely, totally wonderful."

Chapter 18

Heather couldn't sleep.

She'd tried warm milk, melatonin gummies, self-hypnosis, and reading a bunch of comics from her bedside pile—not to mention her brown noise machine, which ran every night—but nothing was working. Sleep was somewhere around the corner, hiding from her.

She got up and made a cup of caffeine-free tea. She turned on her laptop and settled down in front of it. The day's events were circling around in her head like a pack of bush wolves, jacking her stress level through the roof. Maybe if she did a little rooting around on the Internet, she could dig up a couple of things she and Kevin could use tomorrow.

She went to the *Sentinel* website first and found a list of Dorothy Kerr's stories. She sent it to the printer, knowing that Kevin liked working with paper, and then began to skim them, looking for something, anything, to pop out as suspicious or controversial.

She'd covered some serious stuff, including child disappearances, a murder trial, buildings in Perth found to be in violation of the fire code, a local abattoir fined for slaughtering calves that were younger than allowed by the regulations, and a story about local participants in the 2022 Freedom Convoy protest in Ottawa.

Her eyebrows went up when she found Earl Black's name mentioned in this last piece. Seems he'd borrowed his brother-in-law's F-150 and driven to Ottawa with Canadian flags stuck in the box, staying there for several days before coming home when his vacation time at the factory ran out.

Had he become angry at Dorothy for mentioning him by name in the article? It was something to ask him about.

She retrieved the list of Dorothy's stories from the printer and, after scanning it, thought that perhaps she should run another query of the *Sentinel* database to see if Dorothy's name came up in the letters to the editor.

Jackpot. Her piece on the illegal Ottawa protest had generated a huge response, spread across several issues. As she scanned these, one name in particular popped out at her. Someone by the name of Thomas Searle had written a long, bitter epistle that the paper had run in full. In it, he waxed vitriolic against Prime Minister Trudeau, vaccinations of any kind at any time, the deliberate and systematic erosion of freedom in Canada by a corrupt, dictatorial federal government, and so on and so forth.

Heather went back to Dorothy's article and found "Searle Meat and Potatoes, North Burgess" among the list of local participants in the protest. Her sleepless brain seized on the name, and she opened a new tab to take a look at Dorothy's story on the abattoir.

Bingo. The business in question was, in fact, Searle Meat and Potatoes. In her article, it was described as a family business owned by Thomas Searle. His sons and wife also worked there.

Dorothy quoted Searle near the end of her piece. He railed on about government regulations and government interference in small businesses trying to make a living.

Heather flipped back to the Freedom Convoy article and found Searle's business listed among the participants. Dorothy Kerr seemed to have fastened on Thomas Searle as a target for her investigative stories. His participation in the 2022 occupation and regulatory infractions against his meat business had made it into print in a way that he obviously didn't appreciate. Was there fire behind his smoke?

She suddenly felt very tired. Closing the browser, she shut down the laptop and pushed away from the desk. She sat there for a while, unwilling to move.

In the glow of the desk lamp she could see her reflection in the black laptop screen. Her cheeks looked like a chipmunk's. She needed to find a way to lose twenty pounds without changing her diet, her lifestyle, or anything else except the shape of her body. No, thirty pounds.

Right.

She'd been the butt of more than one of Maynard's sarcastic observations around the detachment office. He and Skelton in particular seemed to have something against well-fed women. "I see you've been working out at the gym" was a favourite, along with cracks about her ergonomic desk chair and asking about the current price of corn on the commodities market. Ha ha. Close enough to be harassment, but too lame to take seriously.

She was upset, very upset, that someone had put two into Maynard's brainpan this morning. She'd strongly disliked the guy and preferred never to be in the same room with him, but he was a fellow officer, for chrissakes. Nobody murdered a fellow officer and got away with it. An attack on one was an attack on them all. Pure and simple.

She got up and wandered into her bedroom. As she passed her dresser, she wanted to look at the picture that sat there, front and centre, but she resisted the temptation.

She crawled under the covers and turned off the bedside lamp. She could see the shape of the dresser in the darkness, and that seemed to be enough for now. She rolled over onto her side and closed her eyes.

The picture was a photograph of her late husband, Scott Webster. They'd met when she was going to school in Kingston and he was a cadet at the Royal Military College. It took about thirty seconds for them to click and three months to tie the knot.

A year after he graduated from RMC, Scott deployed to Afghanistan, where he was killed by a roadside improvised explosive device. His death changed her life. She abandoned her vague plans of becoming an English teacher and applied to the OPP. She was accepted, aced all her courses at police college, and was deployed to Prince Edward County as a provincial constable.

The photo on the dresser was the only one of Scott that she kept on display. It had been taken along the waterfront in Kingston, just before his fatal deployment. He was sitting on a park bench, the water behind him, each elbow hooked over the back of the bench, a shit-eating grin on his face. He'd been saying naughty things to her as she tried to take the picture, and it was a miracle she'd been able to hold the camera still long enough to get this one magnificent shot of him.

She looked at the photo only once a day, each morning when she went to the dresser for a pair of underwear while getting dressed. She would look at the picture, hike her eyebrows, and give him that shit-eating grin right back.

It was a ritual. It kept her from going insane, because the pain never seemed to go away.

She figured it never would.

Chapter 19

The next morning, which was Tuesday, Ellie was up early and out on the road thirty minutes after sunrise. She drove to the crime scene and found Inspector Grayson Kennedy on site, on the phone to someone. She waited politely until he was finished before stepping under the canopy and approaching.

"Good morning, Ellie. Did you get any sleep?"

"Some. How are we looking here, Gray?"

Kennedy picked up a take-out cup of coffee and drank. "As you no doubt noticed, we reopened Highway 7 late last night, and we've lifted the shelter-in-place order for the area. Ditches have been swept from one end to the other. Nothing to report. ERT just had their shift change, so they've resumed door-to-doors at the campsite and the Landing itself."

"How long will you keep this road closed?"

"Might be a few days yet."

"What about you? Did you get any sleep?"

He smiled faintly. "A few hours, in my car. The sergeant brought me some breakfast from Mickey Dee's. Haven't missed a beat."

"Call me if anything rings the bell."

"Will do, Ellie. Give my best to the commissioner, will you?"

Ellie gave him a two-fingered salute and left. As she drove to Perth, it occurred to her that she'd neglected to do a breath test on Kennedy. But his eyes had been clear, if tired-looking, and his voice had been rock steady. She didn't think there was anything to worry about at the moment as far as he was concerned.

When she reached the detachment office, she called Dave Martin for an update. Like everyone else, he was essentially available around the clock, but this time his phone went directly to voicemail and she had to call the lab on their direct line in order to reach him.

"Sorry, Ellie, my cellphone conked out. It's still charging. Looking for the latest?"

"Whatever you can give me."

"What I can give you is a summary. Our reports are being posted as we speak, and I'm sending stuff to Alaric that he can share with your team because I can't sit in on your nine o'clock."

"That's fine."

"I've gone over all our tire-track and footprint evidence, and I can give you the following. Earl Black's Jetta pulled over one metre and change from the end of Dorothy Kerr's driveway. Constable Maynard pulled up directly behind him. Maynard walked up to the Jetta, walked back, walked up again, no doubt to give him the ticket, and walked back again. There's no evidence to support the theory that Black got out and walked back to shoot Maynard while he sat in his cruiser."

"No footprint evidence, you're saying."

"Correct. Switching to tire tracks, the Jetta did an awkward turnaround, using the end of the driveway, and left the scene. As he did so, he passed over tracks we've matched to Dorothy Kerr's vehicle plus another set of tracks that I'll get to in a moment."

"There were two vehicles in Kerr's yard at the time of the traffic stop, is what you're saying."

"Correct. Now, that second vehicle is the dually you may have heard about. The evidence shows that it came down the Kerr driveway after Black left. It stopped at the end of the driveway and the driver got out. He walked across the road to Maynard's cruiser and back again. He drove away, passing over Black's tracks."

"Okay."

"I don't know what you're holding Black on, because I'm up to my neck in the lab and can't keep track of current events, but I'm telling you right now he didn't shoot Maynard. The driver of the dually did."

"All right. What else?"

"Ballistics are still pending. The bullets are still inside his head, so we'll get a look at them after the autopsy. It must have been a lower-calibre weapon, like a .22 or something. We'll know for sure soon enough. The sort of thing a guy might use for target shooting. Without a permit, right? We've seen this kind of thing before. The bullets slow down as they penetrate, then tumble and bounce around inside the brain, creating all kinds of fatal damage. Just as deadly as a through-and-through in the final analysis."

"Okay."

"I gotta go, Ellie. It's all in the case file. Give my best to the commissioner."

"Sure."

At nine o'clock the team convened for their morning meeting.

When everyone had arrived, Ellie closed the door and walked around to stand behind her chair.

"Am I going to have to jump up on the table and yell at everyone again this morning?"

There were a few chuckles and wan smiles. They all looked tired, and some were showing signs of stress. Even Heather Hope wasn't her usual, buoyant self. Instead of a comic-themed T-shirt she wore a navy polo shirt with the RMC crest on the left breast.

Ellie sat down. Team morale was not necessarily her purview, and she didn't consider herself particularly adept at the rah-rah stuff, but her heart went out to them.

"It's almost twenty-four hours since Constable Maynard was shot and killed, and we've already made a lot of progress toward finding his murderer. We've got a very busy day in front of us, and I know you're all champing at the bit to get going, but we'll take a few minute for some updates. Alaric, I understand you've been keeping tab on Ident's progress."

Alaric cleared his throat. He'd gone home last night for a few hours' sleep, and after showering had changed into a black cotton shirt with the sleeves rolled up, black denim jeans with a large cowboy-themed belt buckle, and he'd switched from the gold-framed glasses he'd worn yesterday to a pair with thick black frames. All of which matched his black hair and beard.

"Yes," he said, "Kate and I have been reading through their reports as they come in and cross-referencing them."

"They've been working around the clock," the young file co-ordinator confirmed. "There's a lot of stuff to process, but we're on top of it."

"I'm sure you are. Alaric, what are your first impressions?"

"Earl Black's not our guy."

"Please explain."

Alaric walked the team through the footprint and tire track evidence much as Dave Martin had done with Ellie this morning.

Doug Skelton was not happy. "Come on, Johnny Cash. Sounds like they screwed up the sequence of events. Black sure looks good for it to me."

"Well, *Doug*, he isn't." Alaric tapped the table with his finger. "You've got him on assault, sure, but you're going to have to be satisfied with that. He isn't the shooter. Period."

Bob Pierce stirred. "During our search of Black's property and vehicle we found a Browning HiPoint 9 mm, prohibited and improperly stored in the bedroom, and a quantity of ammunition. Are you saying that neither victim was killed with a nine?"

"Not categorically, no, but circumstantially, it sure looks like a .22. Ten bucks says that's what comes out of the heads of both victims."

"I'll take that bet," Skelton growled.

"All right," Ellie said. "Earl Black's off the table as of right now as a suspect. Sonja, charge him on the firearms offences. Doug, I want you and Bob to concentrate on Constable Maynard's past record of interactions with the public. Any recorded threats against him, any complaints, everything. See if somebody else jumps into the spotlight."

She turned to Heather. "Tell us what you know about Dorothy Kerr that we didn't know yesterday. Keep it brief. I'm leaving in five minutes."

"Sure." Heather cleared her throat. "Right now we're looking at a couple of stories she wrote for the *Sentinel* that got some of the readership upset. It's unclear how pissed the guys at Drummond Scrap Metal were about her investigation into stolen copper, but another local business got hit by her twice. Once on regulatory violations at their abattoir, and the other for their participation in the 2022 Freedom Convoy protest."

"Why's the protest relevant?" Ellie demanded.

Heather shifted nervously. "It's not, in and of itself. It's just that this guy, Thomas Searle, who owns the abattoir, turned into quite a letter-to-the-editor guy after she included his business in the list of participants. Libertarian-style rants. When the abattoir got hit with regulatory violations and her story on it ran a few months ago, he started in with the anti-government rhetoric, and *really* wasn't happy that she'd written him up again."

"All right. Follow up on Searle, and see if there's anything else to be had on the scrap metal business." Ellie stood up and looked at Sonja Freeling.

"If something pops, let me know."

"Will do. Give my best to the commissioner."

Ellie rolled her eyes and hurried out of the room.

In the parking lot, she started the Crown Vic's engine to get the air conditioning going. Then she plugged in her cellphone and made the hands-free call to Cecil Dart.

Chapter 20

Parking was almost impossible to find at the arena, but Ellie managed to claim a spot right at the far end of the lot between an OPP cruiser and a black Town Car that had probably made the trip down to Perth from Orillia.

She showed her identification to the uniformed officers screening arrivals at the main entrance and pushed her way through the crowd to Constable Rachel Townsend, who was deep in conversation with an impeccably dressed man in his early forties.

"Ellie," Rachel said, "this is Kerry McGuinness, our regional media co-ordinator. I'm not sure if you've met before. Kerry, Detective Inspector March."

Ellie shook his hand. "Everything set?"

"Yes. I'm going to start things off, then Commissioner Dart will take the floor for his official statement. Chief Superintendent

Malcolmsen will say a few words. Then I'll open it up to questions. Inspector Galvin is available to answer as appropriate. Can I count on you as well?"

"Sure," Ellie said. She hated speaking in public, but there was no point mentioning it here. It was one of the reasons they were paying her the big bucks.

McGuinness patted her on the shoulder, which was another thing she hated, and went off in search of the commissioner.

"He's very good," Rachel said. "He knows his stuff."

"Well, that's a relief." Ellie heard the sarcasm in her own voice, but couldn't help it. The regional commander, Jordan Malcolmson, had brought McGuinness in last year to fill the vacant regional media relations co-ordinator position rather than promote someone—Rachel, say—from within. Civilians often parachuted into middle-management and senior positions on the administrative side of things. Not much was said about it when they came with an impressive résumé and obvious knowledge and skills that fit the job. Kerry McGuinness met all those criteria. A former national newscaster with CBC News in Toronto, he'd defected to CTV to become their Parliament Hill correspondent and occasional political analyst. Apparently he'd been caught up in some internal friction and was looking for a quiet exit. He reached out to Mal and was fast-tracked into place. He was young and ambitious, married with small children, and very, very smooth.

As far as Ellie was concerned, the guy was on probation, and she knew others in the region felt the same way. It was one thing to be able to follow a script and deliver all the talking points and stickhandle around difficult questions, but it was another to do so while representing front-line staff and everyone else in the force without artificiality or phoney showmanship.

Rachel looked at someone over Ellie's shoulder and quickly snapped to attention. Ellie turned around to find the commissioner standing behind her, waiting politely to speak. He wore his Dress Order Number One uniform, including his peak cap with two rows of gold oak leaves, metal OPP cap badge, gold twisted cord, and gold buttons.

"Sir," she said, also coming to attention. "How was the flight down?"

"As tiring as always. No last-second changes, I take it?"

"No, sir. The tracks and treads tell the story. Ballistics will likely confirm it, once we get the bullets from the victims. So the shooter's still out there."

Dart nodded. "I've already told Colleen she can handle any questions on the arrest as she prefers. How's Gray Kennedy doing?"

"Very well, sir. No complaints."

"Ah. Good to hear."

"A number of people asked me to give you their best, including Gray."

"That's nice. Tell them I'm counting on them more than ever now."

"Will do, sir."

McGuinness appeared from the crowd and touched Dart's elbow. "Five minutes, sir."

"Gotta run," Dart said. "Glad you're in the room, Ellie."

"Yes, sir."

Chapter 21

"Good morning everyone," McGuinness said, stepping up to the microphones on the stage that had been set up for the news briefing. "Thank you very much for coming this morning. My name is Kerry McGuinness, regional media co-ordinator for the Ontario Provincial Police East Region, and I'll be moderating this morning's event."

Chatter in the room levelled off as reporters held up their cellphones and recorders, others put pens to paper, and television cameramen trained their equipment on McGuinness. Ellie saw that the national media networks were all represented in the room, along with a score of other journalists of various stripes. The murder of an on-duty law enforcement officer was a big story, and everyone was here to catch it.

"As you can imagine," McGuinness continued, "the past twenty-four hours have been extremely difficult not only for the members of the Lanark County detachment but also friends and family of those who were senselessly shot and killed yesterday. Needless to say, this remains an open and active investigation, and we appreciate the patience and support of the public while we work hard to get to the bottom of what has happened and bring the person responsible to justice."

Ellie decided that McGuinness might have been a good choice for the job after all. He spoke well, his voice was clear and easily audible, and he was poised and professional. He was working without notes, which also made a good impression.

He explained the agenda for the briefing and introduced Commissioner Dart, who stepped up to the microphones with the calm self-assurance Ellie had always admired in him. He began by stressing the importance of being able to directly address all members of the OPP, those individuals personally connected to the victims, and also the public, whose roads and homes it was their sworn duty to protect.

"As you now know, Provincial Constable Terence Maynard was shot and killed on West Shore Drive, Drummond Township, at approximately ten thirty-five yesterday morning, May the first, while performing his duty as a traffic patrol officer. As you may be aware, our constables participate in well over eight hundred thousand interactions with members of the public across the province over the course of the year. As part of this number, they initiate more than a hundred thousand traffic stops and issue in excess of sixty thousand traffic tickets. Constable Maynard had just completed such a stop and was sitting in his vehicle writing up his notes when an unknown individual induced him to lower his window, whereupon he was fatally shot."

Ellie watched as cameras flashed and journalists shifted from foot to foot, searching for better angles. Because she knew Dart well, she could hear the edge of anger, barely suppressed in his voice, that might go unnoticed by others.

"Constable Maynard was a veteran of twenty-two years on the force and was well-respected by his peers. He leaves behind a mother, a sister, and many friends, neighbours, and colleagues. His loss will be grieved by all, here in Lanark County and across Ontario and beyond. Information regarding his funeral will be released when it becomes available.

"You may also know there was a second victim, Ms. Dorothy Anne Kerr, who resided in the house on West Shore Drive across from where Constable Maynard's life was senselessly taken. Please be assured that we will exercise every means at our disposal to bring her killer to justice as well."

After a few concluding remarks, Dart yielded the platform to McGuinness, who introduced Chief Superintendent Jordan Malcolmsen, the regional commander. In his early fifties, Malcolmsen was tall and slender in his dress uniform, his peak cap distinguished by one row of gold oak leaves, as opposed to the commissioner's two. His lantern jaw, square head, and high, greying temples reminded Ellie of the late actor Cesar Romero.

Malcolmsen smoothed out his moustache and began to speak, referring to his notes as he went.

"I want to thank members of the media, and of course our community, for your patience and understanding at this most difficult time. I'd like to thank the members of our Emergency Response and Tactical Response teams for their tireless efforts, as well as investigators of the Lanark County Crime Unit and the Regional Support Unit, and our regional Identification Services team, who are working around the clock as we speak to find the person who did this and bring them to justice.

"This is a heart-breaking time, of course, for our officers who worked alongside Constable Maynard, and on their behalf I'd like to thank members of the community who have left flowers and messages in the lobby of the regional headquarters in Smiths Falls and the detachment office here in Perth. Your thoughtfulness is a comfort to us all at this difficult time.

"I can tell you that the shelter-in-place order for the immediate area of the incident has been lifted and Highway 7 has been reopened to through traffic, although West Shore Drive will remain closed while our investigation progresses. Finally, I'd like to say that we will be continuing our door-to-door canvasses, and a Crime Stoppers tip line has been opened that may be contacted at the number distributed to you. If you know anything or saw anything, please share your information with us. Thank you."

Ellie watched him step away from the microphones and resume his place on the stage next to Dart. This time when his hand went up to his moustache, she could see a faint tremor. Even chief superintendents were not immune to the emotions of the moment.

McGuinness was back at the microphone, signalling the start of the question-and-answer portion of the briefing. The first person he called on, unsurprisingly, was the national CTV correspondent.

"Is it true an arrest has been made? What can you tell us about the suspect and the charges that have been laid?"

Colleen looked at Malcolmsen and stepped up to the microphones, tugging the cuff of her jacket down over the cast on her wrist. "Inspector Colleen Galvin, Lanark County detachment commander. Two arrests were made yesterday during the course of our investigations. Earl Avery Black of Ramsay Township was arrested at his home and charged with assault on a police officer, resisting arrest, possession of a prohibited weapon, improper firearm storage, and other charges. His spouse, Lana Olverson Black, was also arrested and charged with firearm-related offences. Neither is considered a suspect in the double shooting currently under investigation."

A babble arose as reporters vied for the opportunity to ask the next question. Someone shouted, "Inspector Galvin, were you injured during the arrest?"

Colleen looked puzzled for a moment, then held up her wrist, barking a short laugh. "Fell off a ladder at home. Completely unrelated."

McGuinness leaned over to the closest mic and said,

"Linda."

"Linda Taylor, CBC. My question is for you as well, Inspector Galvin. Did Constable Maynard fire back at his assailant?"

"No, he did not. His sidearm remained holstered throughout."

"Was he caught off guard? Was he not vigilant enough to prevent this from happening?"

Colleen frowned. "No, not at all. To build on what the commissioner said, our traffic constables here in Lanark County initiate more than four thousand traffic stops a year, and Constable Maynard was well trained and experienced in how to conduct himself while issuing a ticket. I have to remind you, though, that the assailant approached the constable *after* the stop was completed. It's more than probable that he showed no visible threatening gestures to the officer, who voluntarily lowered his window to speak to the individual. Again, there's no indication whatsoever that Constable Maynard was less vigilant than the situation called for."

Other questions followed. Has the murder weapon been found? Do you have other suspects? What can you tell us about the vehicle driven by the shooter? Colleen handled all of them calmly and with minimal detail, preferring to hold her hand somewhat closer to the vest than the journalists may have wished.

Finally, Malcolmsen recognized a man in his early fifties, wearing a green polo shirt and dark blue jeans.

"Larry Wilson, Perth *Sentinel*. I—"

He hesitated as light amusement rippled around the audience of experienced, seasoned national journalists. A question from the local freebie! This should be good.

"Uh, I just want to remind you that my colleague, Dorothy Kerr, was the other victim yesterday, and I'd like to know if you're considering the possibility that she was the killer's intended victim and Constable Maynard was an innocent bystander."

Another ripple went around the room, this one lacking in

amusement. Ellie stepped forward from her place at the far end of the stage and walked up to the microphones. She caught Colleen's eye, who nodded, and looked at Dart, whose expression was relieved.

"Detective Inspector Ellie March, Criminal Investigation Branch. I'm the major case manager responsible for this investigation and, to answer your question, Mr. Wilson, yes, we are actively considering that possibility. In fact, our detectives are pursuing a two-track process as we speak. In one, we're proceeding under the assumption that Constable Maynard was the primary target and Ms. Kerr was considered collateral damage, and in the other we're also investigating the possibility that the killer was there yesterday morning with Ms. Kerr as his intended victim, and that Constable Maynard was in the wrong place at the wrong time. Rest assured, no stone will be unturned until we get to the bottom of this."

She stepped back to allow McGuinness to take charge of the microphones again. He glanced at Dart, caught the commissioner's nod, and called an end to the briefing.

Ellie left the stage and made a beeline for the exit, desperate for a cigarette.

So much for the management of expectations, she told herself.

Chapter 22

After watching the press briefing on television in the meeting room with everyone else who could fit in there, Pierce made his way to the lunch room, where he stood in line for a cup of coffee from the Tim Hortons carafe and a sandwich from the platters dropped off by the restaurant manager as a gesture of support.

The chatter around him kept to predictable themes—that Dart had done the right thing by helicoptering down from Orillia; that the Dress Order Number Ones were a fine touch; and that he was still nevertheless an incompetent clown by most accounts, just like the rest of senior management.

The woman in line in front of him turned around and smiled. It was Kate Byrnes, the file co-ordinator. "Nice, isn't it? The Timmies, I mean."

Pierce nodded. Since transferring into the detachment from RHQ, he'd learned that the community relations people here worked closely with the restaurant to hold a number of public events, including softball tournaments, barbeques, curling bonspiels in the winter, and other opportunities to increase their community exposure.

"This is the first time we've had a chance to work together," she went on, looking up at him. "I like your writing style. Very simple. No jargon or cop-ese."

"Thank you."

She put a hand on his arm. "Quiet, intelligent men are hard to come by these days."

Pierce smiled. "I guess. My wife always says I never know when to shut up."

Kate removed her hand and turned back as the line moved up to the table.

He poured himself a coffee, picked a sandwich from the platter, and moved to one side. He could tell that the mood had lifted somewhat from yesterday, and it was his belief that Dart and Malcolmsen were responsible. The displays of *esprit de corps* and internal support had helped. Not to mention Ellie's decision to reveal their investigative strategy rather than keep it shrouded in mystery.

A sudden commotion at the door drew their attention. People were moving aside to allow someone to enter. Pierce heard Staff Sergeant Dunn's voice booming above the hubbub.

"Everyone! Please! Quiet! Hey! Turn it down for a second!"

The noise level dropped quickly at the sound of the voice of authority.

"Thank you! Listen up. This is Dr. Ishani Narayan. You saw my e-mail this morning. She's here to provide grief counselling to each and every one of you, under the direct orders of the regional commander. When Dr. Narayan contacts you, I expect you to book a time with her without a bunch of bullshit." He glanced at his watch. "She's going to start filling her calendar in twenty minutes. This won't take long, so no griping. Get it done.

That's all."

He and the psychologist disappeared, and the grumbling started. Pierce was disappointed that the mood in the room had suddenly changed so drastically.

Chapter 23

Pierce's nickname was "The Face," although few people called him that any more. Like many nicknames, it was fun for a while to tease him with, then the humour grew thin, and after a while the whole thing was dropped.

Nevertheless, his face had been his meal ticket for several years before he entered law enforcement. After graduating from high school he'd bummed around Toronto's theatre district, picking up parts on a fairly regular basis until he finally attracted the attention of a good agent, who got him into television commercials. After that there were bookings as a background actor on Canadian TV programs, where he had no lines but the camera might find him for a moment or two. The next step up the ladder was to speaking parts as what's known in the business as a day player, someone appearing in one or two scenes, enough for a screen credit and longer exposure to the camera.

His break came through one such part, where he played a witness in a made-for-TV mystery movie, a guy who lived in the apartment next door to the murder victim. The lead detective was a woman, and a few sparks flew between them. Audience response afterward was very positive and, striking while the iron was hot, his agent landed him a part as a principal actor.

For two years he played the role of Detective Brian Anderson on CTV's ill-fated series *The Badge*, a police procedural set in Toronto. Detective Anderson's primary characteristic was pessimistic negativity, a smouldering moodiness that darkened his outlook and upset the people with whom he interacted. He served as a foil to the main characters, Detective Bill Barnes and Detective Aretha Ross, who were upbeat and easy going. When the series was cancelled, they'd just finished filming the season-ending cliffhanger in which Detective Anderson was forced to choose between saving his own life or saving the lovely Detective Ross.

He never found out what the writers had had in mind for him.

During his two-year run on the show, he made friends with Sergeant Charlie Watkins, retired from the Toronto Police Service, who'd been brought in as a technical consultant. Watkins was a hard-assed old gasbag who constantly berated the writers and directors for their errors, misconceptions, and stereotypes, but Pierce saw an opportunity in front of him and didn't hesitate.

Once Watkins realized that Pierce was a receptive audience, he began to regale him with an endless supply of war stories, complaints about restrictive departmental policies, and detailed explanations of correct procedures in the field. Pierce peppered him with questions, which Watkins seemed to enjoy answering, and most of it went into Pierce's notebook after hours.

He had an ulterior motive, of course.

His father, Ronald Pierce, was a watchmaker who'd operated a clock and watch repair shop in a mall in Burlington in the 1980s and 90s. He was the kind of guy who wore a short-sleeved shirt and a tie to work year round, and he kept his eyeglasses with their owlish magnifiers perched on his forehead when he wasn't using them. He loved timepieces, large and small, and seemed to have an infinite store of patience for them.

Young Bob spent many Saturdays sitting with his dad in the shop, not because he was interested in clocks or in business, but because he worshipped his father, and it gave him a chance to talk to him. Ronald was as patient with him as he was in his work, and these were great times for a boy and his father to spend together.

When Pierce was thirteen, his father suffered a heart attack at the shop. Pierce rushed out into the mall, looking for help, and spotted a Halton Regional Police officer walking by. The officer immediately called for medical assistance and performed CPR on Ronald until paramedics arrived. There was no doubt that the police officer saved Ronald's life, and Pierce never forgot it.

It remained in the back of his mind that some day he would become a police officer himself.

When Pierce received the call from his agent that *The Badge* was being cancelled and he was once again out of work, he knew it was now or never. Watkins had repeatedly recommended that if he wanted to get into real police work, he should try the OPP rather than the TPS, because the opportunities were greater and their reputation was generally somewhat better, at least as far as public relations were concerned.

Pierce took that advice and was hired twelve years ago. Posted to Rainy River, he served three years as a traffic cop on lonely northern roads before receiving a transfer to Lansdowne in Leeds County, where much of his work involved joint-forces operations with the Canada Border Services Agency around the bridge across the St. Lawrence River into the United States.

He was bumped up to detective constable and eventually ended up at RHQ with the regional support unit, from which Sonja Freeling plucked him as a transferee to the Lanark County Crime Unit last year.

The odd thing was that Pierce occasionally suffered from bouts of impostor syndrome. He berated himself for not being a real police detective but merely acting out the role of one. It took him quite a bit of effort to remind himself that any job performance involves a certain amount of role playing, since people are not necessarily the same person at work as they are at home. After all, he was no longer an actor acting like a cop, but a cop acting like a cop.

Big difference.

For one thing, the bullets were real now.

As Terry Maynard had discovered.

Not that Pierce lacked self-confidence. He had just as much as Doug Skelton, sitting next to him in the passenger seat as they drove to Barrhaven, the Ottawa suburb where Cheryl Hutton, their first person of interest, lived. Skelton was a sheep farmer acting as a detective, and he was proud of the fact. He cultivated the image of a slow-talking, slow-moving good old boy who knew everyone and everything in Lanark county. In Pierce's opinion he was full of sheep dip, but he reminded himself he was no longer playing the role of Detective Anderson the pessimist but rather Neutral Bob, the flexible, responsible everyman.

As they turned down Hutton's street, Skelton coughed up phlegm. He lowered the window and spat. "I got this," he said.

"Help yourself." Pierce was a good note taker, and he didn't really care one way or the other.

"I don't like all this digging into a brother officer's past. Like he was responsible for his own death and not the goddamned shooter."

"I don't think that's what this is all about. We're looking for someone with a grudge against him, not something to hang on Maynard himself. Her complaint's already part of the record, so it's not like we're digging up fresh dirt on him."

When she answered the door, Cheryl Hutton grimaced as she waved them in. "Ignore the barking; it's just the dogs in the kennel out back. They'll quit in a minute."

"Detective Constable Skelton. We spoke on the phone."

"Yes," she said, squinting at his identification. "You're a few minutes early."

Pierce shut the door behind him. Skelton was already on his way to the living room, so when Hutton looked at him, he introduced himself.

"Have I seen you somewhere before?"

"Not likely. I only recently transferred into the detachment."

"It's not that," she said, following him into the living room and settling down on the couch. "Your face looks very familiar."

"I get that a lot."

"Ms. Hutton, as I said on the phone, I've got a few questions about Terence Maynard."

"Yes. Can I get you guys something? Coffee?"

"We won't be long," Skelton said, answering for both of them. "Walk us through your complaint against Constable Maynard."

"All right." She settled back on the couch and crossed her legs. "It started out with lewd remarks and off-colour jokes. Not when others were around; just when he and I were alone."

"You were an administrative clerk, is that right?"

"Yes. I worked in the general office with two other clerks. He'd wait until I was alone in the room and come in for a 'friendly visit,' as he called it."

"According to your complaint," Skelton said, "there was physical contact."

"Yeah. First it was just what they call frottage, incidental contact and rubbing against me that he could claim was accidental if I called him on it. I made the mistake of trying to ignore it, so he began to grope me, squeeze my rear end, and all that. Finally I got sick of it and went to the staff sergeant."

"How did you feel about it?" Skelton gave her a long look.

"Violated."

"Angry?"

"Yes, of course, angry. Wouldn't you be?"

"I'm not a girl, so I couldn't say."

"That's three-quarters of the problem. I felt like I was working in some kind of men's club. Like I was a Playboy bunny or something. It was demeaning."

"Were you pissed when it was dismissed?"

"Well, duh, detective. I guess maybe I was. Not surprised, though. 'Lack of evidence' told me that my side of the story was meaningless to them. It was damned hard to take."

"And you held a grudge against Constable Maynard."

She smiled at him without humour. "Now we're down to it, aren't we? No, I didn't hold a grudge. I got out of there. Clerk jobs are a dime a dozen. I found something else pretty quickly, and that was it. Screw Maynard, screw the OPP, and screw you, pal."

"Where were you yesterday at ten thirty in the morning?"

"I was sleeping in. My husband had the day off. We took advantage of it."

"Did you have any contact with Maynard after you quit?"

"Are you insane? No."

"Did he try to contact you?"

"No. Thank God for small mercies, eh?"

"We'll be contacting your husband to verify your story," Skelton said, standing up.

"Feel free. Here." She went over to a hall table and took a business card from a tray. "Call him right away. Get your mind settled that I had nothing to do with Maynard's death. It's unfortunate somebody shot him in the head. That's no way to go. But it wasn't me, it wasn't my husband, and I hope I never see or hear from you again. Have a nice day."

She opened the door and held it for them until they were outside. After a long look at Pierce, as though she were still trying to place him, she closed it firmly behind them. They heard the deadbolt click into place.

Interview over.

Chapter 24

Alaric Quinn was just ending a call on his cellphone as Kevin and Heather walked into the comm room. He put the phone in its wire holder guy and smiled up at them.

"Thanks for coming. I've got something interesting for you."

The data entry assistant, Simon O'Connor, was busy on his headset, his eyes on the computer monitor in front of him.

Kevin pulled over a couple of chairs. Heather sat down on one and said, "Was that your spy phone?"

Alaric laughed. "No, it was my mom. She didn't want me to come in to work today. She wants me to find another job."

"Did you tell her you were safe behind these solid cement block walls?"

"She wants me to get a job at Amazon. She thinks I could be running the fulfillment centre inside of a year."

"There's an ambition."

"How's your dad doing?" Kevin asked.

"Good. He just nailed down the patent on a double-sized hiking tent that folds up into a fanny pack. He's happy."

"So, what have you got for us?"

Alaric switched his monitor to one of the PCs in front of him and handed Heather a set of headphones. "Something to listen to. A call to Crime Stoppers that came in early this morning. So far it's been the usual junk, hate messages and kids having fun, but this one I'd like you guys to follow up on."

Kevin took another set of headphones and slipped them on. As primary investigator, Alaric's responsibilities not only included auditing and reviewing information related to the case as it came in but also assigning tasks where warranted.

Alaric clicked on a button, and the voice of a Crime Stoppers tips co-ordinator could be heard answering a call. A woman identified herself as Sue Pembroke and readily gave her address, adding, "I also own the bookstore, According to Type, here in town."

When asked about the tip she wished to leave, Pembroke said, "I'm a friend of Dorothy's. Dorothy Kerr. I was, I guess I should say. This is very upsetting. She's in my quilting group."

"What's the nature of your tip, Ms. Pembroke?"

"Mrs. I'm a widow. I wanted to tell you about seeing Dorothy on Sunday night. I was at the Northlands Mall, eating a hamburger in my car."

"What time was this, Mrs. Pembroke?"

"Uh, early in the evening. A few minutes before seven. Anyway, as I was saying, I saw Dorothy walking to her car with a take-out pizza from Mario's. I didn't even know she was parked there. She walked to her car. I'm getting a bit ahead of myself, because before that a bus pulled off the highway and parked in the front of the McDonald's. Two men got out, and while one went inside the other started escorting these women into McDonald's two at a time. He waited for them to come out, took them back to the bus, and took another two women in. I guess the second man was inside watching them. Just before Dorothy came out of Mario's there was a mix-up at the bus. Too many women tried to come out, and while the man was getting them to go back inside a woman came out of McDonald's alone. She ran across the parking lot and hid behind Dorothy's car."

"What happened next?"

"Well, that's when Dorothy came out of Mario's with her pizza. She went around the side of her car to put the pizza on the passenger seat and saw the woman. The woman looked like she was trying to explain what was going on, her hands going up and down. Dorothy got the woman into her car, gave her the pizza to hold, and drove away."

"What did you do, ma'am?"

"Like I said, I ate my hamburger."

"All right. Do you have anything else to add?"

"I can't think of anything right now."

"Detectives may visit you to discuss your tip, Mrs. Pembroke."

"That's fine. Did I give you my address? Yes, I did. But I'll probably be at the bookstore."

The call ended, and they took off their headsets.

"I know her," Heather said. "Nice but nosy."

"I ordered a book last week," Kevin said. "Maybe it's come in by now."

Heather smiled sweetly. "Shall we inquire?"

Chapter 25

Sue Pembroke greeted Heather enthusiastically as they walked in the door of the According to Type bookstore.

"We've got some new graphic novels in I think you'll like," she said, coming around from behind her counter and walking over to a shelf. "Right over here."

"Sorry, Sue, we're here on business. This is Detective Constable Walker. We want to talk to you about your Crime Stoppers call."

"Oh. Okay. Yeah. Dorothy." She went back behind her counter and sat on a stool.

"Walk us through it again. What you saw." Heather took out her phone. "Do you mind if I record this?"

"No. Not at all." Pembroke described what had happened in the mall parking lot, repeating what she'd said in the tips call, but this time she ended her narration a little differently. "When the black truck pulled out after her and followed her onto the highway, that's when I got a little upset and decided to call."

Heather leaned her hip against the counter. "What black truck was that, Sue?"

"The one that was watching her."

Heather glanced at Kevin, who said, "Let's start with the bus. Was it already there when you got to the parking lot?"

"No, it pulled in off the highway as I was getting out of the car to get my hamburger. I saw the two men get out and the women starting to go into McDonald's."

"What did it look like?"

"It was an old school bus, the big yellow kind, with the names spray painted off."

"Did you see the licence number?"

"No, sorry."

"Okay. I'm confused about something. Didn't you go into the McDonald's as well for your hamburger?"

"Oh, no. I don't like their food. I went into Jimmy's instead."

"That's the restaurant in the mall next to the pet store," Heather explained to Kevin, who pretended it was news to him.

"So you got your hamburger in Jimmy's and came back out to your car to eat?"

"Yes. I was hungry, so I didn't want to wait until I got home."

"Okay, fine. And the women were still coming and going from the bus when you came back out?"

"Yes, they were."

"And what about Dorothy? When did you first see her?"

"Well, technically, I saw her car first. When I got back from Jimmy's. She must have gotten there while I was waiting for my burger. I know her car from seeing it around. It was parked a few rows in front of me and up a couple of spaces."

"But you could see it clearly."

"Oh, yes."

"The next thing is that you saw the woman running from McDonald's to hide behind Dorothy's car."

"Yes."

"Can you describe her to me?"

"Small. Straight dark hair. Chinese, or at least Asian. She was wearing a white T-shirt and jeans."

"About how old?"

"Young; maybe a teenager, maybe early twenties."

"Not a child, though?"

"No."

"Why did she hide behind Dorothy's car in particular?"

"Because it was there. She looked over her shoulder as she was running away. The man inside McDonald's was coming out, and she didn't want him to see her, I guess, so she ducked down behind Dorothy's car."

"Then Dorothy came back to the car with her pizza and found her there?"

"Yes. And they got in and drove away."

"And a black pickup truck left the parking lot behind them?"

"Yes."

"Okay." Kevin glanced at Heather's cellphone, which she'd put down on top of the counter. It was still recording. "Let's stop for a minute and rewind. When did you first notice the black truck?"

"After I came back with my burger. Before Dorothy came out with her pizza. It was a couple of spaces above mine. I only noticed it because I saw a man get out of the passenger side and walk up to the bus. He stood there for a minute and talked to the man who was bringing the women back and forth. When the mix-up happened with the extra women trying to get out, he was in the middle of the tangle, pushing them back onto the bus."

"Did he see the Asian woman running from McDonald's and getting into Dorothy's car?"

"I don't think so. But the man who was driving the black

truck must have, because he honked the horn when Dorothy got into her car with the woman."

"What happened?"

"Well, the man at the bus mustn't have heard him, because the driver got out and called him over. Then they got back in their truck as Dorothy pulled out of her parking spot."

"Was it your impression they were following Dorothy, or was it just that they left at the same time?"

"Like a coincidence? No, I don't think so. I think they followed her."

"Can you describe them? Start with the man who got out on the passenger side and went up to the bus."

"He was an older man, maybe in his sixties. Stout. Big huge white moustache that curled up at the corners. Blue flannel shirt and jeans."

Kevin nodded. "Very good. What about the other man?"

"Younger, in his thirties. Tall. Just a bit of a pot belly. I never saw his face, though."

"But you'd be able to identify the older man if you saw him again?"

"Oh, yes. Absolutely."

"Can you describe the truck for me?"

"Oh, just one of those big black pickups people drive around these days. I don't know what kind, or what year, or that. It looked like it was nearly new, if that helps."

"Did it have a double set of wheels on the back?"

"I couldn't say. Now I remember you, detective. You ordered a copy of Mr. Heron's new book."

"Yes, that's right." He looked at Heather. "Anything else?"

Heather shook her head and turned off the voice recorder app.

"Is it in?" Kevin asked.

"Not only is it in," Pembroke said, "but Mr. Heron came in and very kindly autographed all ten in the order. So you get a signed copy, no extra charge."

"That's great!" Kevin reached for his wallet.

"While you're busy with that," Heather said, putting her phone in her pocket, "I'll be over here." She made a beeline for Pembroke's graphic novels shelf.

Chapter 26

Their first stop at the mall was the McDonald's, where they spoke to the manager on duty. She'd been working on Sunday and remembered the bus-load of women shuttling in and out. Unfortunately, she couldn't offer much of a description of the man who'd stayed inside to watch them, and who occasionally barged into the washroom to herd them back out when he thought they were taking too long.

"White, thirties, needed a shave, medium height, dark hair. That's pretty much all I remember."

Heather's eyes roved around the ceiling. "Security cameras in the lobby and behind the counter, right?"

"Yes, that's right. Plus one outside monitoring the drive-through and the garbage corral."

"You'd still have the footage from Sunday? From about four in the afternoon on?"

The manager's face grew cautious. "Yes, but—"

"Arrange for a copy of it to be made, will you? All your cameras? We'll be back for it with a warrant."

"I can do that."

"Thanks."

Outside in the parking lot, they strolled toward the mall and stopped about two-thirds of the way down. They turned to look back at the McDonald's.

"Pembroke was probably parked about here," Kevin said.

"Man, I can taste that hamburger. Jimmy's is a good restaurant."

"Yeah. Good take-out. Janie loves it."

Heather smiled.

"Bus over there." Kevin pointed at where the drive-through wrapped around.

"People in their cars coming through would have seen them." Heather folded her arms. "Sometimes you have to wait a minute for service. Time to sit there watching women being ushered back and forth in front of you."

"All Asian, do you think?"

"I wonder. Possibly."

"Security camera out here would have caught it."

They fell silent for a moment, thinking it through.

"Pizzeria," Kevin said, turning to his right.

"Take her, what, forty-five seconds to walk from the front door to her car?"

"Yeah. Maybe thirty."

"Want me to time it?"

Kevin shook his head. "So she sat about here," he motioned with his hands, "and the black truck was up a few spaces, maybe where that Audi is."

Heather pivoted to look back at the mall. "Wonder what kind of cameras we've got out here."

"Let's go see."

A CIBC bank with an ATM occupied the unit on the end.

There was a camera mounted on the corner, but it was aimed at the front entrance and wouldn't be of any help. The camera on the ATM might be useful, but it lined up rather close to the pizzeria and might not have enough of an angle to show them what they wanted to see. Besides, banks were notoriously difficult to negotiate with when it came to security-related information.

Next door was a large dollar store, then a dry-cleaning outlet, an insurance company, and Jimmy's Restaurant. Their video surveillance was all internal, showing the front counters and entrances only.

They walked down to the large grocery store that anchored the far end of the mall.

"Jackpot," Heather said, pointing.

They looked at cameras on the near corner of the building, two on either side of the front entrance, and one on the other corner.

"The ones at the ends will give us the whole damned parking lot," Heather said.

They went inside and asked to speak to the manager, who told them that the corner cameras didn't belong to them.

"Mall security," he said. "You'll have to talk to them."

"Do you have a phone number?"

The guy rolled his eyes, as though when God handed out brains, cops were still stuck in line at the doughnut shop.

"You just walked by their office. Next to the hobby store?"

"Chee, thanks, boss," Heather said in an exaggerated cartoon voice.

The manager in charge of the mall office was a tall drink of water in a suit one size too small for him. When they told him what they were looking for, he sat down on the corner of his receptionist's desk and took out a pack of cigarettes.

"Shouldn't be a problem," he said, smiling. "We don't have it here, though. You'll have to get it from head office." He rotated the pack in his hand without removing a cigarette.

"I see," Kevin said. "Where's it located?"

"Vaughan."

"Vaughan, Ontario."

"Yep." He slipped his free hand inside his jacket. "This is my card. Tony here will give you the particulars so that you can reach the powers that be, but feel free to call me any time. You plan on getting a warrant, I take it?"

"That's the idea," Kevin said, putting the card in his pocket.

"Good." He stood up, nodded at Kevin, winked at Heather, and went out the front door, using his shoulder so that he could draw a cigarette from the pack and stick it into the corner of his mouth.

Tony held out another business card. "This is your contact with head office. Mr. Jim Giordano. You should be able to make the arrangements for what you want through him."

The card bore a logo of a bridge and river in silhouette and the initials BWR in the corner. The company name was Bridgewater Realty. An address in Vaughan and a telephone number were printed below that. On the back of the card, Tony had written Giordano's name and a different telephone number.

"Thanks."

Outside, they gave the manager a little wave and crossed the parking lot to Kevin's Charger. When they got in, Heather buckled up with a loud snort.

"If that isn't a satellite office for Murder, Incorporated I'm Lara Croft, Tomb Raider. What the hell's going on here? A bus trafficking in Asian females makes a pit stop at a mall in Perth owned by a company in Vaughan owned by the mob?"

"Don't jump to conclusions, Heather. Just because it's Vaughan doesn't mean that it's 'Ndrangheta."

"I can't even pronounce that, but I know an OC front when I see one."

"Seen a lot, have you?"

"Well, maybe not personally. On TV."

Kevin laughed.

"I thought maybe we'd get something connecting Tom

Searle the slaughter king to this bus thing, but now it looks like something completely different. Don't you think?"

Kevin started the engine and shifted into drive. "I think we need to run this past Alaric while the warrants are being written, that's what I think."

Chapter 27

Daniel Troy Senior was a short, squat piece of work with a receding hairline, a wide mouth, and big fists. He was driving an old red tractor across the dooryard as Pierce and Skelton drove in, and when he saw them pull up he shut off the engine, slid down, and strode over.

"Help you with something?"

They got out, and Skelton held up his badge. "OPP, Detective Inspector Skelton. Are you Daniel Troy?"

"OPP? What the hell do you want?"

"Got a few questions for you." Skelton looked around. "Nice place you got here."

When Pierce had run Troy's background before setting out, he'd learned that the Troy farm encompassed a full two hundred acres on Roger Stevens Drive in Montague Township. He ran beef cattle and he cropped hay and soybeans. The farm was free of liens or other encumbrances, and it had belonged to the family for five generations. To all appearances it was a well-run, profitable business.

"Yeah. Ask your questions and beat it. I got work to do."

"Tch tch." Skelton tipped back his Smithbilt ten-gallon hat to scratch his forehead. "A little politeness never hurts. We're investigating a double homicide, Mr. Troy, and we want to talk to you about the complaint you filed on Constable Terry Maynard back in 2022."

"Maynard? Don't know the guy."

"Are you sure that's the answer you want to give us?"

"Complaint. Wait, you're talking about Danny."

"Pardon me?"

"My son. Danny. He's the one filed the complaint against that cocksucker cop."

Skelton shook his head slowly, as though greatly disappointed. "That cocksucker cop you're talking about was shot twice in the head yesterday morning, and I'm very much interested in knowing where you and your son were when it happened."

"Shot. Ungh. Yeah, yeah, right. Saw it on the news. Didn't know it was that guy."

"So where were you yesterday morning, Mr. Troy?"

"Here, working. Where the hell else would I be?"

"Who can verify that?"

Troy stared at him. "Let's see, I spent the entire morning up in the back pasture helping a cow give birth to a calf that was tangled up and didn't want to come out. Couldn't move her, so I stayed with her until it was done and they were okay. Do livestock count as witnesses?"

Skelton, who'd been there and done that, only with sheep rather than cattle, shrugged. "What about your son?"

"Why don't you ask him yourself?" Troy pointed with his chin. "He's in the garage. That's where I'm taking this old girl for her weekly maintenance."

Skelton followed him over to the tractor and watched him

climb up into the seat. "Massey Ferguson 135," he remarked. "Diesel?"

Troy started the engine and rolled off toward the garage.

"I've got one myself," Skelton said to Pierce as they followed Troy across the yard. "Nice little hobby tractor."

Daniel Troy Junior was banging away at a partially disassembled bailer, muttering and cursing to himself. He was his father's opposite, tall and lanky, with a scraggly beard and longish blond hair. When his father rolled up beside the bailer and killed the engine on the Massey, Junior fired his hammer into a stack of tires along the far wall.

"Not gonna get to that fucking thing until tomorrow," he snarled. "This son of a bitch needs to be blown up with a fucking stick of dynamite." He looked at Skelton and Pierce. "Who the hell's this?"

Skelton badged him. "We're going to ask you a few questions."

"Are you now." Junior wiped his face with a rag. "Come back some other time. I'm working."

"Where were you Monday morning, Mr. Troy?"

"Same place I always am, in this fucking garage. Why do you want to know?"

"We're investigating a double homicide, Mr. Troy. Can anyone verify your whereabouts all morning?"

"Homicide? Who got snuffed?" Junior threw the rag aside and looked at his father, who was bent over, inspecting the bailer.

"A police officer. Didn't you see it on the news?"

"Don't watch the shit. If it was a cop, it's no skin off my fucking nose."

"The officer's name was Constable Terry Maynard. Ring any bells, son?"

Junior spat on the floor and picked up a thermos. "No. Wait. Yeah, that son of a bitch. He got offed?"

"He was shot yesterday morning. Was that you, Troy?"

"Fuck," Junior said, laughing. "Looks good on him." He took a drink from the thermos and wiped his mouth with the back of his hand.

"You filed a complaint against Constable Maynard in 2022, is that correct?"

"Fucking right. Son of a bitch violated my first amendment rights to freedom of speech, man. Figures a cop would get away with that bullshit."

Pierce had his eye on Troy Senior, who'd drifted toward the garage door and was talking quietly on a push-to-talk phone.

"You're thinking of American law, kid." Skelton shook his head. "You anarchists get it wrong every time."

"American, Canadian, no difference. You vampires sucking on taxpayers' hard-earned money are all the same. Trying to take away our freedom."

Skelton held his tongue. As a provincial civil servant sworn to protect the public, he believed in this country's system of government, its judiciary, and its laws. Despite the fact that he normally voted for the local Conservative Party of Canada candidate at election time, he disliked libertarians and anarchists and the just plain stupid, particularly those who had begun to infect the good, old-fashioned conservatism he'd always supported over the years. They held out their hands whenever there was something they wanted from government, then spat on it instead of saying thank you.

"Constable Maynard issued you a ticket for speeding. He also warned you about the flags on your truck as a hazardous distraction to other drivers that could have gotten you another ticket."

"He hit me, man. I'm not going to take that shit. Not off of anyone, cop or no cop."

"Oversized flags like that are a hazard to traffic, son."

"I'm a patriot. I'm proud of my flag. It's our symbol of freedom."

"Constable Maynard maintained in the complaint process

that at no time did he make physical contact with you."

"He's a fucking liar. I had the cuts and bruises to prove it."

"He stated that you already had those injuries when he pulled you over."

"He tried to beat the shit out of me, man. Deal with it."

Pierce had drifted over toward the garage door. He'd unobtrusively brought out his notebook and pen and had been taking notes, but now as a vehicle pulled up outside and a door slammed he put them away and rested his hand on his holstered sidearm. Troy Senior stepped forward to meet a young woman who entered the garage, arms folded defensively.

"What the hell are you doing here?" Junior snapped.

"Officers," Senior said, "this is my daughter-in-law, Tip. She can tell you that Danny was here on Monday morning."

"That's right," Tip said, looking at Pierce. "I brought him his ten o'clock thermos of coffee like I always do. He was changing the oil on Dad's truck."

"Oh?" Skelton looked at Senior. "What kind of truck?"

"F-150."

"Do you own a dually, Mr. Troy?"

"Used to. Got rid of it. Why?"

"Could we see some identification?" Skelton said to Tip.

Looking confused, she took a wallet out of her jeans pocket and handed over her driver's licence. Skelton glanced at it and handed it back. "You're Daniel Junior's wife, is that correct?"

"Yes. Dad says you need to know where Danny was Monday morning. Well, he was here."

"When your husband attended the Freedom Convoy occupation in February of 2022, did you accompany him?"

She shook her head. "That's Danny's thing. I've got the kids to look after and chores to do."

"What the hell's that got to do with anything?" Junior took a step toward Skelton. "We're done here, mister. Time to leave."

Skelton gave him a long look, then nodded at Pierce and walked away.

Chapter 28

"You're eating too fast. You'll get indigestion."

Kevin swallowed a mouthful and frowned at Caitlyn, who sat across the breakfast table from him. "I always eat like this."

"That's what I mean. You should chew your food slowly, enjoy the taste, and then swallow. Breathe, and then take another bite."

"It's oatmeal, Cait. Who chews oatmeal? Anyway, I've got to hit the road."

She thoughtfully considered the last piece of toast on her plate. "I'd like your opinion on something."

"Sure. What about?"

"I've been trying to make a decision, and I'd like your input."

"I'm all ears."

"I—"

Janie burst in. "What are you doing just sitting there? Did you see the time? If you're going to ride your bike to school you need to get out of here earlier than this."

"Okay, Mom. I'm coming."

Janie was already gone, back down the hall to see if Brendan was having any luck getting Josh ready to leave.

"I don't need you to say anything right now," Caitlyn continued, "but if you could think about it I'd—"

Kevin's cellphone, which was sitting on the table in front of him, began to vibrate. He looked at the call display and picked it up.

"Sorry, Cait, I have to answer this. Walker."

"It's Bob, Kevin. Ellie's moved the meeting up an hour."

"Shoot. Okay, thanks for the heads-up." Kevin turned around to stare out the kitchen window at the driveway where his car sat, waiting for him.

"No problem. Everyone else is already here. Do you want me to tell her you'll be a few minutes late?"

Kevin agonized over it for a moment. He'd never forgotten the verbal thrashings he'd received from Scott Patterson, his former supervisory sergeant, on the rare times he arrived late at a crime scene.

"No, I'll be there. Thanks." He ended the call and turned around again. "I have to run. Can we talk about this when I get home, sweetheart?"

She'd already left the room.

Sonja Freeling gave him a look when he hurried into the meeting room eleven minutes late, but Ellie ignored him, her attention on Doug Skelton, who sat at the far end of the table from her.

"You were about to update us," she said. "Go ahead."

Kevin sat down next to Heather, opening his notebook and

clicking his pen.

She leaned over and patted his arm. "You should consider moving into town so you'll be closer to work."

"Ha, ha."

"Cheryl Hutton's not of interest to me," Skelton said. He sat ramrod straight in his chair, his hands folded on the table in front of him. "While it's true her only alibi is her husband, I don't get the kind of vibe from her I'd expect to if she'd shot Maynard, no matter how much she hated him."

Kevin could see that he wasn't going to let Pierce get a word in edgewise, and Ellie seemed to sense the same thing.

"Bob? Is that your feeling as well?"

"Yes, Ellie. I agree with Doug."

"Danny Troy's another matter," Skelton said, as though he'd never been interrupted. "The guy's a loose cannon, plenty of hatred and anger, plenty of motive, and yeah, sure, his alibi is his wife, but I believe Hutton and I don't believe Troy for a second."

"What's Troy's alibi?"

"That he was working in the farm garage all morning, and his wife brought him coffee at ten o'clock."

"Any chance of shaking it?"

"We'll need contradictory evidence of some kind."

"How do you plan to go about finding that?"

"Not sure yet, but I think if I widen the scope of our interviews we might be able to find someone that saw Troy some place else that morning. Plus, they claim to have gotten rid of a dually they owned a while ago. That'll have to be looked into, too."

Kevin saw Ellie glance at Pierce, whose expression remained carefully neutral. She decided not to ask him for an opinion this time around.

"Follow up on it, then. Heather?"

"Right now we're looking into a witness report on suspicious activity involving Dorothy Kerr early Sunday evening. She might have gotten involved in some kind of human trafficking operation at the Northlands Mall. We're in the process of getting access to surveillance video from the McDonald's and also from the mall's outside cameras. The property's owned by a company in Toronto called Bridgewater Realty, so it may take a bit of time. Vaughan, actually."

"Oh?" Ellie looked at Alaric.

"I've left voice messages, sent an e-mail, and texted them. Waiting for a response. Interestingly," he paused for effect, "the building Terry Maynard lived in traces back to them as well."

Kevin could see that Ellie's interest had been piqued. They'd dealt with businesses in Vaughan before, businesses of the 'Ndrangheta variety.

"Keep me informed," she said. "Doug, let's get going."

Skelton gathered his things together and stood up.

"Doug and I will attend Constable Maynard's post-mortem," she said, turning off her tablet and slipping it into her bag. "Heather? Still good for this afternoon?"

Kevin watched an expression of revulsion slither across her face before she nodded. She'd been tabbed to attend Dorothy Kerr's autopsy at one, after Maynard's had been completed and Dr. Kalman, the forensic pathologist at the Ottawa Hospital, had had a chance to grab a quick bite to eat. Heather had confided to him that she'd never been to an autopsy before, and he'd suggested she might want to skip lunch.

As they filed out of the meeting room, Dunn tapped Kevin on the arm.

"Don't you read your e-mail? Dr. Narayan's waiting for you."

"Oh, blast. Sorry, Staff."

The truth was, he'd seen it sitting in his Inbox and had avoided opening it. Feeling as though he were about to be lined up in front of a firing squad, he made his way across the floor to Staff Sergeant Dunn's office.

Chapter 29

"Come in and sit down," Dr. Narayan said from behind Dunn's desk. "Please close the door, if you don't mind."

Kevin did as he was directed, settling into the visitor's chair and folding his arms across his chest.

It was his first close look at her, and he found himself interested despite his reservations. A very small person, she wore her long black hair in a braid over her left shoulder, a long-sleeved dress with small flowers on it, and a pearl necklace. Her Ghandi-style glasses, round-rimmed and silver framed, caught the light from the overhead fluorescents as she looked down at the open file in front of her and then back up at him.

"I should talk for a moment," she said, her voice lightly accented, "and explain myself, if that's all right with you. Then it's your turn."

"Okay."

"I work for a Toronto company, Cage Intelligence Services. We do a variety of work, some of it intelligence-related, yes. Our clients include the federal government and other entities. I'm part of the Behavioural Sciences Division, which provides consulting services related to everything from criminal profiling to handwriting analysis, industrial and organizational psychology and," spreading her hands, "grief counselling."

"I don't think I've heard of you before."

"Our contracts with the OPP have been few so far, and mostly in the Central and West regions. Personally, I specialize in grief counselling, as you have no doubt deduced, and I also consult when large organizations encounter problems related to interpersonal dynamics and that sort of thing. Mostly I work within the GTA. Boring work to most people, I admit, but fascinating to me. Plus, it puts food on the table and clothing on the backs of my children."

"I see."

"Your turn to talk is coming up. First, may I call you Kevin rather than Detective Constable Walker?"

"Sure. That's fine."

"My first name is Ishani, but please call me Dr. Narayan. It's not an ego thing, you understand, but a reminder that I have a role to play which I take very seriously, and I want you to be able to trust me in that role and not think I'm trying to win you over with a bunch of fake friendliness. Everything we share should be honest and genuine. Does that sound all right to you?"

Kevin thought for a second and then nodded.

"Now it's your turn. Feel free to talk about anything you like."

What on earth was he supposed to say? There was nothing he felt comfortable discussing with her, no matter how disarming she might be.

"I've been informed that you recently lost your father. Would you like to talk about that?"

"No."

"Are you upset about it?"

"No." As she waited, he felt that she deserved a little more than just monosyllables. "We were estranged. He didn't like me very much. I went along with it because my mother would have wanted me to, just to preserve the peace."

"But you would have reconciled, if he'd been willing?"

Kevin grimaced. "I don't know. He was really unlikeable. It was a lot simpler this way."

"You have your own family now."

"Yes."

She waited.

He said nothing, his guard still up.

"You adopted your wife's two children, according to the file. And you have had a third child with her."

"And another to come," he blurted.

Her face lit up. "Really! Congratulations. Do you know yet if it's a boy or a girl?"

"No, not yet. We're hoping for a girl, though."

"Well, there you are. Let me ask you about Constable Maynard. Did you know him well?"

Kevin shook his head. "Never met him. I recently transferred into the detachment from Leeds. There are still a few people I don't know. Particularly in Traffic."

"I see. Did his death upset you?"

After a moment, Kevin nodded. "You could say that."

"Even though you'd never met him?"

"Too close for comfort. It was a reminder of how dangerous the job is. Plus, it really upset my family."

She raised her eyebrows. "Did you talk to them about it?"

"Last night. Josh, our youngest, was the most upset. He's only six. Caitlyn's the oldest—she's sixteen—so she helped with the other two."

"Do you get along with your wife's two children?"

Kevin couldn't help but smile. It was one of his favourite topics of conversation. "Oh, yeah." Then he thought about

Caitlyn at the breakfast table this morning, and the smile faded.

"What are you thinking about right now?" asked Dr. Narayan.

"This morning Caitlyn wanted my advice on something. I don't know what it was. Before she could explain, Bob called to tell me the meeting had been moved up an hour. When I hung up, she was gone."

"Which bothers you?"

"Yeah. I probably shouldn't admit to a psychologist that I feel guilty about something, because it'll probably mean another hour at least, but, yeah. I try to keep them at the top of my priority list, but sometimes I screw up."

"Children are quite a responsibility, aren't they?"

"They sure are."

Dr. Narayan removed her glasses and polished them with a handkerchief she slipped out of her sleeve. "Please continue to examine your feelings about the loss of your father and the loss of a fellow officer. Grief has a way of hiding in small places in the back of our mind and emerging unexpectedly to upset us. You talk about it with your wife? Yes? Continue to do so. And feel free to see me again at any time while I'm still here in Perth."

"That's it? We're done?"

"That's it," she said, smiling.

Chapter 30

Ellie was eastbound on Highway 417 heading into Ottawa. Skelton was somewhere behind her, driving his own vehicle. She was thinking that traffic was a little heavy for this time of day when her hands-free buzzed. The incoming call was from Bridgewater Realty, according to the call display, with a long-distance number. The name had just come up in the team meeting this morning, so she answered.

"March."

"Detective Inspector Ellie March. How very nice to hear your voice again."

The speaker was male with a light baritone and perfect diction. He sounded very familiar, but for a moment she couldn't place the voice.

"To whom am I speaking, please?"

"Leonardo Arcuri, Ellie. I trust you're well these days."

The name clicked. "Mr. Arcuri. Why are you calling?"

A soft chuckle. "Well, I believe, actually, your people called my people, so I thought I'd find out personally what I can do to help you out."

"I see." Ellie tried to hide her surprise. Four years ago she'd been snowed in at the village of Westport while investigating the homicide of a *contabile*, or money man, for Dante Tassone, the head of a prominent 'Ndrangheta family based in Woodbridge, near Toronto. Leonardo had been there as Tassone's personal attorney and chief counsel for his holding company, Wooden Bridge Investments. Before the storm had finally blown itself out, Ellie had shot and killed Tassone's rebellious son, ending an internal power struggle that had threatened the safety of everyone in the village.

"First of all, please accept my sincere condolences on the loss of your officer. This is a terrible thing to have happen."

"Thanks." Ellie had no use for career criminals, especially those at the top of organizations that profited from illegal activities such as extortion, racketeering, and the drug trade. Leonardo, however, had impressed her as a man whose word was good and whose moral code was, in its own way, honourable. She knew, for example, that it included prohibitions against harming law enforcement personnel, sworn and civilian, and that the murder of Terence Maynard would truthfully bother him.

"How can I help?" he asked.

"I don't know, Leonardo. How can you help?"

He laughed softly. "Always the same Ellie March. You may be interested to know I've moved over to the business side of things. Or maybe you already know. Your young analyst, Ms. Charlotte McKinley, impressed me quite a bit. At any rate, as president and CEO of Bridgewater Realty, I'm now on the board of a new holding company called Skybird Investments. A fresh start on things for me, you might say."

"I see. So, are you calling to tell me you're going to fight our warrant to release the Perth mall security tapes?"

"On the contrary. We have everything listed on the warrant ready to send to your Detective Constable Quinn. I just have a couple of questions for you first."

"Questions. I'll just bet you do."

"Simple questions. Hopefully you'll be able to answer them without any discomfort. We can treat it as an exchange of information."

"Ask your questions."

"Very good. First of all, when Detective Constable Walker spoke to our employee in Perth, Mr. Anthony Petrulli, he asked whether our cameras would cover the entirety of the mall parking area. The answer, of course, is yes, which leads me to guess that it's not the grocery store that interests your people but the parking lot itself. Is this a correct assumption?"

Ellie sighed, her eyes on the highway in front of her. "Yes."

"Naturally I've reviewed the footage from the time period requested in the warrant. Would I also be correct to assume that the bus containing young Asian women is the focus of your interest?"

"Why do you ask, Leonardo? Do you know something about this that you should tell me?"

"Well, Ellie, I'm just a simple real estate executive, you understand, but I can assure you this bus does not belong to us or to anyone I know. We're in the real estate business, not the human trafficking business, which is what that very much looks like."

Ellie said nothing.

"For another thing, our vehicles are of a much better quality than the clunky converted school bus in the video. Very amateurish. So. Do you believe this bus, in particular the men, might be involved in the murder of your constable? And the other person? The woman?"

"I can't comment on that, Leonardo."

Silence for a moment. Ellie eased her foot off the accelerator as the highway merged with the 416 and traffic began to edge over into her lane.

"I think these men may be known to us. Would it be helpful if we looked at photographs of the ones you're particularly interested in, to assist in their identification?"

Ellie lifted her foot from the accelerator to change lanes, giving her a moment to think. Although normally cynical when it came to criminals who assured her they would like to be helpful, since altruism wasn't a part of their make-up, Ellie believed that Leonardo Arcuri was an exception. Since he already had the video, he obviously examined the images of the men. Her best guess was that he wanted to see who *she* was interested in. Why not play along and see where it went?

"When your people send the video footage to Detective Constable Quinn," she said, "have them make the arrangements with him for the photos."

"I will. Glad to be of assistance. By the way, Dante sends his regards."

"I thought he was in Italy."

"Oh, he is. He is. Enjoying retirement in his villa on the coast with his olive groves, his ocean breeze, and the slower pace."

"Glad to hear it. He should stay there. I'm surprised you didn't follow him."

"Mmm. Well, for one thing, Ellie, I'm my own man. I don't necessarily 'follow' someone else. And for another thing, I'm a native Canadian, you know. Born and raised. This is my home, not Italy."

"No offence meant, Leonardo."

"None taken. Stay well, Detective Inspector March."

"And you. Keep your nose clean."

"I'll do my best."

The line went dead.

Chapter 31

Heather Hope from Keene had never attended an autopsy before. It wasn't something she'd ever tried to find an excuse to sit in on, nor was it anywhere on her bucket list of things to do before she ended up on the slab herself, another in the endless chain of corpses extending back into the gloom of prehistory and forward into the darkness of oblivion.

She was in a funk.

The operating room, or whatever they called it, was not very big. It was outfitted the way you'd expect it to be, with a dissection table, scales, movable lamps and mirrors, sinks, rolling tables with pans and tools and other stuff, a forensic pathologist, and the pathologist's assistant, referred to by Dr. Kalman as "Claude, my denier."

Oh, hello, Claude. How very nice to meet you.

Gowned and garbed so that only his eyes were showing, it

was impossible to tell if he looked like the reincarnation of Igor or if he was just some guy with a really weird and horrible job. At least he didn't seem to be a hunchback.

Trying to see the lighter side, though, wasn't working. The room was crowded with people. In addition to Dr. Kalman and Claude were Constable Raines, the responding officer who'd accompanied Dorothy Kerr's body to the hospital in order to maintain chain of custody, Identification Constable Jane Witten, who'd attended the victim at the scene, Detective Sergeant Sonja Freeling, who'd hung around after Maynard's autopsy to attend this one as well, and little ol' Heather, sitting on a stool in a corner trying to disappear.

She didn't actually have to be leaning over the damned table watching every organ and gobbet of flesh being removed, photographed, weighed, bagged, and tagged. All that mattered was that she was in the room, fulfilling her duty. It was necessary for Raines to be here for legal continuity, but Ellie's requirement that an investigating detective also attend was just her own policy, a belt-and-suspenders kind of thing that would let the detective inspector sleep at night but was guaranteed to have Heather staring at the ceiling at three o'clock in the morning for the foreseeable future.

She struggled to put her finger on exactly what was upsetting her so much about the procedure.

It wasn't that she'd never seen a dead person before. She'd attended fatal traffic accidents, unexpected deaths at long-term care homes and hospitals, and a couple of suicides so far during her career, so she'd been around corpses enough to be used to them.

She wasn't particularly squeamish, either. She could tolerate the sight of blood and body wastes and all the other revolting Final Indignities that accompanied death, so her stomach was fine. In fact, she'd never lost her lunch once while on the job. Kevin had confided in her that he'd barfed at his first autopsy, and he'd worked hard to get used to them so that it wouldn't happen again, but a weak stomach had never been a problem for her. After all, she'd been born and raised a farm girl. So it wasn't the sights and sounds and smells that were bothering her.

Of course, she'd taken the precaution of bringing nose plugs with her, and they were firmly in place, thank you very much. Heather understood that the pathologist paid close attention to odours during the course of her post-mortem examination, as they might convey to her important information about the victim's physical state, but that didn't mean that Heather had to get in there and sample the air along with her. To hell with that.

It wasn't physical, this thing that was upsetting her. It came from the unavoidable fact that Heather Hope from Keene lived an extended portion of her waking life in the world of her very active imagination.

At the centre of that world was this very crazy worry that the body should remain intact after death so that the soul could still use it on its journey into the Hereafter. She remembered reading once (okay, it was probably in a comic book, but likely a *Classics Illustrated*, which earns extra points for trying) that the ancient Egyptians believed in this sort of thing. It was why they mummified their dead—to preserve the corpse for the journey into the next world.

It had stuck in her head all these years and devolved into a sort of superstition about the body and the afterlife. When her husband's remains had returned from war in a casket that stayed closed until it was lowered into the ground and covered over, because they'd told her they'd had to basically shovel him into the body bag, he was so horribly torn apart, it had made her that much more upset. How would he find her when it was her turn to pass over?

It was why she'd never signed up to be an organ donor. The superstition. Selfish, she admitted, and not necessarily what she'd recommend to anyone else. God, it was so screwed up.

However, it bore noting that she wasn't some gristle-brained lunkhead with eccentric ideas about reality that didn't exactly align with the understanding of so-called normal people. Far from it. She was a university graduate with a Bachelor's degree in English literature, and her grades from the Ontario Police College, first in Basic Constable Training and later in Criminal Investigation Training, consistently placed her in the top 5 per cent of her class. She was bright, self-aware, adaptable, and empathetic.

She just had this thing about death and the human body.

So she sat in a corner of the room, eyes down, nose plugs firmly in place, breath hissing in and out through her clenched jaw, very, very miserable as they dissected the cadaver that had once been a person named Dorothy Kerr.

Chapter 32

Kevin spent the afternoon on the road, driving down to Tay Valley Township. Located at the southwestern tip of Lanark County, it was rocky, hilly country laced with narrow back roads and dotted with legacy farms, small lakes, and pastures filled with boulders and stunted shrubs.

Although Kevin had served in the detachment now for almost two years, there was still much of Lanark County he was unfamiliar with, so he was glad to get out of the office and drive down to North Burgess, one of the three former townships that had amalgamated several decades ago into Tay Valley.

His destination was Searle Meat and Potatoes on Lally Road. He followed Scotch Line Road out of Perth and turned left onto County Road 14, Narrows Lock Road, just before Stanleyville. He'd been on this highway before, but only at the southern portion where it crossed the Rideau Waterway into Leeds County at Narrows Lock.

He'd never been up here, and so on a whim he turned off and drove in to take a look at Stanleyville. It was a small, quiet little hamlet whose primary feature was a large, impressive-looking Catholic church named after St. Brigid, an Irish saint, and an accompanying cemetery across the street.

He sat for a moment, engine idling, and Googled the place. It was named after Michael Stanley, an immigrant from Forkhill, County Armagh, Ireland. The church was built in 1864, one hundred and sixty years ago. The place was originally called Micaville, after a nearby mica mine that provided employment to local immigrants and their families, but eventually the powers that be decided it was better to name the place after a person than a mineral. No doubt Stanley, who'd become a political heavyweight over the years, provided appropriate input.

On a whim, he Googled St. Brigid and learned that she was the patroness saint of Ireland, closely associated with the Celtic goddess of the same name. There was some question as to whether or not she had actually existed, or if she were another Christian version of a Celtic concept, like Halloween and mistletoe. According to Wikipedia, both Brigids, Christian and pagan, were associated with healing, poetry, and dairy cattle. Something Heather might be interested in, he mused.

He drove back out to Narrows Lock Road and continued south. It was a beautiful afternoon. The sun was bright and the sky was blue. He switched to stronger sunglasses and dawdled along at the speed limit, catching glimpses of Black Lake through the trees on the right, until he reached the intersection where Lally Road began.

He turned left and followed it, a narrow, winding lane with trees pressing close on either side. Murphy's Point Provincial Park, a popular spot for tourists and boaters, was somewhere up ahead, and he was glad that there was no other traffic at the moment, because there was little room for two vehicles to pass without losing a side mirror or scraping a fender.

As he drove along a stretch in the road where the edge was a bit higher on the right, exposing rock and sand, he caught several flashes of light out of the corner of his eye. Being curious by nature, he wondered what it was. Being Kevin, he pulled over, shifted into park, set his hazard warning lights, and got out for a look.

He soon spotted several large stones with amber-coloured crystals embedded in them. Intrigued, he picked up a couple and dropped them into his pocket. Back in the car, double-checking behind him to make sure he wasn't holding up traffic, he took a photo of the best-looking specimen. He then used a rocks-and-minerals identification app on his phone to discover that the mineral was phlogopite, a type of mica. Another quick search informed him that the Silver Queen Mine had operated on this very road at the beginning of the previous century, producing phlogopite, apatite, and mica that was sold to markets in Europe, England, and the United States.

They were cool-looking stones, and he thought the kids would get a kick out of them, particularly Brendan, who was currently adding geology to his growing list of interests. He found a plastic bag, dropped them in, and put them on the back seat for later.

Not too much farther along the road he came to a clearing on the left that extended back to accommodate a large working farm. Close by were two buildings. One had a parking area in front and a large sign over the entrance proclaiming to all and sundry that this was Searle Meat and Potatoes. The other was a featureless structure that Kevin assumed was the abattoir.

Kevin parked and went inside the shop.

It was set up like a small general store, with a few aisles stocked with canned goods, dog food, and snacks, but the main attraction was the bank of freezers and coolers at the front on the left and the pallets of bagged potatoes on the right.

The prices on the potatoes struck him as a little high, so he drifted over to the meat. Frozen or fresh? As he lingered in front of a cooler of freshly wrapped steaks, stewing beef, and hamburger, a woman came out of the back room and stood behind the counter.

"Nice day," Kevin said.

"That it is." She was about sixty. Her grey hair was held back by a pale blue bandanna that matched her watchful eyes. She wore a neat green apron over denim coveralls.

"I've never been here before. Do you produce all this beef?"

The woman shook her head. "Locals."

She didn't seem to be much of a talker, but Kevin persevered. "Is that your abattoir next door?"

"Yes."

"So you do everything over there and sell it here."

"We kill, cut, and wrap for customers who bring their stock to us. We buy sides from some of them who need a little help with their payments. That's what you're looking at now."

Kevin picked out three packages of steak and took them over to the counter, thinking he'd surprise Janie with them. He wasn't sure if she had anything particular in mind for dinner, but if not tonight, she might like to grill them up tomorrow. The barbecue was now her territory, and hers alone. He'd tried a few times to cook on it, but he'd soon discovered that grilling wasn't among his skill sets, and Janie had declared it off limits. Thankfully, she knew what she was doing out there and always came back inside with delicious food for everyone.

As he reached for his wallet, his arm brushed back the corner of his jacket. He saw the woman look at his sidearm and freeze.

"Cop," she spat.

"Yes, ma'am. OPP. But right now just a customer buying supper."

Jaw clenched, she rang it up and put the card reader in front of him. As he tapped, she bagged the steak, tore the slip from the reader, tossed it in, and left the bag on the counter.

"Beat it," she said.

Kevin picked up the bag, smiling. "Have a nice afternoon."

Outside, he unlocked the Charger and put the steaks on the back seat next to the stones. He closed the door and walked over to stand in the middle of the gravel driveway that ran between the store and abattoir up to the farmhouse and outbuildings sitting on a slight rise toward the back of the property.

It was a nice spot. The hayfields on either side between here and the house had been mown. Several round bales squatted here and there in the shorn fields. Behind the store he saw the back of a passenger car, a silver Honda, that the woman had probably driven down from the house.

He had a better view of a black Ford F-150 that was parked behind the abattoir, no doubt belonging to the person working inside. Not a dually, though.

He took several photos of the place. As he was walking back to the Charger, an older model pickup truck rolled in and parked. A woman got out and gave him a long, aggressive stare before going into the store.

Kevin started the engine, and then took a moment to send the photos to Alaric for inclusion in the target report he was assembling on the Searles. Then he drove away, feeling very pleased with himself.

Chapter 33

Back at the office, Kevin went looking for Alaric in the comm room. He wasn't there, but Simon was sitting at his desk, headset around his neck, refastening his ponytail with a black scrunchie.

"How was your road trip?" he asked. He was a civilian in the second month of a six-month term contract brought in by Sonja to help out with a backlog of reports in the digital dictation system or in handwritten form, transcribing them into the Records Management System.

"Fine. Nice country." He described where he'd gone.

"Ha, ha. I live down there, and I don't think it's so darned nice."

Kevin sat down in Alaric's visitor's chair. "Is that right? Whereabouts?"

"You passed my place on Narrows Lock. Two-storey

apartment building with white siding. Number four."

"Just before Long Lake Road. Sure. I remember seeing it."

"A palace. Living in the lap of luxury."

"It didn't look too bad to me."

Simon laughed. "It's okay, but once my financial plan works out, I'm going to see if I can find something a little better."

"Plan?"

"Lottery tickets."

Kevin's cellphone buzzed. He took it out and checked the call display. "Hey, Alaric. I'm sitting at your desk right now, waiting for you."

"I'm with Sonja, in her office. Can you join us?"

"Be right there." He slipped the phone into his jacket pocket and stood up. Simon was busy with something on his screen, but he must have seen him peripherally as he moved toward the door. He raised a hand and waggled his fingers.

There were two visitor's chairs in Sonja's office and Alaric was sprawled in one, so Kevin settled down into the other and crossed his legs.

"Alaric's been bringing me up to speed on the Searle angle," Sonja said.

Kevin nodded. Sonja had brought the shaggy detective constable into the crime unit almost two years ago from the Ottawa detachment, at the same time that Kevin was transferring in from Leeds County. Alaric and Sonja had known each other before that, but Kevin wasn't exactly sure how or in what capacity, other than that Sonja was familiar with Alaric's work, including his expertise in forensic accounting and also his connections within various intelligence networks. At a time when the regional intelligence co-ordinator position was vacant due to ongoing resourcing problems, Alaric's ability to work in that area was something she valued very highly.

It helped that they got along well, and Kevin had found that Alaric was hard to dislike. Completely tone deaf when it came to his personal appearance, Alaric's wardrobe tended toward corduroy jackets with elbow patches, twill work trousers with elastic waistbands, and a collection of ties bequeathed him by his late grandfather, a mechanical engineer who'd owned and operated his own tool and die plant.

His beard was trimmed, as per OPP policy requirements, but his eyebrows seemed to have a mind of their own. His footwear consisted of either sandals over black sports socks or Reeboks sneakers (it was a question of brand loyalty). His eyes were friendly, though, and his manner of speaking was direct and honest.

"We got the mall video," he said. "We've also got the McDonald's security footage. You can look it over later, but in a nutshell, here's what we have. The bus is owned by a numbered company which is in turn owned by a company called Freedom Enterprises Ontario L.L.C., the majority owner of which is a guy named Peter Humbert. Ring any bells?"

Kevin frowned at Sonja. "The Freedom Defender guys?"

"Interesting, huh?"

"FEO," Alaric continued, "owns a small fleet, along with heavy construction equipment they rent out, a few transport trucks, and other assorted stuff."

"And they run a little human trafficking business on the side?"

"Looks like. I've passed this on to people who are interested in this sort of thing—"

"Miss Drillon," Sonja interjected in a stage whisper.

"—and they'll do what they do, but at the moment our interest is limited to something else. Something immediately relevant to our investigation."

Miss Drillon, Kevin was aware, referred to Brooke Drillon, Alaric's girlfriend. She was an intelligence analyst with the RCMP and a match for Alaric when it came to IQ *and* eccentricity. Kevin had never met her. But he'd seen pictures. Apparently she loved *Dungeons and Dragons*, including the cosplay that sometimes went with it.

"Which is?"

Face red, Alaric tried to ignore Sonja's teasing. "The black truck reported by your witness? The one in the parking lot that followed Dorothy Kerr after she picked up the woman?"

"Yeah?"

"The licence plate is registered to Searle Meat and Potatoes."

"Shit."

"Yeah. The link you were looking for, eh?"

"You said it."

Alaric adjusted his glasses, which today were red frames to match his red Reeboks, and looked thoughtful. "We've pulled stills from the external video and blown them up, but we're still looking for a match. Same with the two guys in and out of the McDonald's, which we've got from their security cameras." He raised his eyebrows. "Ellie's arranged for a little outside help."

"What kind of outside help?"

Sonja cleared her throat.

"An individual named Leonardo Arcuri," Alaric said. "Apparently you've met him before."

Kevin stared at him in surprise.

"He's president and CEO of Bridgewater Realty," Alaric explained, "the company that owns the mall and supplied the video."

"Well, I'll be—and you're saying he's going to identify these guys for us?"

Alaric glanced at his watch. "I'm expecting a response in about, uh, ninety minutes."

"They work for him? They're 'Ndrangheta?"

"That's the thing. Apparently they're not. According to Ellie, Arcuri claims the real estate company is above board, and his, um, organization isn't involved in human trafficking. At least not up this way."

Kevin thought it through. "Freelancers, maybe. Operating without permission from organized crime. We're playing with fire, here."

"I trust that Ellie knows what she's doing," Sonja said.

Alaric grunted. "In the meantime, we'll be handing off this part of the investigation to FIS, who'll take it from there."

The Field Intelligence Section's unit in Ottawa would co-ordinate with their joint forces partners in other law enforcement agencies, including the Ottawa Police Service and the RCMP.

Kevin bit his lip. "Okay, fine. That leaves me with the black truck and the Searles."

"Correct. Thanks for the pics of the store and abattoir, by the way. Better than what you get from Google Street View."

"What I'd like to do," Kevin said, "is talk to the guys who patrol down there. Get their take on the family, how they fit in the community, that sort of thing."

"Talk to Bridges," Sonja said, referring to the sergeant commanding the Lanark Patrol unit.

"Recon," Alaric said. "Always a good idea."

Kevin found Andy Bridges in the lunch room, pouring himself a cup of coffee.

"You're in luck, Walker," he said, sipping the black brew cautiously. "Pound's still in the building. Even better, he seems to be in a good mood today. Don't piss him off, okay?"

Provincial Constable Ron Pound stood in front of his locker with a towel around his waist as Kevin walked in and sat down on a bench opposite. He ran an electric razor around his face as Kevin explained what he was looking for.

"Sure. Tough bunch. They like to throw their weight around." He put away the razor and slapped aftershave on his cheeks. "Every now and again Dan and I get called out to a farm or something where one of the Searle boys is causing trouble."

"What kind of trouble?"

Pound removed the towel and pulled on a pair of Montreal Canadiens boxer shorts. "You name it. They show up, and pretty soon the wife or girlfriend or mother's calling 911. We get there, and, hey, it was all just a big misunderstanding. And the woman who called it in is nowhere to be seen."

"Hunh."

"And they're equal-opportunity shit disturbers." Pound climbed into a pair of black denim jeans and tugged up the zipper. "Sometimes it's a squabble over some young guy's car, but like as not it's older people they're hassling about selling their property and clearing out. The Searles are ambitious sons of bitches, that's for sure."

"I don't suppose anybody would be willing to talk about it?"

Pound made a noise. "Not likely. A lot of guys walking around down there with permanent limps." He ducked his head into the neck hole of a black golf shirt, turned it around until it was facing the right way, and tugged it down over his muscular torso.

"You might try old MacDuff. He's the local farrier. Crusty old geezer. Nothing much seems to scare him."

"Thanks." Kevin stood up and left the locker room as Pound sat down to lace up a pair of black Nikes.

Chapter 34

At the team meeting the next morning, which was Thursday, Doug Skelton leaned back in his chair and studied the patterns made by old water stains on the ceiling tiles as Bob Pierce went over their activities from yesterday. They'd re-interviewed Maynard's neighbours, who'd been covered during the widespread canvass on Monday, but they had nothing else of interest to offer. In the afternoon, they'd looked up a couple of his fishing buddies, a used-car salesman and an electrician, but neither seemed inclined to talk about possible enemies Maynard might have had, husbands whose wives he might have been caught with, or any other likely candidates for closer scrutiny.

"The electrician, Brookfield, talked about Maynard's problem with boating and drinking, but made it clear he himself was the one who did the driving, or whatever you call it when it comes to boats. Maynard sat in the middle, drank beer from the cooler between his legs, and talked."

"What did he talk about?" Alaric asked.

Pierce rolled his eyes. "Sports, women, immigration, women, celebrities, female celebrities, his female neighbours, movies he liked to watch on DVD, and women." He glanced at Skelton. "Did I miss anything?"

Skelton shrugged, not particularly interested.

"MacRae," Pierce added, "the used-car salesman, said that afterwards, in the cottage, he'd ramble on about politics and how much he hated anarchists and all the rest, but it didn't last long because he'd pass out and make them the gift of a couple hours' peace and quiet before it was time to go home."

"Doesn't sound like they were close friends," Ellie observed.

"I don't think Constable Maynard had any close friends. We also checked up on Maynard's ex-wife. She's accounted for; and it's unlikely she has enough money to have paid someone to kill Maynard for her. She's paycheque to paycheque."

Skelton suddenly came back down to earth. "I understand you've made progress with the mall video," he said to Kevin.

"It's a work in progress," Heather said.

"What's the name of the company again that owns it?"

"The mall?" Heather glanced at Ellie. "Bridgewater Realty."

"Organized crime?"

"It looks that way."

"Human trafficking?"

"We've passed the information on to FIS," Alaric said. "They're looking into it."

"Are you thinking that's the connection to Kerr? That she was the primary target because she stumbled across their operation?"

"We're not there yet."

"Doug," Kevin interjected, "what do you know about the Searles? In North Burgess?"

"Are you talking about the meat and potatoes family?"

"Yeah."

"Not much. I don't get down there very often. You think they're involved with this?"

"Yeah, they showed up on the video."

Skelton said nothing, his face a careful blank.

When the meeting ended, Kevin was about to say something to Heather when Sonja Freeling interrupted. "In my office."

Heather nodded wordlessly.

Left alone in the meeting room, Kevin realized that Heather had been far from her usual buoyant self this morning. She'd arrived at the detachment office in navy twill trousers and a pale blue golf shirt, obviously chosen from the boring and conforming end of her closet, and the usual wisecracks and sarcasms had not been in evidence.

Kevin waited for her outside in the parking lot, perched on the front fender of the Charger, watching traffic roll past in the street. His mood was a little down. He realized that Skelton was sniffing around for something, and it bothered him.

Kevin was also concerned about Heather. What did Sonja want with her? Was there some kind of problem?

Here she was now, emerging from the back door and trudging toward him, head down, hands shoved in her pockets. He mulled over his options and decided to wait for her to speak first. They got in the car and Kevin took them down Sunset to Christie Lake Road, where he turned right and slowly accelerated up to highway speed.

She cracked her knuckles, staring straight ahead, until Kevin slowed for the left-hand turn onto Bowes Side Road. She adjusted her sunglasses, thumped a fist on her thigh, and hissed. "Stupid. Stupid, stupid."

"What is?"

"They had a meeting. To pick the delegation. Sonja gave me the news. Malcolmsen wanted a woman from the detachment. Everybody else already had their lists—all men, of course—so I was elected. Jesus.""

It took Kevin a moment. "You're talking about the funeral."

"Yes, I'm talking about the funeral. Skelton's going to be extremely pissed."

"He probably wouldn't want to leave his farm and the animals. It's going to be a couple of days, altogether."

"I know. But it's yet another reason for him to hate my guts."

"He doesn't hate your guts, Heather."

She gave him a sidelong look. "Ground control to Major Tom. Can you hear me?"

"It's an honour to be chosen. Congratulations."

"Maynard was a despicable troll. Some honour."

They wound their way into North Burgess. Heather was familiar with the area, but she set the GPS on her cellphone anyway so that Kevin could follow its directions until they arrived at Pike Lake Road. Before long, he turned into the yard at civic number 1973 and they got out.

The house was an old log cabin with updated windows and a tin roof. There was an extension on the side, shaded by a mature Manitoba maple tree, with a vinyl exterior, a single window covered with drapes, and a side door. On the right was a large barn with big double doors and a people-sized entrance, above which was hung a painted sign that said "Farrier."

There were two vehicles in the yard, an older model Grand Cherokee and a Nissan pickup truck with a white cap and a magnetic sign on the door advertising "J. MacDuff, Farrier."

They'd come to the right place.

They found the old man organizing tools on a workbench next to his forge. A small man in stained coveralls and work boots, his white hair stuck out from under a battered driver's cap in a shock across his forehead. He stared at their warrant cards and badges with worried brown eyes before leading them out the back door to a small area with a picnic table, a burn barrel, and a fenced-in chicken coop with hens poking around in the dirt and grass.

He took out a pack of cigarettes, offered them around, then lit one for himself. Tossing the spent match into the burn barrel, he put the pack away and blew out a cloud of smoke.

"What can I do for you folks?"

Kevin parked his haunch on the edge of the picnic table. "We understand you work as a farrier for the farmers around here, is that right?"

"Farmers, yup, and horse folks who ride and breed and that sort of thing." He worked his cigarette. "Did I do something wrong?"

"No, not at all. We thought you might be able to help us out with a few questions about some of the people who live in the area."

He squinted at Kevin through a veil of smoke. "Like who we talking about?"

Kevin smiled, as though caught in a poor attempt at subterfuge. "The Searles, for example."

"Thought as much."

"Why's that, Mr. MacDuff?"

"Any time the police come around here asking questions, like as not there's a Searle behind it somehow. What've they done now?"

Heather gave him a bright little smile. "How long have you been in business, Mr. MacDuff?"

The old man lit a fresh cigarette off the one he was smoking and threw the butt into the burn barrel. "You can call me Jock. Everybody does, except Revenue Canada. I've been doing this for nearly sixty years. What'd you say your name was, again?"

"Heather."

"Now there's a fine Scots name for you."

"My great-grandparents came from Scotland."

"Lovely!"

"Sixty years?" Kevin repeated.

"Near about. Learned the trade from my uncle, my mother's

brother. Andrew Burns. Mean-spirited old crabbit, but he gave me the gift of a lifetime's work, and I'm grateful for that."

"I'm a farmer's daughter myself," Heather said. "I grew up on a dairy farm. We had a couple of horses, but nothing much to speak of."

"Where was this, dear?"

"Keene. In Peterborough County."

"I know of it, although I can't say I've been there."

"Do you know Constable Pound? He patrols this area for us."

"Sure. Decent guy. Good family man, I hear. Four or five kids."

"He suggested we might want to talk to you about the Searle family."

"Did he, now?"

Heather looked concerned. "Was he wrong about that?"

"No. No, he wasn't. But it's never a wise policy to get too deep into the affairs of people like them. Not good for the health."

"Have they threatened you before?"

MacDuff moved over to the picnic table and sat down. Heather sat down across from him.

"I'm their tenant, you see." He chain-lit a fresh cigarette, stubbed out the butt, and dropped it into the turned-up cuff of his overalls. "The land and buildings here belong to them. I've been renting for over twenty years, now."

"Have there been problems?"

The old man shrugged. "At first. The missus liked to come over looking for trouble. I had to set her straight. Haven't seen her for years now." He shook his head. "The boys drop in every month to collect the rent and sometimes wanting me to fix something for them, like my forge is their personal property. I do it when I have the time. Don't get paid for it, though."

"Any rough stuff?"

MacDuff chuckled. "No. Not with me, anyways. Rough

language, yeah. Pretty foul-mouthed bunch, and they love talking tough, but I don't give them any excuse to push me around. Rent's always ready and waiting when they come looking for it."

The chuckle became a snort. "Not that I couldn't stand up for myself if they did. I've always got a hammer or a pair of tongs within quick reach, you see."

Kevin repressed a smile, imagining the elderly bantamweight in front of him mixing it up with young, work-hardened men. "But they get that way with other people, do they?"

The farrier tapped his cigarette. "Yeah. Now and again."

"For example?"

"Ohhh, I don't like going over old ground. Don't see the point."

"We're trying to get a sense of the sort of things they're capable of doing to other people," Heather said.

He looked at her. "What do you think they've gotten into now?"

Heather glanced at Kevin. "We're investigating that double homicide that happened in Drummond on Monday."

"No kidding. Where the cop was killed." He nodded. "One of yours."

"One of ours, yes. And another person, Miss Kerr."

"And you think the Searles are mixed up in that?"

"We haven't gotten that far yet," Heather said. "Right now we're just running down leads, gathering information, all that stuff. The Searles were seen in the same place as Miss Kerr the night before she was shot, so that's what we're looking at right now. Whether it means anything, or it was just a coincidence."

MacDuff thought about this for a long moment. "There was an older couple named Shonfeld, lived on the next line over from here. This was back when I first came here from Quebec, the Eastern Townships, after my wife passed away. They were a couple of ex-hippies from the city who bought a small plot of land and tried to make it as itinerant farmers. Had a bunch of kids, a few milch cows, that sort of thing. Pretty hopeless. They made butter and maple syrup and stuff like that to sell at the farmer's market in town, and they raised some beef cattle as their main source of income. Trouble was, they had to take the animals to the Searles for slaughter and dressing, because they couldn't afford to haul them farther, and Shonfeld couldn't always pay the bill.

"Tommy got tired of it after a while and came around with one of his sons. The official story was that Shonfeld had an accident with his tractor, that it rolled over and smashed his leg, and Tommy found him that way and pulled him out, but everybody knew better. Gary, the youngest, is a mean sonofabitch with a baseball bat in his hands."

Heather shook her head. "Pretty cold."

"They left a month or two later. Sold everything to Tommy and disappeared. That's the place where his second oldest, Bert, lives now."

"You think the Searles are capable of killing people? Is that what you're saying?"

"Oh, I don't know if I'd go that far." MacDuff stubbed out his cigarette on the picnic table top and left it there. "They're capable of a lot of bad things, though."

Heather leaned her elbows on the table, wanting to hear more.

"You have to appreciate this is hardscrabble country," MacDuff said. "Just look around you. Rock covered with scrub; abandoned mines that haven't been worked in decades; poor, thin soil. Animal husbandry is the only way to make any kind of living at all unless you're lucky enough to have a piece of the tourist business along the Rideau. Their place is a legacy farm. Know what that means?"

"Sure," Heather said. "It goes back generations to the original settlers of the property. With a heritage designation. We lived down the road from a couple of them when I was growing up."

"From what I've heard," MacDuff said, taking out a package

of chewing tobacco and stuffing a wad under his lower lip, "Keene's good farm country. Place like this, though, people need a certain mentality to persevere for two centuries in the same spot, like they've done. The earliest Searles didn't take too long to figure out their government grant wasn't much good for growing crops, so they got into beef. Ended up controlling that whole business in the area until Tommy's old man, Hank, ran into financial troubles thanks to liquor and carelessness. Had to sell off chunks of the farm and other properties the family had added to their little kingdom along the way until all he had left was the original house and ten acres."

He leaned over and spat into the grass. "That's when Tommy, who was in his twenties at the time, started up the abattoir."

"You seem to know all about them," Heather said.

MacDuff laughed. "Nothing wrong with my ears. And you know country folk, they love to talk. I spend half my time shoeing their horses and the other half drinking their tea and listening to their stories. And the Searles have always been a favourite topic around here."

"Thomas Searle would be in his middle sixties now," Kevin said.

"That's right. And he's spent his whole life rebuilding their little empire. A lot of folks around here have had financial trouble now and again, what with the economic downturns and recessions and all the rest. As I say, the youngest, Gary, is his leg-breaker when he wants to teach a lesson, but sometimes he just arranges to pay off their debts in exchange for their land. They become his tenants, and he can do whatever the hell he wants to them after that."

They listened to the sound of a vehicle slowing down and turning into MacDuff's driveway. He led them back through his shop and out the front door just as a big black pickup truck pulled up and the engine was shut off.

Kevin glanced at the licence plate, memorizing the number. He noticed that the truck wasn't a dually.

"Speak of the devil," MacDuff murmured, standing next to Kevin, "and he's sure to appear. The one behind the wheel's Gary, the knee-capper, and the other's Bert."

"Think they've got a horse that needs shoeing?" Kevin asked.

"Not damned likely."

Chapter 35

Kevin was not the kind of police officer who went out of his way to look for trouble. Although he had the size to handle it and a former hockey player's appreciation of the subtleties of rough play, he preferred not to let matters devolve to a physical level if he could possibly help it.

Just the same, when a situation called for him to step forward and assert himself, he didn't hesitate. It helped that he possessed the courage to place himself in harm's way if necessary, and it also helped that he had a fairly high pain threshold.

"What can I help you boys with today?" MacDuff stopped a few paces short of the truck.

Kevin took a few extra steps to place himself slightly ahead of the old man.

Gary Searle was the first one out of the truck. His green T-shirt stretched tight across his muscular torso, a white ball cap covered his shaved head, and his eyes were hidden behind Wayfarer-style sunglasses. He wasn't carrying a gun, but the sheath looped on his belt told Kevin he was armed with a knife that looked like it might be a KA-BAR USMC combat knife with a seven-inch blade. Legal to carry in Canada.

Gary leaned his haunch against the fender of his truck and folded his arms. His clean-shaven face was expressionless.

One tough dude.

His brother strolled toward them, hands loose at his sides. Bert Searle was five or six years older than Gary, and not quite as hard-edged. He wore a pale blue short-sleeved shirt, jeans, and dark brown moccasins. No knife. He showed them crooked teeth in a fake friendly smile.

"Jock, my man. You're late. What's going on?"

"You didn't come around on Monday," MacDuff replied. "I was expecting you, since it was the first of the month. You'd didn't show on Tuesday, either."

"Well, we were here yesterday, and guess what? No Jock. You know how annoying that is?"

"I was on the road. Working. People make appointments, I show up."

Bert frowned. "Where was this, now?"

"McGill's farm."

Gary barked a laugh, and Bert shook his head. "Goats, for chrissakes."

"Goats have hooves too, you know."

"Any fool can trim a goat's hooves," Bert scoffed. "Nothing to it."

"Some people prefer to have a professional do it, thank you very much."

Bert spat on the ground. "Shut up and go get the money."

"Sure, Bert. Be right back." MacDuff walked away in the direction of his house.

"So what were you boys busy doing on Monday?" Kevin asked, as though making polite conversation.

"None of your fucking business. Why don't you fuck off out of here while you can still walk on both legs?"

Kevin moved his jacket aside to show his holstered weapon.

Gary laughed. "Shit, Bert. He's a cop. Show a little more respect."

"And his girl partner." Bert stared at Heather, who was holding up her badge. He suddenly frowned at Kevin. "Hey, now. You wouldn't be the cop who was harassing my mother yesterday, would you?"

Kevin shrugged. "No. But I did buy some pretty good steaks from her."

Gary slowly straightened up.

Bert pointed at him. "Be smart and don't show your face on our property again."

"Let's try not to write cheques your ass can't cash, eh, Bert?"

At that point, MacDuff came out with a manila envelope in his hand. He shuffled past Kevin and gave it to Bert, who opened it up and looked inside.

"It's all there," MacDuff growled.

"Sure. Thanks." Bert closed the envelope and stuffed it under the waistband of his jeans at the small of his back. "Make sure you're home next time we come around."

"You make sure you come around next time when I'm home. How about that?"

As they watched them turn around in the yard and drive back down to the road, MacDuff muttered, "Damned bastards."

"Seem like fine, upstanding young men," Heather said.

MacDuff gave her a long, withering look.

Chapter 36

That afternoon, Pierce was at his workstation writing a report when Alaric tapped on the divider. "Got a sec?"

"Sure. What's up?"

"There's a Crime Stoppers call I've logged into your Inbox. Would you do me a favour and check it out?"

"No problem." Pierce saved and closed his report.

"It's called 'Parashar-underscore-oh-one.' Some lady called to say her boarder's acting up and talking about cops getting what they deserve. We need to follow up on it."

"I'm on it," Pierce said. He slipped on a headset as Alaric disappeared with a wave. He found the file and opened it.

The caller was a woman named Elaine Parashar. She lived on Birch Street in what she described as a "nice three-storey craftsman home" that was a bit too big for her now that she was a widow and retired from her job as a bookkeeper. She rented a second-floor suite of rooms to a man named Dan Keegan who was "a bit of a drinker." He'd gotten rowdy the night before and was yelling about "cops getting what they deserved," and she was getting a little scared.

Pierce called her up and arranged to stop by for a chat. Then he went looking for Skelton. He wasn't at his desk, and his hat wasn't on the coat hook. The guy in the next workstation, DeBrees, told him that Skelton had gone over to the feed store to settle some kind of dispute. Apparently they'd delivered the wrong order to his farm and overcharged him for it.

"Chicken feed instead of sheep chow," DeBrees said. "He was a little pissed."

"I thought they just grazed," Pierce said.

"I just eat them. I don't dish out their supper, so don't ask me."

Pierce texted Alaric that he was going to check out Mrs. Parashar and follow up on the call. Alaric immediately replied that he was fine with that and would let Ellie and Sonja know what was happening.

Before leaving, Pierce hit the washroom. At the sinks, he washed his hands, checked his look in the mirror, and left.

The Parashar house was indeed a fine old craftsman, well kept with a neat lawn and a cement driveway. He parked behind an older model Saab and rang the doorbell.

Elaine Parashar was a white-haired woman of east Indian descent dressed in blue jeans and a green-and-gold paisley top. She brought Pierce inside with a quick look at the street, in case Keegan might appear in the driveway at any moment.

"He's at work, like I said on the phone, but I'm a little worried." She led the way into the living room, where Pierce sat down on an oval beige sofa. Coffee or tea was offered and politely declined.

"As I said on the phone, he's usually a quiet man, no trouble at all. No loud music, no parties. No visitors at all, actually. It's just when he drinks that the problems begin."

"Does he get violent, Mrs. Parashar?"

"He stays in his room, for which I'm grateful, because I'm not sure what would happen if I tried to confront him in any way. When he's sober, he's polite and quiet, pays his rent on time and never complains about anything, but when he starts to drink it's like he becomes a different person. A bad person. He breaks things and swears loudly. So, I suppose you could say he's violent that way."

Pierce was taking notes. He finished scribbling and looked up at her. "Where does he work?"

"At the wire factory on the edge of town. He said something one time about having had a long day on the forklift."

"How does he spend his time when he's home?"

She thought for a moment. "I can hear the TV up there sometimes, but he keeps it turned down low so it's not a problem. He probably has it on while he cleans his guns."

"Guns?"

"I can smell the gun oil. And when I clean his rooms, which is every Tuesday and Friday morning, I find wadding and things like that in the waste paper basket when I empty it out. He keeps the suite locked, but we have an understanding that I'll go in at those times to vacuum and dust and take out the garbage."

"I see."

"He has a gun safe up there, so he must keep them in that because I never see them sitting around, but it makes me nervous knowing they're in the house. I don't like guns. My late husband bought one for himself, but I made him get rid of it. Mr. Keegan said one time that he has a collection, so I assume that means several. It must be because he was in the army when he was younger."

"Does he talk about that kind of thing? His guns, or his military background?"

She shook her head. "Not really very much. He doesn't talk to me often. He's . . . solitary."

"Tell me about last night. When you decided to call Crime

Stoppers."

"Well, I wasn't eavesdropping." She laughed without humour. "He was so loud, I didn't have to, anyway. I was passing in the hallway, on my way to the stairs to go up into the attic. I keep books up there out of the way, and I was looking for one I wanted to read again. At any rate, I could hear the television in his room, turned to the news about the police funeral that will happen on Monday. I heard glass clinking, like he was pouring a drink, and suddenly he started swearing at the broadcast. Yelling that the cop had gotten exactly what he deserved and there was more where that came from. 'Who's next?' he kept saying. 'Who wants a piece of this?' And I could hear a snapping sound. I think it was an unloaded gun being fired. It was very upsetting."

"I can imagine." Pierce hesitated, not sure how to frame the question. "Did he say anything else about it? Suggesting that he might have been personally involved in the shooting?"

She sighed. "It was mostly incoherent. Loud cursing and rambling. The only parts I could understand, I've already told you about. I'm sorry."

"Please, don't worry." Pierce checked his notes. "I take it that parking's included with his rent."

"Yes. He usually parks his truck far enough over to the side that I can get by him when I have to go out, but sometimes I need to ask him to move it a bit so I can get out of the garage. He gets a little testy about it."

"Oh?"

She looked down, embarrassed. "You know. Bad language. Not necessarily directed at me, and not loud. Under his breath. That sort of thing."

"What kind of truck is it?"

"I'm not sure, but it's on the lease he signed for me."

"Could I see it?"

"Of course. Let me just go get it."

Pierce watched her leave. He considered asking to see Keegan's room, but was hesitant to look around without a warrant, given that the man kept his possessions behind a locked door. If Keegan were their shooter, everything would have to be done just right, by the numbers and completely clean.

Mrs. Parashar returned and handed him a large manila envelope. Pierce pulled out a three-page document, typed and stapled, based on a common lease form found online. Keegan had filled out most of the blank fields in a blue ballpoint pen, and other details such as the amount of rent and start- and end-dates of the agreement were written in another hand, no doubt Mrs. Parashar's.

Keegan had taken the room on the first of November, 2022, and when the term had run out last year, Mrs. Parashar had written "and monthly thereafter," which both parties had initialled.

Turning to the second page, he found where Keegan had filled in the blanks related to his truck, a 2016 Ford F-150. Balancing his notebook on his knee, he jotted down the information, including the licence number and colour—black. He had no idea if F-150s came with dual rear wheels or just single, but he'd find out soon enough.

The third page contained the signatures of both parties, the date, and the signature of a witness—T. Maloney.

"Who's this?"

"Tom Maloney. He was here cleaning the furnace while Mr. Keegan was looking at the apartment. He was glad to help us out."

Pierce hesitated, trying to recall the law as it related to documents found without a warrant. If he used his camera to take photos of the lease agreement, and they turned out to be important evidence in a case against Daniel Keegan, would they be disallowed because he'd obtained them without a warrant? Mrs. Parashar had handed him the document of her own free will, yes, but Keegan was also a signatory to the thing and he wasn't around to give his permission. Pierce clenched his teeth, trying unsuccessfully to sort through what he remembered on the subject.

Best to err on the side of caution. They could always come back with a warrant if the lease agreement turned out to be important. He put it back in the envelope, stood up, and handed it to Mrs. Parashar.

"Thanks very much for your help." He took out a card and gave it to her. "Call me at any time, particularly if you're still worried or if he gets out of control again."

"I have a portable phone," she said. "I'll carry it around with me, in my pocket. With your number on speed dial."

Chapter 37

That evening, Ellie was in her home office, logged in through a secure connection on her laptop, reading reports that were filling up the folders in the Maynard/Kerr case. She picked up her cup, but it was empty, and as she was absent-mindedly setting it aside Reggie kicked at the kitchen door to be let in.

It was past eight o'clock and the sun had already set, so when she moved aside the curtain and looked out, she could see the big German shepherd grinning up at her in the yellow porch light, his tail wagging. She let the curtain fall back and did nothing, just to tease him.

Reggie kicked again, harder this time.

She opened the door and stepped aside as he barged into the kitchen. As she closed the door and turned around, he head-butted her thigh and trotted off into the office, thumping down on the rug.

She made herself a fresh cup of coffee, stirred in a teaspoon of honey, and grabbed a new chew bone from the cupboard. Reggie's tail beat a steady rhythm as she set down her coffee and bent over to scratch his ear.

"Anything interesting out there tonight? Raccoons or porcupines hanging around?"

Reggie growled, his tail slowing a little. He didn't like porcupines, having gotten a muzzle full of quills last fall. They were Public Enemy Number One, as far as he was concerned.

"Here." She handed him the rawhide bone. "Gnaw on this and forget your troubles."

At that moment her cellphone began to vibrate. She sat down and picked it up, frowning. It was Grayson Kennedy.

"Hello, Gray. Anything wrong?"

"Hi, Ellie." He sounded nervous. "How are you this evening?"

She decided immediately to cut to the chase. "Are you drinking?"

"No, actually. No, I'm not."

Knowing that alcoholics routinely lied about their consumption when they were off the wagon, she didn't necessarily believe him. She'd know for sure, though, in a moment or two.

"What can I do for you, Gray?"

"Well, I've just been sitting here, thinking."

"I see."

"Sober, Ellie. You have my word. Sitting at the window, smoking cigarettes, watching the traffic in the street. Thinking about all the things I've done wrong in my life and how I'd really like to make amends. Before it's too late."

"We all have regrets, Gray," she said, deciding to believe him. His voice, although low and soft, was even and under control. No slurring, no stumbling. "It goes with the territory. It's what makes us human."

She looked at Reggie, chewing industriously on his bone. No regrets there.

"I felt rejuvenated, Ellie, coming off the bench like that. Being in the field again, handling a big responsibility, being in command. I still have that in me, you know? I'm not washed up yet."

"You did an excellent job, Gray. Everyone thought the crime scene was very well managed."

"Thanks. I appreciate it." He sighed and shifted around in his chair. "Look, I don't want to waste your time. You're probably sitting there reading interview transcripts and crime scene reports. I'll get to the point."

She waited, sipping her coffee.

"I know that the crime unit's going to be down a couple bodies this weekend. Because of the funeral. Two from the crime unit, isn't it? And personnel from RHQ also going. I'd like to volunteer my services. To you. To help out for the next few days."

Ellie was surprised. It wasn't at all what she'd expected him to come out with. "Help out in what way?"

"With the investigation. Assisting the crime unit. Interviews, surveillance, whatever."

"Christ, Gray."

"I know, Ellie. It's a big ask."

She hesitated, trying to decide how to put her concerns into words. He anticipated her with a sigh.

"I'm more than two years sober. I started out with AA, but I didn't like their program and switched to a secular one that meets once a week here. In Smiths Falls. They give you a little badge you can wear with each milestone. I've got my two-year one in my hand right now, looking at it. That's what gave me the courage to call. That and a couple of cigarettes first."

"Look, this is gnarly, to say the least," Ellie said. "What you're asking is nowhere in your job description, not by a long shot. If something happens, the association will crucify Colleen, Malcolmsen, Ron Belanger, and everybody else right up the line. Including me."

"The Association and I are not exactly on speaking terms right now. They pissed me off, and I stopped paying my dues. Quite a while ago. They've delisted me, as I understand it."

The OPP Commissioned Officers Association was an organization that served as a link between officers at the rank of inspector and up. It was the senior equivalent of the Ontario Provincial Police Association, the union representing the rank and file.

"I see." Ellie closed her eyes and rubbed her forehead, listening to Reggie's molars grind against tough rawhide.

"You're not my first call tonight," he went on. "Ron and I are still friends. He owes me a couple, going back to our Middlesex days. So he called Mal, who called me. He said I'd have to run it by you before it'd go anywhere. So here I am, asking if you think there might be a possibility I could be involved in your investigation."

She opened her eyes and tipped back her head, staring at the ceiling. He was putting her in a hell of a spot. If he'd already gone over her head to a deputy commissioner and a chief inspector, and they were at least entertaining the idea, what the hell was she supposed to say? "Sorry, Gray, it's a wacky idea and those guys should've known better"?

"I've agreed to sign a waiver of liability," he said. "If you green-light it, Mal will sign off. If you deep-six it, we forget the whole thing."

"Shit." She knew a liability waiver was worth less than the piece of paper it was printed on, if they ended up in court. It was an enormous risk.

He had enough sense to stop talking and let her think.

She flipped over to Text, found Jordan Malcolmsen in her Contacts list, and typed:

Talking to Gray.

Within seconds, as though he were waiting for her message, he responded:

Sorry, El. Ron owes him a few.

A waiver?? Wtf.

I know. Your call, El. I'll take the hit if it goes south.

You sure?

Then Ron will owe me one. Big time.

She closed the app, gritting her teeth. She could hear Gray's rapid breathing.

"Your rank is a problem," she said after a moment. "I could pair you with Walker, for example, but we couldn't have you overriding his decisions and pulling crap like that."

"Understood." There was a slight lift to his voice, as though he could tell she was working her way through the problem he'd dropped in her lap. "I'd have observer status only. I could make suggestions and offer advice, if he's open to it, but the call would always be his."

Ellie was never adverse to taking a risk when the situation called for it. Gray had gauged the situation well; they would be shorthanded over the weekend, and the investigation was gaining momentum, particularly along the track focusing on Dorothy Kerr. Kevin needed a helping hand, and at one time Gray Kennedy had been a well-respected, valuable member of the OPP.

"Okay. Take a day to think it over. Think very carefully. If you still want to do this, I'll see you Saturday morning, nine o'clock sharp, in my office."

She pretended not to hear the sob of relief as Gray hung up.

Chapter 38

It was Friday, and Doug Skelton's morning had not gotten off to a good start. When he went out to the barn after breakfast, before leaving for work, he discovered that the power was off. A quick search revealed that a rat had become interested in the wiring and had done enough damage to shut everything down (and electrocute himself in the process). Very grateful that a fire hadn't started as a result, Skelton was obliged to repair it on the spot, muttering all the while about barn cats that were supposed to take care of vermin like this instead of goofing off outside in the woodpile.

As a result, he was late getting into his cubicle and logging in. His butt was barely in his seat after a quick trip to the washroom when someone poked their head in his doorway to tell him that Sonja wanted to see him in her office.

Christ, he thought, expecting that he was going to hear it about having been late.

"Come in, Doug. Close the door."

He was surprised to find that her tone was light and her smile was friendly. He knew that she didn't particularly like him, and having expected to receive a hand slap for lateness, he was caught off guard. Sitting down, he crossed his legs and folded his hands on his knee.

"As you're aware," she said, "our delegation is travelling to Collingwood tomorrow, but we've run into a bit of a snag. Lapointe has come up with a bad case of food poisoning and won't be able to go. Staff Sergeant Dunn wants to know if you'll fill in for him."

"Sure," Skelton said automatically, still processing the sudden turn of events.

"Great. Tomorrow is your travel day, as I said. Sunday you'll have meetings and a rehearsal, and then Monday's the funeral. Staff will send you the full details."

"Fine. I'll need today off to organize things at home. I can't just leave the animals to fend for themselves. I'll have to make arrangements. On short notice."

"Understood."

"I've got plenty of leave."

"That's fine, Doug. I'll let Staff know."

I'd better check the rest of the wiring this afternoon while I'm at it, Skelton thought, heading back to his cubicle.

About time they came to their senses and went with the senior man.

Chapter 39

As the rocky pastureland of North Burgess rolled past on either side, Kevin glanced over at Heather, inscrutable behind black butterfly-framed sunglasses.

"I hear Doug's attending the funeral too," he said.

"Yeah. So I hear."

"That should make you feel better. That you're not bumping him out of something he thinks is rightfully his."

She lowered the sunglasses on her nose and looked at him. "I have to spend the weekend with Doug Skelton. Think about that for a minute."

"Sorry." He smiled as he watched the road for a while, then turned his thoughts to the upcoming confrontation.

"It's Thomas I want. The others we've seen, but not him. I want to look him in the eye when he hands us his bullshit."

"Geez, you sound pretty tough, Kev."

"Yeah."

The fact of the matter was that Kevin was developing a strong dislike for the Searles and was reaching the point where he was ready to start throwing his weight around. Too much time had passed since Dorothy Kerr and Terry Maynard had been shot, as far as he was concerned, and it was time for things to start breaking in the case. He was determined to shake Thomas Henry Searle's tree and see what fell out.

When they pulled into the parking lot and got out, they saw a truck parked at the far side of the abattoir with its gate down. A young guy was leading a steer down the ramp into the back door of the building, supervised by Al Searle, the oldest son, who wore green protective coveralls, blue gloves, and a blue hard hat.

Inside, they found Thomas with an older man, leaning against a support post as they watched the animal being jockeyed along a chute into the room where its life would be terminated.

Kevin and Heather badged him. He pushed away from the post and tipped back his white hard hat.

"I'm in the middle of something. Could you give us a few minutes, please?"

"We'll wait outside," Heather said. "Don't be long."

"Yes, ma'am."

"I was always glad I grew up on a dairy farm," Heather said as they strolled over to the store and sat down on a park bench. "At least I could look the cows in the eye every morning and not feel guilty as hell."

Kevin said nothing. He was a townie, having grown up in Brockville, and the closest he'd ever come to this sort of thing was the grocery store.

After a while she said, "I know those guys."

"Who?"

"The farmers. Gerald Vesey and his son, Todd. They live on Bolingbroke Road, near Little Silver Lake. The kid was accused of trying to steal somebody's deer during hunting season a couple years ago. When we got there he was waving a crossbow around with booze on his breath. His father was trying to calm him down and make peace. It all got settled without any more trouble."

"Drinking and hunting."

"Yeah. Gerald promised to take him home and keep him there. We settled for that."

"From what I could see," Kevin said, "the kid doesn't look like a drinker."

"Must have cleaned up his act."

They waited almost fifteen minutes before an engine started. They heard the ramp being thrown in the truck bed and the tailgate slamming shut. After a few moments Vesey *père et fils* rattled around the corner and headed down to the road, both of them staring straight ahead, obviously aware that the police were on the premises and not wanting to be involved in any way, shape, or form.

The front door of the abattoir opened and Thomas Searle stepped out. Kevin and Heather got to their feet and started over, but Thomas waved them back. He limped across the yard, a short man with long white hair and an enormous white walrus moustache that curled up at the ends. He'd left his hardhat and coveralls inside.

"Sit down. No sense going back inside. Better to let Al do his work without any distractions."

Kevin stepped aside so that the old man could sit. Thomas eased his haunch down and, looking at Heather, patted the bench beside him. She ignored the gesture.

"Mr. Searle," Kevin began, "you're no doubt aware that we're investigating the murders of a police officer and a resident of Drummond Township. We've spoken to two of your sons, Bert and Gary, and now we'd like your side of the story."

Thomas took out a small case and lit a cigarillo. "Just so things are clear right up front." He slipped the case back into his pocket. "I know what you're doing; there's no story and no side, and I don't like the way you bothered my wife day before yesterday. It upset her quite a bit, and I don't want it happening again."

Kevin refused to take the bait. "One of the murder victims, Ms. Dorothy Kerr, was at the Northlands Mall the night before she was shot. A witness places you in the same parking lot at the same time. What were you doing there?"

"When was this? I'm at that mall quite often, son."

"Last Sunday. Late afternoon."

Thomas dragged on his cigarillo and tipped back his head to let the smoke escape in a slow curl. "I don't remember. Too long ago. Probably picking up some take-out at the restaurant. Sunday's Winnie's day off from the kitchen."

"You were seen talking to a couple of men with a bus that pulled off the highway to let their passengers use the washroom in McDonald's."

"I was talking to them?" He smiled. "I talk to a lot of people. I'm that way inclined. So it's more than likely."

"Did you know them?"

"I seriously doubt it. Where were they coming from?"

"Our witness says you followed Dorothy Kerr when she left the mall," Heather said. "Why'd you do that?"

Thomas ignored her, studying the tip of his cigarillo.

"Please answer the question," Kevin said.

"What? What question?"

"Why'd you follow Ms. Kerr when she left the mall?"

He shrugged. "I don't know the woman. I'd have no reason on God's green earth to follow someone I didn't know, other than through a complete and total coincidence."

"Despite the fact that she wrote several articles for the *Sentinel* about regulatory infractions by your business, not to mention your participation in the Freedom Convoy protests in 2022?"

"Really? That was her? I had no idea."

"Did you resent her for what she wrote about your business

and your family? And you?"

He flicked the cigarillo butt into the gravel. "Freedom of speech is a precious thing in this country, and by extension that includes freedom of the press. I expressed my opinion, and she reported on it. Two-way street. The government doesn't like that, though, despite their fancy rhetoric. They'd rather I didn't speak up at all. I suppose," he slowly got to his feet, "that's why they send their police lackeys around to check up on me. Wasting taxpayers' hard-earned money. My money."

"Where were you on Monday morning?"

"Here at the abattoir." He struggled to his feet and stared up at Kevin from an eight-inch deficit in height. "Gilles Bertrand brought a couple of sheep around. They're still hanging, if you want to see them. They come down to be cut tomorrow morning."

Kevin glanced at Heather, who nodded microscopically. She knew Bertrand; they could check out the story with him later if they found it was necessary to do so.

"What about your sons?"

"Al was here, working like always. The other two, I expect you've already asked and they've answered."

Kevin glanced at Heather, who made a rude noise at the back of her throat. He turned to leave and then turned back. "You've got a black truck, a dually. Where's it at right now, Mr. Searle?"

"Not sure. Around here somewhere, I expect."

"I'd like to take some pictures of the tires, if you'll tell me where I can find it."

"And I'd like to retire to the Bahamas and drink rum punch all afternoon, but that ain't likely going to happen either. Beat it, now, before my blood pressure starts to rise."

As Kevin and Heather walked to the car, Thomas spat on the ground.

"Son, you pay attention to what I said about bothering my wife," he called after them. "Happens again, you'll be sorry."

Chapter 40

Pierce was hard at work on his computer, so he barely heard the ruckus as Hope and Walker bustled past his workstation on their way to the comm room, where Alaric was waiting for an update.

He was busy running a series of systems checks on Daniel Thomas Keegan, DOB 26-10-1976, current address 17 Birch Street, Perth, Ontario. Each check added more pieces to the picture he was building of a solitary and very unhappy man.

Keegan was born in Collingwood, Ontario—Terry Maynard's home town as well. They lived two blocks apart and attended the same high school, which caused Pierce to wonder if they'd known each other and perhaps had been friends.

After graduating, they moved in separate directions. Keegan joined the army, while Maynard put in a year with a private security firm before being hired by the OPP. Keegan was deployed twice before suffering a head injury, apparently a concussion, and he ended up in a series of administrative positions, the last being an assignment to the service unit at Garrison Petawawa that was responsible for transporting weapons and equipment. He was discharged twenty years after joining and found a job with Federated Parcel Service as a driver.

Seven years later FPS fired him. After a few months, he found work at the wire factory just outside Perth.

Eventually Pierce leaned back and folded his hands behind his head to stretch his arm muscles. It gave him a track to follow—from Collingwood to the military to FPS to the factory. Along the way, he'd no doubt find more pieces of the puzzle to fit into place.

He began with Keegan's high school. An online search found the website for Lester B. Pearson Secondary School, but it was strictly focused on the present and had no archives of any sort. Another search, this time for yearbooks, was also fruitless. After a moment's thought he called Ident to ask about the inventory that had been taken in Maynard's apartment. Was there a high school year book somewhere among his things?

No, there wasn't.

He pondered for a moment, wondering whether it was important to establish a solid connection between Keegan and Maynard reaching back to high school, and decided to park it for now. He remembered Charlie Watkins, the retired TPS sergeant who'd spent so much time with him on the set of *The Badge*, saying once that momentum was a precious commodity in a homicide investigation. "Do everything you can to build it and everything it takes to maintain it right through to the end."

He moved on to Keegan's military service. His last assignment was with 2 Service Battalion, which provided support services to 2 Mechanized Brigade Group at Garrison Petawawa. He picked up the phone and bounced around different extensions on the base, waiting on hold and hoping that being transferred to yet another person wouldn't result in his call being dropped, so that he'd have to begin the whole process all over again. Finally, however, he spoke to a Chief Warrant Officer Trent Mendenhall, who'd been part of the command team during Keegan's service and was willing to talk to him about it.

Pierce made an appointment for tomorrow after lunch, and hoped it wasn't the beginning of a wild goose chase.

Okay, good. Next?

Keegan's employment record for FPS, his next stop after the army, told Pierce that he'd worked out of their hub warehouse in the Ottawa suburb of Barrhaven, in the city's southwest end. A call to their human resources department informed him that the person who'd supervised Keegan was no longer working for the company. He was transferred to the manager, a friendly sounding woman named Tammy Wharton. Yes, she remembered Daniel Keegan. Very clearly, as a matter of fact. No, she didn't work on weekends, but she was willing to come in tomorrow and meet with him at her office, given the fact that he was a police detective, and so on.

At that moment, Sonja put her head in and spoke his name. Lost in thought, he jumped, swivelling his chair around.

"Sorry," she said. "Didn't mean to startle you."

"No problem. What can I do for you?"

"I just wanted to let you know that I'm working hard to line up someone to partner with you this weekend while Doug's in Collingwood. So far, everyone I've asked about is heading up there, too. But I'll keep trying."

"I'm fine," Pierce said. "I'm running down a few things, lining up some interviews. All stuff I can handle myself."

"You sure? We've got someone coming in to give Kevin a hand. I'd prefer to see you guys working in pairs."

"Understood. If someone turns up, that's fine. Meanwhile, I'll keep on keeping on. Okay?"

She tapped the doorway. "All right. If you need help at any point, call it in immediately. Got it?"

"Got it."

Chapter 41

Ellie's work space at the detachment office was a small cubicle on the second floor at the back, facing north. During the winter months, the wind thumped snow and sleet against the big window overlooking the parking lot, and it was made very clear that the construction company had installed product that skimped on the R-factor or whatever it was that measured the insulating properties of windows. In January, the glass was cold to the touch, and warmth rising from the baseboard heaters curled up against its surface to immediately die a quick and silent death, leaving the room frosty and uncomfortable. In the summer, it was the opposite, as the air conditioning laboured in vain to conquer the waves of heat radiating from the window.

Government contracting work. She wasn't a really big fan.

The office was set aside for her use whenever she was managing a major case in Lanark, and while it had little elbow room, it had the virtue of a door that closed whenever she required privacy. It was her practice to leave it open whenever possible, however, hoping that the summer heat wouldn't build up inside and roast her while she sat at the desk, trying to work.

May had gotten off to a very warm start this year, and in anticipation of discomfort on this sunny Saturday morning she was already removing her jacket as she came down the corridor. When she saw a pair of legs in her doorway, jutting out from the visitor's chair crammed back against the wall, she hesitated a moment before realizing who it was.

"Good morning, Gray." She edged past him, hung up her jacket on the hook stuck to the back of the door, and went around her desk to sit down. "Can't say I'm surprised to see you."

"I appreciate this, Ellie." He straightened in the chair, a file folder balanced on his knees. "You can't imagine how much."

"Oh, I think maybe I can." She turned on her computer. "There's probably coffee in the lunch room. Want some?"

"No, I'm fine, thank you." He opened the file and passed a document to her across the desk. "This is the waiver, which I've signed. Mal's waiting to hear from you, and he's got McFadden ready to go."

It was a boilerplate release of liability form that he'd probably downloaded from the Internet, an "activity participation" type of waiver in which he acknowledged the risk involved in what he wanted to do and agreed not to take legal action if he sustained an injury. Included was a brief description of the tasks involved in participating in a homicide investigation. Again, all copied and pasted into the document.

Gray had signed and dated it.

Sighing, she took out her phone and texted Malcolmsen:
Gray's here. Signed waiver??

Once again he must have had his cell handy, for his reply came through in a few seconds:

Legal hesitated but green lighted. Gloria's standing by.

Gloria McFadden was the director of Human Resources for East Region. She would also have to give it the green light.

Ellie bit her lip. *Thx.*

"Okay, Gray." She stood up. "I'll walk this down the hall and get the HR ball rolling, and when I come back we'll talk about how this is going to work."

"Sounds fine to me."

The word had been passed down the line, and the HR office door was open when Ellie got there. A civilian clerk, pulling a few hours of Saturday morning overtime, took the form from her and promised to let her know when everything was ready for Gray to sign.

Back in her office, she closed the door and sat down. "I'm sure you're aware of how off-the-wall this is."

"Yeah." He smiled wanly. "I'm sorry, Ellie, to put you on the spot. It's just, I saw an opportunity and couldn't let it go by."

"We're going to have you pair with Kevin Walker, as we discussed on the phone. He's following the track that has Dorothy Kerr as the primary target. I'll let him explain it to you. Let me see if he's in."

She put her cellphone on speaker and punched in Kevin's number. "I'm in my office with Grayson Kennedy," she said when he answered. "Can you come upstairs and meet with us?"

"Sure. I'm with Sonja right now."

"Ask her to come with you. We'll be in the break-off room down the hall."

At that moment the HR clerk knocked on the door and entered at the sound of Ellie's voice. Gray signed the documentation she put in front of him, and at that point it became an official thing.

God help us, Ellie thought.

She led Gray out of the office and down the hall. It was her habit when meeting with more than one person—other than team meetings, which she held downstairs on the main floor—to commandeer a break-off cubbyhole across from the training room. It was outfitted with a round table, chairs, whiteboard, and flipchart stands, and when training was not being delivered, it was normally available to her. It was supposed to be booked with one of the administrative clerks, but Ellie usually skipped annoying details like that.

"Please close the door," she said when Kevin and Sonja joined them. She watched Kevin shake Gray's hand and sit down next to him. Typical Kevin, she thought. Open and adaptable.

"The powers that be have cleared Gray to assist us this weekend with the Kerr investigation. We need to go over the ground rules now, before things get started."

Sonja nodded. Kevin glanced at Gray, gauging his mood.

Ellie thought the man looked nervous.

"Given Gray's rank, a few things need to be spelled out up front. Even though he's coming from staff into line on a temporary assignment, he won't have decision-making powers. Functional authority over this case rests with me, of course, while Sonja's command of the crime unit and its personnel doesn't change. Alaric Quinn hands out assignments as primary investigator, and as far as you're concerned, Gray, he gives them to Kevin, whose lead you'll follow at all times. Clear so far?"

Gray swallowed. "Yes, Ellie."

"You'll report to me," she said. "If Sonja needs you to do something, do it. I don't want her coming to me with stuff like that. This is too important for us to waste time on trivia."

"Understood." He swallowed again.

"Sonja?"

"Fine, Ellie. It sounds like the best way to handle it."

Ellie nodded. So far, so good. "Kevin, Gray will be paired with you as an observer. I want him to provide you with advice and guidance, because at this point in his career he's earned the right to be listened to, but all decisions will be yours. Comments?"

Kevin shook his head. He turned to Gray. "Looking forward to it."

That makes one of us, Ellie thought.

Chapter 42

Travel day.

The bus picked them up at the detachment office at eleven o'clock in the morning, a 56-seat motor coach with climate control, reclining seats, tinted windows with shades, footrests, and all the audio/video system features you'd expect (and need) on a long trip.

Heather was shown to her seat by Sergeant Gibbons, who was in charge of the show. She'd left a garment bag containing her dress uniform and accessories with the driver for stowage below, along with her large and rather overstuffed knapsack, so she only had a combo purse-and-travel-bag to carry aboard and shove under the seat ahead of her. She'd been assigned a window seat, so she shuffled over and settled in, wondering who her travel companion would be. Collingwood was well over four hundred kilometres away, and the bus ride would take almost five hours, so she hoped it would be someone interesting.

She leaned over on her haunch and pulled out an *Archie Comics Digest* issue. At a trim size of around four inches by six, it was small enough to fit into the hip pocket of her jeans. This particular issue was number 21, which came out in 1976. The cover featured Archie daydreaming at his desk while the teacher, Miss Grundy, glowered at him. Also on the cover were big Moose hammering Reggie on top of the head, Little Archie scampering off somewhere, Li'l Jinx running to school with an umbrella in her hand, and Betty and Veronica sitting together waiting for something to happen. All her favourite characters. Heather thumbed it open and began to read, ignoring the hubbub around her as the rest of the party found their seats and settled in.

She turned a page and glanced up as Sergeant Gibbons stopped at the empty aisle seat next to her.

"Here," he said to the person standing behind him.

It was Skelton.

He screwed up his face at the sergeant.

"Sit," Gibbons said. "Stay."

Heather kept her nose in her comic as Skelton thumped down. She stared at the page without seeing it, silently cursing her bad luck. Of all the possible seatmates, she was condemned to sit next to the one who disliked her more than pretty much everyone else in the detachment.

Great.

Skelton sat bolt upright, back straight, knees together, his ten-gallon hat still firmly settled on his head. When Heather turned another page, he slowly unbuttoned his shirt pocket and took out a roll of peppermints. He peeled back the wrapper and held it out to her.

Using a finger to mark her place, she reached over and pried out a mint. "Thanks."

He took another for himself, popped it in his mouth, returned the roll to his shirt pocket, and buttoned the flap. "You're welcome."

As the bus jerked into gear and began to move, she watched out of the corner of her eye as he removed his hat and set it on his knees, brim up.

"I've heard," she said, "that when people take off their hat they put it down like that to keep the luck from spilling out."

He rolled the mint into one cheek. "I don't believe in luck."

"Oh."

"It helps the sweatband dry more quickly."

"Oh. Okay."

She went back to Archie and Veronica, who were bouncing through town in his jalopy, setting off on another fun adventure.

Skelton stared up the aisle, watching the road ahead of them through the big front windshield.

She made it halfway through the comic before he stirred and looked over at her. "This is quite an honour. To represent Lanark at such a momentous event."

"Yeah, I guess so." Heather figured from his tone that he was testing her. Baiting her to say something he could pounce on and tear to shreds. She wouldn't give him the satisfaction. She'd never hidden her dislike of Terry Maynard, and there was no way she'd categorize his funeral as a "momentous event," even if the King of England were scheduled to show up. But she wasn't going to give an inch to Skelton. Not an inch.

She'd just gotten into the next story, in which Reggie was misbehaving without knowing that Moose was standing right behind him, ready to pound him one, when Skelton picked up his hat, ran a finger around the band, and settled it back on his head.

"They're sparing no expense for this, as I understand it."

Heather grunted, not particularly caring.

"I checked. This bus alone costs over fifteen hundred a day, plus tax. For three days, it'll cost the taxpayers more than five grand."

"Tch."

"Our salaries, overtime, shift premium—I'm talking everyone who'll attend from the force—will total almost two hundred thousand. Then there are the hotel bills, meals and incidentals, and whatever they're soaking us to use the arena. It'll rack up around a quarter of a million dollars before it's done."

"Out of our existing budget, Doug. It's not like we're stealing from the hospitals or something to pay for it."

"Money that could be spent on something else."

She lowered the comic and gave him a look. "But you just said it was a momentous event, Doug. Which is it? Besides, I thought you were an organization man. Senior management always knows what's best, and all that horseshit."

"They do. But I can't help but dislike the politics in all of this."

"Doug. Jesus. Our total budget as a law enforcement agency is over one-point-two billion dollars. *Billion.* Of course there's politics. Politics is the gravity well of *all* public cash, man. Sucks it all down into one small, tight little spot no one else can see but them. The singularity known as the dollar. So what? Who the hell cares? As long as they continue to pay our salaries, why should we care about the premier and the commissioner and all their nefarious ulterior motives?"

He gave her a tiny little smile. "I suppose you have a point."

She went back to her comic, determined not to say anything else.

A few kilometres passed in blissful silence. But Skelton just couldn't leave her alone.

"Why'd you join up, Hope?"

"Oh, ferfucksakes."

"I'm serious. You're not the LEO type. I'm just trying to understand you better."

"Understand me better?" She closed the comic over her

finger again. "Are you kidding me? You, the guy who's a sheep farmer first and a cop a distant second? Phfft."

"And you grew up a farm girl, so don't blow smoke up my ass, Hope. You and I haven't partnered up yet, but if it ever came to that, I'd want to know I could trust you to have my back."

"Screw you, Doug. Okay? Just screw you."

She wasn't the law enforcement officer type as far as he was concerned because she wasn't an organization man, she wasn't a hardass, and she wasn't male. End of story.

She went back to her reading, and this time he was content to leave her in peace, having poked her with a stick enough to get under her skin, like an annoying sliver that would bother her afterward whenever she thought about it.

After what felt like an eternity, the bus pulled up under the porte-cochère of the hotel. They slowly disembarked, tired and stiff, and lined up to retrieve their luggage. The hotel had four floors, a spacious front lobby, and a friendly staff determined to make their stay as comfortable as possible, given the circumstances. Heather checked in, received her key card, and waited for her turn at the elevators.

Room 217 was down at the end of the hall, on the left. It had a queen-sized bed, a dresser, a TV, a mini-fridge, and a little coffee machine with all the fixings. She closed the door behind her, engaged the deadbolt, and secured the flimsy-looking chain lock.

Silence. After more than four hours on the road, her body felt like it was still vibrating. It was a nice room, with heavy drapes drawn across the window, a matching bedspread, and pot lights that you could dim if they were bothering your eyes.

She sat on the edge of the bed for a few moments, looking around. She checked the time on the bedside clock radio against her Sonic the Hedgehog wristwatch: synchronized. She kicked off her shoes and tried to scrunch her toes in the carpet, like

Bruce Willis in *Die Hard*, but the pile was too short and tight. She picked up the little card on the bedside table, took out her phone, and entered the free wifi password. Yep: connectivity.

She slowly got to her feet and unpacked her knapsack. She carried the garment bag containing her Dress Number Ones over to the little rack just inside the door. Unclipping it so it fell out to its full length, she hung it up next to her white blouses and pantsuit. Finally, she unzipped her combo purse-and-travel bag and pulled out the ziplock bag containing her toiletries, which she took into the bathroom.

Everything was nice, neat, and clean. She arranged her stuff around the sink and unpeeled the paper from the courtesy bar of soap. It smelled pleasant, like vanilla and cream. Slowly, deliberately, she stripped, folding her clothes in a pile on the toilet seat. As always, it took a moment to figure out how the shower fixtures worked—clockwise or counter-clockwise? pull it out or leave it in?—and once the water was flowing from the shower head, nice and hot, she stepped in and drew the curtain.

After shampooing her hair and rinsing it out, she spent a few minutes with her head down, crying. After a while the hot water calmed her, and she was done with it.

It's just another role to play, she reminded herself. *Like cosplay, only very serious. Your Dress Ones are the costume, and you play the role of grieving police detective, solemn and all tightly buttoned up.*

Piece of cake.

Chapter 43

Kevin knew that Gray Kennedy was a veteran of surveillance work when he saw him bring out a box of Smarties and pop a few into his mouth.

"Want some?"

"No thanks." Kevin patted his jacket pocket. "Double Bubble."

Surveillance work was often a long and very boring proposition, with limited movement and constant attention to one's surroundings, and it tended to wear on the nerves after a while. Being able to do something small, like eat candy or chew gum, took the edge off and made the sitting and watching feel a little less arduous.

"So tell me," Gray said around a mouthful of half-chewed Smarties, "why'd you decide to go overt instead of covert?"

Kevin watched a red pickup truck pull into the parking lot of

Searle Meat and Potatoes. When a grey-haired man got out and went into the store, Kevin took a picture with his cellphone.

"Couple reasons. One, there's nowhere really to sit and watch where they wouldn't see us. Too open, and no cover. Second, I *want* them to see us. I'm getting on their nerves, ratcheting up the tension, trying to force them into a mistake."

"What kind of mistake?"

"Who knows?" Kevin grinned. "Half the fun's in being surprised." He took a photograph of the pickup's licence plate and watched as the man came out of the store with a plastic shopping bag.

"That was fast." Gray put the box of candy back in his pocket.

"Picking up an order for his wife, maybe." Kevin snapped another picture of the man through the back window of the truck as he reached over to put the bag on the passenger seat.

They'd been here for about twenty minutes so far, and traffic in and out of the store had been fairly steady. Not surprising, given that it was a Saturday and people were either picking up the meat and potatoes portions of their weekly shopping or were grabbing something good to put on the grill for dinner tonight.

On the abattoir side, things were much more quiet. No visitors had shown up so far. However, watching through the binoculars, Gray had reported intermittent movement behind the lone window in front. Someone was inside, it would seem, working a weekend shift.

"I've missed this," Gray said, watching the red truck pull out and drive past them, the driver giving them little more than a quick glance.

"Surveillance?"

"Field work." Gray pointed as a dusty blue Hyundai approached from the direction they were facing and turned into the parking lot.

"How long have you been sitting behind a desk? If you don't mind me asking."

A young woman and a small boy got out of the car and went into the store. Kevin added them to his collection, along with the Hyundai's plate, which was barely legible under a thick coating of road dust.

"At RHQ? Eleven long, agonizing years. Before that, five years as a staff sergeant and detachment commander, South Bruce, including the bump up to commissioned rank."

"Sixteen years since you've worked in the field?"

"Seems like an eternity, eh? And the last five years of that was at the rank of sergeant, which had more than its share of desk work."

"Wow."

"Twenty-five, this fall. But I doubt they'll give me a plaque or a certificate signed by the premier. I think they're waiting for me just to go away."

Kevin digested this in silence.

"As for you," Gray said, "I hear you should have made a sergeant's list quite a while ago but won't apply. What the hell's up with that?"

Kevin shrugged, feeling his face grow warm. "I like what I'm doing, I guess."

"I can understand the sentiment," Gray said, "given that I'm sitting right next to you doing the same damned thing and getting a hell of a kick out of it. Just the same," he pointed at the shop door, which had opened and closed, affording a quick glimpse of the little boy who apparently wanted to leave before his mother was ready, "you do understand, don't you, that the pay gets better the higher you go?"

"We're doing okay. My wife has a beauty salon in town, and she's raking it in right now. I don't need the extra money. And the grief that goes with the job."

This time when the door opened, the boy held it for his mother, who carried several plastic bags of stuff around to the back of the car.

As she was popping the trunk lid with her remote, two

vehicles arrived in quick succession—a black Audi driven by a white-haired woman in jeans and a black polo shirt, and a gold-coloured van with a "Davidson Plumbing and Heating" logo on the side, out of which tumbled a young guy wearing a baseball cap and a gold-coloured T-shirt with the same logo.

Kevin clicked away.

"Just as long as it's not one of those fear-of-failure things." Gray studied the van with his binoculars.

Kevin didn't answer. He hoped the older man wasn't going to start psychoanalyzing him or something. He got enough of that from Caitlyn as it was.

"God knows I've been through that shit enough times in my life." Gray lowered the binoculars and rubbed an eye with his thumb.

The plumbing guy emerged from the store and jogged over to his van, a package of meat wrapped in brown paper clutched in his hand. He backed out of the lot and drove away in a cloud of dust.

"Not that I want to bring up a bunch of old news," Gray went on, "but I've heard your dad just passed away. Was it sudden?"

"No. Cirrhosis."

Heavy drinker?"

Kevin grunted, not wanting to talk about it.

"My problem started right after the death of my wife. Boy, I hit it hard and didn't look back."

"I'm sorry," Kevin murmured.

The white-haired woman came out with five pounds of potatoes and a full shopping bag, which she put in the trunk of her Audi and drove away.

It was suddenly quiet.

"I was a Mountie back then, working highway traffic in Manitoba. Which is where I'm from. I was called to the scene of a bad accident and there she was, barely recognizable in the wreckage. I thought I'd die, right on the spot. We had two young girls. What the hell was I going to do without her?"

He fell silent for a moment, fiddling with the strap on the binoculars.

Kevin checked the time on his phone.

"That was '98. Not long after that I got pulled over by a guy I knew. He let me off with a warning, but I didn't quit. I couldn't. Things had to feel fuzzy, all the time. It went downhill from there."

Kevin nodded uncomfortably.

"I don't know what your dad was like," Gray said after a moment, "but I drank every day. Couple of swallows before I brushed my teeth; the odd nip here and there when I had a minute to myself; a drink while I was fixing supper; and then full out to put myself to sleep at night."

"Sounds like him," Kevin said. "They didn't call him Johnny Walker for nothing."

"It's what's known as a functional alcoholic. Maybe you know about this already. Someone who has an alcohol use disorder, to use the new fashionable term for it, but can still go to work, do the job, act more or less normally, and hide their problem. Maybe that's what your dad was. It's definitely what I was."

"But you don't drink now." Kevin said it as a statement, but it was actually a question.

"Not for more than two years. Which is a pretty short time in the life of an alcoholic, but not bad, considering." Gray took a moment to check out the abattoir through the binoculars. Nothing much to see.

"I always think of what that guy said in *West Wing*. The chief of staff; I forget his name. 'I don't want just one drink, I want twelve.' He was trying to explain to the kid that when you stop drinking, you don't stop being an alcoholic. The memory of how it feels to be drunk is always there with you. You're an alcoholic for life. The objective is to become an alcoholic who doesn't drink. That's what I am now. A booze hound who lives without the booze."

A black 2014 Audi Quattro eased into the parking lot, and a short, middle-aged man sauntered into the store carrying a smallish black duffle bag with leather handles. He spent ten minutes inside the store, and when he came out he walked over to the abattoir and disappeared inside.

Kevin and Gray waited through fifteen minutes of complete inactivity before the man reappeared, still carrying the duffle. He put the bag in the trunk, backed out of the lot, and left.

"Interesting," Gray said.

After another ten minutes or so of peace and quiet, the abattoir door opened and Bert Searle, the middle son, sauntered out. He leaned against the wall and lit a cigarette. Kevin snapped industriously, glad for something to do.

His cigarette half-smoked, Bert suddenly looked up and noticed them. He stared for a moment, as though trying to figure out what the hell they were doing. Kevin took his picture again and showed him a thumbs-up.

Bert threw away the rest of his smoke and started across the parking lot toward them.

"Uh oh," Gray said.

Opening the centre console, Kevin took out his sidearm, still in its holster, and put it on his thigh.

Bert stopped. He fished his cellphone out of his back pocket and went through the motions of taking *their* picture several times. Then he flipped them the bird and went back inside.

"I think you've gotten under their skin," Gray said.

Kevin put his gun away again. "Mission accomplished."

Chapter 44

"Thanks for seeing me." Bob Pierce sat down in the chair indicated by Chief Warrant Officer Mendenhall and took out his notebook.

Mendenhall settled in behind his desk and folded his hands. "You wanted to talk to me about Danny Keegan. Do I have that right?"

"Yes, sir. That's right." He jotted down the date, time, and place. Garrison Petawawa, formerly known as Canadian Forces Base Petawawa, operated with about six thousand armed forces personnel and another thousand civilians employed by the Department of Defence. It served as the home base for the 4th Canadian Division Support Group and 2 Canadian Mechanized Brigade Group, within which was situated the 2 Service Battalion, where Keegan had served for four years.

"You were his sergeant in the weapons service unit, is that

right, sir?"

"That's correct. You don't have to call me 'sir'."

Mendenhall was now the regimental sergeant major, second-in-command of the battalion responsible for second-line support to the Mechanized Brigade Group, including transportation and supplies. He was a formidable man in his late forties, his head shaved bald and his laser-beam eyes a dark brown.

"I don't want to take up too much of your time," Pierce said, trying not to appear intimidated. "I appreciate your seeing me."

Hours of operation for the battalion were Monday to Friday, but Mendenhall had left orders for Pierce to be shown inside and escorted to his office.

"Not a problem. What do you need to know?"

"What were Keegan's responsibilities?"

"He came in first as a support technician before qualifying to drive in transport. That's where he was when I was promoted, and that's where he stayed until his discharge."

"What was his service record like?"

"Spotty."

"Oh?"

"Disciplinary problems. Off-base scraps; instances of insubordination. As a driver, he needed a clean record and that sort of stuff didn't help. Also, he had a problem with substance abuse. Before long, he'd worn a groove in my office carpet, and I had to take him off the road and put him back behind a desk."

Pierce glanced up from his notebook. "What kind of substance abuse?"

"Alcohol."

"Otherwise, what kind of guy was he?"

"A gun enthusiast."

"Oh?"

Mendenhall nodded. "He knew as much about the weapons he was transporting as the techs themselves. The C7A2 5.56 mm automatic rifle, for example. And the C8A3 carbine rifle. At that time, the Browning nine was the handgun issued to personnel, and he spent a lot of his free time on the firing range with one. Very proficient."

Pierce took a moment to digest this information. An unstable individual with an interest in firearms. A red flag for sure.

"Any history of violent behaviour? Fighting with others, that sort of thing?"

"They're soldiers. There's always fighting of some kind or another. But yeah, his self-discipline was at a lower level than others, I'd say, when it came to controlling his temper."

"Anything serious?"

Mendenhall shook his head. "No. Nothing egregious. The usual bar fights in town, scuffles with other soldiers here on the base. Enough to have him sent to me on a regular basis for discipline, but not enough to have him arrested."

"Is he capable of shooting someone?"

Mendenhall stared at him for a long moment before replying. "Before transferring to service support he deployed to Afghanistan, where he saw combat. In a military context, he was quite capable of shooting someone. But in a civilian context? I'm not qualified to answer that question. Sorry."

Pierce thanked him for his time and left the base. Driving south on Highway 17, he crossed over the bridge spanning the Mississippi River that was dedicated to the memory of OPP Constable Kenneth Swett, who was killed in a collision with an impaired driver while on duty in July, 1981.

As he drove, he built a picture in his head of Daniel Keegan as a plausible suspect. His landlady's remarks about his gun collection were reinforced by what CWO Mendenhall had told him about Keegan being a gun aficionado and proficient shooter. The fact that he and Terry Maynard were both the same age and were born and raised in Collingwood, with the strong possibility that they'd known each other growing up, lent further weight to the theory that Keegan might have had a motive for shooting Maynard.

If he could turn up evidence that they were personally

connected, he might be able to find that motive and take the case forward from there.

They'd already turned up one guy, Earl Avery Black, in possession of a prohibited handgun. Would Keegan turn out to be another one?

When he finally reached the outskirts of Ottawa and merged onto Highway 416 southbound, his thoughts turned to the next interview in front of him. After leaving the military, Keegan had found a job as a driver with FPS without too much delay. Wanting to keep busy, apparently.

Tammy Wharton met him at the front entrance. They rode an elevator up to the top floor, and when she showed him into his office he looked around in surprise. It was huge, tastefully furnished, and the big picture window behind her desk provided a clear view of the highway and the forest on the other side.

She led him over to a seating arrangement in the corner and poured them coffee from a silver pot. She used matching tongs to drop two cubes of brown sugar into her cup, gestured for him to fix his own the way he wished, and leaned back, stirring.

"Daniel Thomas Keegan," she said, setting her spoon down on a napkin and sipping carefully. "We fired him six years ago. I still remember him, though."

Pierce sampled his coffee, which he took black. It was hot and good.

"That's his file." She looked at a manila folder with multi-coloured numbers on the tab that sat on the table between them. "I went through it to refresh my memory before you got here. Sad guy. Very sad."

Pierce set down his coffee and brought out his notebook. "What makes you say that?"

"Oh, I don't know. We gave him about six second chances, if you know what I mean. He just came across as a really sad guy. Not happy."

Pierce nodded. "How long have you been manager here?"

"Two and a half years. I was senior HR specialist before that, and a junior assistant when Mr. Keegan's name started showing up on my desk." She looked around the room over the rim of her coffee cup. "This is a great job. I have a Master's degree and certification from Cornell. Tuition was really expensive, but thanks to this place I'm finally paying off all that debt."

She was in her mid-thirties, and her shoulder-length blond hair was held back behind her right ear with a pearl hairpin. Good humour brimmed in her large blue eyes. She was friendly and likeable.

"You said he'd been given second chances. What for?"

"Oh, several times he reported to work smelling of alcohol. His supervisor—who no longer works here by the way, did I mention that?—stepped in and made sure he didn't get behind the wheel. Several times it was bad enough that they involved me before they put him in a taxi and sent him home. A shame, really. He was a good driver."

"Did the company offer him any help?"

"Oh, yes. Of course. We have an excellent employee assistance program. We offered counselling, paid leave for detox, and a spot in a recovery program, but he turned it all down."

"What about customer complaints?"

She looked uncomfortable. "Not until the one that got him fired."

"Tell me about it."

She sighed, her eyes falling to the file between them. "His route took him to Smiths Falls, Perth, and back again. A lot of territory to cover, but he was very reliable."

Pierce nodded.

"He had a delivery in Perth that caused all the trouble. Seems he knew the addressee. A man named Maynard. It was an apartment. When he came to the door, Mr. Keegan started arguing with him. Punches were thrown. Someone down the hall came out to intervene, and Mr. Keegan left. Mr. Maynard called us to complain, and it went from there."

Pierce's pen froze over his notebook for a moment. He

realized he was holding his breath. "What was Maynard's full name?"

She picked up the file and opened it. "Uh, Terence Maynard. The address was 2117 Concession Street, Apt. 9." She watched him scribble it down. "Do you need the postal code?"

He shook his head. Tammy had either not paid attention to the news lately, or hadn't connected the name in Keegan's file to the double murder he was investigating.

"Were the police called?"

"Apparently not. Mr. Maynard told us he wanted it handled privately.

"In his complaint, did Maynard say what he did for a living?"

"No, we never get into that sort of thing." She closed the file and put it back down on the desk. "Poor Danny. I swear, that man, if it wasn't for bad luck he wouldn't have any luck at all."

"Why do you say that?"

Tammy retrieved her coffee and took a long draught. "Well, it was my understanding that things turned really bad for him after the death of his girlfriend."

"How so?"

"When we first hired him, there weren't any problems. It was only after she died that he started getting into trouble with impairment issues."

"What can you tell me about the girlfriend?"

She stared into her cup for a moment. "I'm trying to remember her name. It's somewhere in the file . . . Simmons. Susan? No. Stephanie. That was it. Stephanie Simmons."

Pierce wrote it down. "You said she passed away?"

"She was a regular addressee, in Perth. We delivered a package to her every Tuesday. Medicinal CBD. That's how Mr. Keegan met her in the first place, since she was always on his route. She was battling cancer, and the CBD helped. They became friends."

She made a face. "He told me this during his exit interview.

There's no confidentiality restrictions, you understand, for HR like there is for lawyers and doctors. Oh, you'll have to get a warrant for records from pay and benefits or leave and extra duty, that sort of thing, but what he told me in conversation I can repeat, especially since you're investigating a murder."

"If it gets to that point, I'll be back with one."

"I'm trying to follow all this," she frowned. "Do you think Mr. Keegan is somehow involved with this murder?"

"Two murders, actually. You do understand, don't you, that Terence Maynard was one of the victims?"

Her jaw dropped. "The man we've just been talking about? Oh my god oh my god. And you think Danny Keegan did it? Is that what's going on?"

"Right now we're following a number of leads," Pierce replied. "We're still at the information-gathering stage. Can you tell me how serious the relationship was between Keegan and Ms. Simmons?"

"Oh my god. This is terrible. Oh my god."

Pierce gave her a moment to gulp her coffee and wipe her mouth.

"I'm sorry," she said. "It's just pretty shocking."

"I understand."

"Did you ask me a question?"

"How serious do you think the relationship was between Keegan and Ms. Simmons?"

"Oh. Yes. Well, it was pretty serious. They got engaged and everything. Even though she was really sick and didn't stand much chance of recovering, as I understand it, they were going to get married while she, you know, while she was still alive to do it. She didn't make it. It really wrecked him."

"Could you let me have her address? Where the shipments went?"

She hesitated, taking a deep breath. "I'm sorry. We deal with some pretty serious stuff in HR, but I have to admit this one has thrown me for a bit of a loop. I'm okay now. Just a sec." She dug through the file and found the address.

After jotting it down, Pierce closed his notebook and put it in his jacket pocket. "I really appreciate your help, Ms. Wharton."

"Oh, Tammy, please. It's not a problem. I'm just sorry one of our employees, a former employee, is mixed up in it."

"He's a person of interest at this point. It may not go any further than that."

She nodded, wanting to say something else.

He waited.

"Um, I feel silly, but, uh, could I ask you a big favour?"

Pierce stood up. "It depends on what it is."

She slipped a brown envelope from the back of Keegan's file and took out an eight-by-ten colour photograph. He realized, with horror, that it was a publicity shot of him in costume and makeup as Detective Brian Anderson. He remembered it being part of the show's press kit, along with shots of the other cast members.

"My sister is your biggest fan. When you called to set up the meeting I wondered if it might be you, and when I told Stacey she was sure of it. She knew you'd become a real police officer; she just wasn't sure where. She's binge-watched *The Badge* something like three times. Would you mind signing this for her? She picked up a media kit at a comic book convention a couple years ago. It's from that. She's sick right now, a bad respiratory infection. It'd really cheer her up."

He laughed, embarrassed, and used the Sharpie she gave him to autograph the photo:

> *To my biggest fan Stacey:*
> *Get well soon!*
> *"Detective Brian Anderson"*
> *Robert Pierce*

It was, he had to admit, one of his best-looking head shots. And although he was very well aware that it was putting a crease in his professionalism as a detective constable of the Ontario

Provincial Police, he also had to admit that it never grew old—the fans; the recognition; the pleasure it gave people to meet him in person.

She thanked him, still embarrassed, put the photo back in the envelope, and stood up to show him out.

She paused at the door. "Oh, yeah. I almost forgot. One quick question."

He laughed. "Isn't that supposed to be my line?"

"Pardon? Oh, right. Yeah! *Columbo*. Anyway, Stacey wants to know about the cliffhanger. At the end of the last episode. She said to ask you if you were going to save the woman and get shot, or if you were going to save yourself."

Pierce laughed. "I have no idea. They never told me."

Chapter 45

That evening, Kevin got home at a decent time, early enough that they were able to eat supper together. Caitlyn served a very nice sausage pilaf and Caesar salad her grandmother had made for them this afternoon. Janie was in a good mood, relating the story of a new and rich client who'd tipped her a hundred dollars after having a perm and colouring done to her exact specifications. Brendan was filled with questions about the double-murder investigation, which Kevin answered with vague generalities, and Josh was entranced by the sausage in the pilaf, his new favourite thing in the whole universe.

Caitlyn talked about something she'd seen while bicycling home from school. A flock of birds appeared above the rooftops, swirling and twisting in perfect formation. Starlings, she thought they were. When she got home she looked it up and found that this behaviour was called a murmuration, when dozens or even hundreds of birds flew together in a tight, whirling pattern, twisting and turning back and forth.

It was the sort of thing, she explained, that she never would have seen while riding on the school bus. Thanks to her bike, though, she was now free to observe the world around her and find all sorts of new and fascinating things to record in her journal.

Because she was sixteen, Caitlyn was able to begin the process to obtain her driver's licence, but Kevin and Janie had held a little family council with her on the subject and she'd assured them she wasn't particularly interested in learning to drive a car right now. Kevin could see she was already leaning toward the green side of the social spectrum, and might prefer to stick with her bicycle for several more years yet.

Thank goodness for small miracles.

When supper was finished, everyone went their separate ways. Caitlyn disappeared into her room to do her homework. Brendan went next door to return Barb's dishes and watch a little television with her. Josh sacked out on the couch in the living room to play on his Nintendo Switch. Janie went into the bedroom to do some online banking on the laptop.

Kevin had washed Barb's dishes by hand so that Brendan could take them back, and now he loaded the rest into the dishwasher and started it up. He made a cup of coffee in the machine, intending to take it outside to watch the evening gradually settle in.

His cellphone buzzed. He looked at the call display: *Private Number."*

"Walker."

"Hello, Detective Walker. I hope things are well."

The voice was distorted, as though voice-changing software was being used to disguise it. Kevin had installed a call recording application on his phone a while ago, but he'd never had occasion to use it. He hastily flipped to it now and opened it. Unfortunately, it went directly to a notification instructing him to download an update before he could proceed to use the app.

"Who is this?" he said, closing the recorder down again.

"Never mind who it is. Just pay attention to what I'm saying to you. I won't say it twice. You need to leave honest, hardworking people alone. Stop harassing the Searles. They've done nothing wrong. Back off. Just back right off."

Kevin leaned against the doorframe. On the couch, Josh was absorbed in his game and not paying attention to anything else around him.

"Is this you, Mr. Searle? Thomas Searle? Where are you at right now, Mr. Searle?"

"I told you, never mind who this is. Just do what I'm telling you, or else."

"Or else?"

"Bad things could happen, Detective Walker. They happen all the time. They could happen to you and that nice young family of yours. So do what I tell you to do. Understand? Back off. Right now."

Kevin lowered his voice. "Is that a threat?"

"No, son. It's a promise."

The line went dead.

Chapter 46

"Sit down," Sonja Freeling said as Kevin appeared in her doorway bright and early on Sunday morning. "Take me through it again."

He closed the door and dropped a completed form on her desk before lowering himself into her visitor's chair. "As I said last night, the caller was using a voice changer app or something like that, but I'm pretty sure it was Thomas Searle. Heather and I talked to him on Friday, and the last thing he said before we left was a threat. 'Don't bother my wife again, or you'll be sorry.' Words to that effect."

Sonja was taking notes. She scanned the form, which was an *ER037 – Threatening Call Report*, which all personnel were required to complete when receiving the sort of phone call Kevin had informed her about last night. "And you weren't able to record it."

"No. Alaric tells me it's a burner phone. Probably at the bottom of a lake somewhere by now."

"You haven't indicated any background sounds." She tapped the form.

"There weren't any. He could have been calling from his bedroom closet, for all I know."

"And his language was 'well-spoken, educated.'"

"Searle's a polite man and a careful speaker. No obscenities, no extreme emotions. Called me 'son,' which he also did on Friday when Heather and I talked to him."

"All right. I'm sending Patrol out to bring him in for questioning. Giles will handle it. I want you and Kennedy to stay clear for the time being."

Detective Constable Sharon Giles was another resource on temporary loan from regional headquarters to fill in during the current shortage of badges.

"Speaking of Kennedy," she went on, "have you heard from him this morning?"

"Not yet. I was going to call him when we were done here."

"We're done here." She watched Kevin spring out of his chair and head to the door. "It was *supposed* to be my day off, you know."

"Sorry about that."

"Give this thing some time. Let Giles lean on him."

"Will do."

Back at his workstation with a fresh cup of hot coffee, Kevin sat down and called Kennedy's number. After six rings, it went to voicemail. Instead of leaving a message, he cut the call and dialled again. This time, Gray answered, his voice thick.

"What time is it?"

"Eight forty-one. Are you coming in this morning?"

"Yes, I'll be there. I'm sorry, I slept in."

"No problem. I'll see you when you get here."

"I'll pick up some breakfast on the way. Do you want anything?"

"No, I'm good, thanks."

"See you soon."

Wondering what to expect when the inspector finally showed up, Kevin logged in and opened the case file. He'd already uploaded the photos they'd taken during yesterday's surveillance of Searle Meat and Potatoes, but he hadn't yet had a chance to analyze them.

He cropped the photos to headshots and ran them through an image comparison application to look for driver's licence matches in the provincial Ministry of Transportation database. One by one, he identified them, queried them in other systems, and added them to his list.

The grey-haired man driving the red pickup truck was John Bennett, fifty-nine, a welder who lived on McVeigh Road. The young woman who drove up in a dusty blue Hyundai with her small boy was Mary Ann Cullen, twenty-eight, a registered nurse practitioner living on Scotch Line Road. The white-haired woman in the black Audi turned out to be Faye Roberts, sixty-four, a Perth resident, and the young guy driving the Davidson Plumbing and Heating van was Scott Davidson, owner and operator of the aforementioned business, which he ran out of his home at Numogate, the little crossroads hamlet in Montague Township.

None of these folks seemed to offer anything of interest, but the next face rang the bell for him. The guy who'd gone into the store and then over to the abattoir turned out to be someone named Ronald Robert Barlow, forty-six years old, a resident of Smiths Falls and a known fence who specialized in smaller items such as jewelry, coins, watches, and miscellaneous gold pieces that could fit into a hand-held duffle bag, say, for easy transportation.

Kevin toggled back to the photos of Barlow that he'd taken yesterday. If he'd purchased something in the store, he wouldn't have put it into his expensive-looking leather duffle bag, he'd have carried it out in one of their plastic shopping bags. So it was a safe bet he'd gone in to touch base with Winnie Searle before going next door. It made Kevin wonder how much of the shot-calling she did, as opposed to her husband.

Since he came back out still carrying the bag, it led Kevin to wonder if Barlow had made a pickup, rather than a delivery. Did the bag look any heavier or lighter? Impossible to tell.

Barlow wasn't a known drug dealer, so it wasn't that kind of a cash-for-product type of thing. Considering the type of merchandise Barlow dealt in, it would hardly be a delivery, would it? A birthday present for Mrs. Searle? A stolen string of pearls or a nice diamond-studded brooch? Unlikely, since he consulted with her first in the store before strolling next door to do business with Thomas.

A pickup, then.

Did the Searles have a stolen-goods sideline to go along with their meat and potatoes business?

At that point Gray appeared in his doorway. "You look busy."

Kevin waved him in.

Gray sat down and began to unpack his breakfast takeout bag on Kevin's desk. "You don't mind, do you?"

"No, not at all." To Kevin, Gray's voice sounded normal, if a little tired. He smelled of shampoo, deodorant, and cologne. No whiff of alcohol. No obvious signs of a hangover.

The inspector unwrapped a sausage and egg muffin. "I should explain."

"No need." Kevin had logged into CPIC and was running a query on Barlow.

"I take a lot of medication," Gray said, biting and chewing.

"Sounds like fun." Kevin kept his eyes on the monitor, where a series of hits began to populate the screen.

"An anti-depressant; trazodone, to sleep at night; buspirone to address all the anxiety issues; and lots of other stuff. It was the traz that did me in this morning. I woke up at one-thirty and couldn't get back to sleep, so I took two more and it worked a little too well at the back end. Sorry about that."

"No problem. I've been going through the surveillance pics and found something interesting. Check it out."

Kevin pushed the monitor around. "Look familiar?"

Chewing, Gray squinted at the mug shot on the screen. "Yeah. Yesterday. The store and then the abattoir. Mr. Duffle Bag."

Kevin nodded, not embarrassed at having given Gray a morning memory test. Either he'd be helpful or he wouldn't.

"Ronald Barlow. A.K.A. Ronnie the Rock Man. Fence. Specializes in smalls, especially diamonds, hence the nickname. Lives in Smiths Falls but works Ottawa, Kingston, Belleville."

"Interesting." Gray wadded up the wrapper and tossed it into the wastepaper basket. "You thinking he may run a pickup service for some of his clients. The Searles, say?"

"I like it as a theory."

Gray nodded, sipping his coffee, which was still hot. "Leverage."

"Exactly."

"Going to bring him in for a little chat?"

"You bet your ass I am."

Chapter 47

The firing range of the Osprey's Nest Gun Club was located on the appropriately named Carbine Road in Mississippi Mills Township, about a kilometre west of the village of Pakenham. Pierce had frequented the place before, so he knew what to expect.

The club operated three outdoor ranges, including a 200-yard rifle range; 50- and 100-yard ranges for rifle and shotgun shooting; and a combination skeet- and trap-shooting field. There were two indoor ranges, one for handguns with ten shooting stations and another for pistols that was reserved exclusively for law enforcement officers. Pierce had used the latter before, and found it an adequate facility for training, practice, and re-qualification.

The owner-operator was a no-nonsense former police sergeant from Sarnia named Donny Olsen. Pierce found him in the lounge, serving four men at a table, all retirement age, all exuding an air of habitual wealth and privilege.

Olsen recognized him and waved him over to the bar, which was deserted. "Can I get you something?"

"I'll have what they're having," Pierce quipped.

"You won't be sorry." Olsen set up a china cup, saucer, and napkin, then poured from a steaming carafe. A silver tray of cream and brown sugar cubes followed.

Pierce inhaled. The aroma was fantastic, and the coffee was hot and delicious.

Olsen pulled over a stool and sat down across from him. He was in his early sixties, a redhead going grey, with a pale face and grey eyes. He wore a server's apron over jeans and a blue plaid shirt.

"Condolences on the loss of your brother officer."

Pierce nodded.

"Happened to us once, something similar. Traffic stop in a bad part of the city; kid panicked because the car wasn't his and his licence was suspended. Killed a married man with three kids."

"Damn."

"Yeah. So, do you like the coffee?"

Pierce nodded, sipping.

"Specialty single-origin coffee, from a region in Brazil that grows some of the best in the world."

"Impressive." Pierce liked coffee and drank more than he really ought to, but he knew next to nothing about it, other than what he liked and didn't like.

Olsen reached under the bar and took out a laminated piece of eight-by-twelve cardboard. "Coffee, I mean really good coffee, has what they call tasting notes, just like wine and single-malt scotch. Flavours and afternotes that come out when the beans are roasted. Different, depending on the beans, the environment they grew in, how they're roasted, and how they're brewed. It can be very complicated."

"I had no idea."

"Yeah. I didn't either until I got into it. Now I guess I'm what you'd call an aficionado. With an educated palate. Sort of like a well-trained border collie."

Pierce smiled.

Olsen tapped the card. "This is what they call a coffee tasting flavour wheel. See? You've got fruity, spicy, chocolate, earthy, nutty. The whole nine yards. Then you move out toward the edge of the wheel. The coffee you're drinking right now is here," he pointed at a spot on the wheel labelled "Nut" and looked at Pierce closely. "Now, which spoke would you say it falls in?"

Pierce took another sip and concentrated. "I'm not sure. Sort of like almonds, but also like, um, hazelnuts I guess."

"There you go. The group over there, a millionaires club or something from the city, went through a bunch of different varieties before settling on this one. They tried sweet and sugary, with caramel and maple sugar notes," he pointed, "but it was too sweet for them. They went in the opposite direction," he moved his finger, "over to earthy with notes of soil and fresh wood, but two of them didn't like that one at all. Finally, they settled on our best Brazilian, with hazelnut and pecan notes, the two side-by-side on the wheel. Thank God. I was getting tired of guessing."

Pierce lived in Kanata, the suburb on the west end of Ottawa, and it was a relatively short drive to Pakenham, so he'd found Osprey's Nest convenient to get to, and a well-run operation worth the cost of a membership. He'd come out often enough to have formed an acquaintance with Olsen, mostly revolving around handgun preferences, ammunition, and that sort of thing. Before now, he'd never bothered coming into the lounge after shooting, because he was always alone and preferred not to socialize with strangers if it wasn't necessary.

He had no idea that Olsen was lurking in here with specialty coffee, tasting wheels, and millionaire patrons.

"You said you wanted to talk about one of our club members," Olsen prompted.

"Yeah. Daniel Keegan."

"Keegan. Sure." His expression changed from affability to something else as Pierce watched him slip the tasting wheel back under the bar. Caution? Dislike?

"How long has he been a member?"

"About six years. A handgun guy. Gunsmith, as I understand it. Makes his own ammo; refurbishes old weapons."

"Really?"

"Yeah. He brought a few pieces in for me to look at, back when he was probationary. Pretty good work."

Pierce was aware, as a member himself, that probation lasted a year. Strict adherence to all the club's rules and regulations was an absolute must in order to be approved as a member.

"Any problems with him during that time?"

Olsen shook his head. "Came out once a week for the first while, once the pandemic restrictions were lifted, then a couple times a month after that. Kept things quiet and low key. Too bad it didn't stay that way."

"What happened?"

Olsen reached under the bar for a towel. He wrapped it around his hand and unwrapped it again. Stood up and began to wipe the bar down.

"Got into a dust-up. Started in here, actually. They bumped into each other. Apparently they were old enemies or whatever. Wasn't their only run-in, either. The last time, the fists started to fly, and that was it. I had to throw them both out and suspend their memberships."

"Who was the other guy?"

Olsen stopped wiping and stared at him. "What? I thought you knew. I thought that's why you wanted to talk to me."

Confused, Pierce put down his coffee. "I don't understand."

"The other guy. It was Terry Maynard."

Chapter 48

Pierce's next stop was back in Perth. On his way, he mulled over something his wife had said on the air Friday morning. Georgette co-hosted the weekday morning show on FM-92 The Drive, which ran from 6:00 AM to 9:00 AM, and Pierce listened in whenever he could. His wife was blessed with a low, throaty, resonant voice that was perfect for FM radio, and he loved the sound of it.

The program was the usual morning prattle—traffic, the weather, and light chatter about odd stories popping up in the news. Georgette had a Master's degree in public administration and had worked for several years in the federal government as a bilingual senior communications officer with Global Affairs Canada before a random encounter with the FM-92 station manager at a meet-and-greet for the ambassador to Canada from Germany resulted in an audition and a subsequent job offer. She found the light tone of the morning program a welcome, low-stress change from government work.

Her co-host partner, Bob Wierzbowski, was a former weather guy with a nimble sense of humour and an easy-going on-air persona that seemed to fit well with Georgette's more serious approach. In other words, she was the straight man and he was the funny man, and the pairing had owned the top spot in the city's morning show ratings for the past three years.

One of the items in the seven o'clock news was an update on the Maynard funeral, which would take place in Collingwood on Monday. When he was finished, the newsreader lingered for a minute as he often did, and he happened to ask Georgette whether or not her husband was a police officer.

"Yes," she said. "He's a police detective, actually."

Wierzbowski leaned in. "How's he dealing with it? He must be upset."

"He doesn't talk about work," Georgette calmly replied. "He's been fine. When he comes home, it's all about us, his family. But I'm sure it's had an effect on every law enforcement officer, no matter where they are. It makes you think. They're all there to protect and serve the public, but at what cost?"

"Anyway," the newsreader said, "our thoughts are with him. Thank him for his service for me, will you?"

"Sure, Steve. I will."

Pierce had appreciated the sentiment, but he knew his wife well enough to know that since the shooting she'd been giving him space out of loyalty and respect rather than out of choice. She'd be thrilled if he came home and announced he was going back to acting and leaving the real stuff behind, but she wasn't going to suggest it herself.

Okay, but what about it? Should he consider it? For her sake? And for the girls?

Things were very good for their family right now. Georgette loved her job. They had a large, beautiful house in Kanata, two cars, a kayak, and they were seriously considering buying a cottage in the Gatineau Hills from one of Georgette's friends at the station.

The girls, Judy and Joy, were twelve-year-old twins. Bob liked to joke that they were the same age as the twins who played the ghost girls in the horror movie *The Shining*.

"Sure," Joy liked to retort. "We're naturally spooky."

Being identical twins, they enjoyed confusing people as to which was which. As hard as they tried, though, they could never fool Pierce.

"I'm a detective, and one of you has a tell."

They begged him to spill his secret, but there was no way he would surrender his only means of maintaining the upper hand around them. (It was Judy, and her left ear wiggled right before she laughed.)

Pierce knew it wouldn't be long before they figured it out and started using it against him. After all, they were very bright little girls. They shared a burning interest in robotics, and had already picked out the engineering school where they planned to get their degrees before going into business together.

Pierce, a humble actor-turned-cop, knew better than to try to match wits with the likes of that.

He pulled up in front of the bungalow on Dufferin Road corresponding to the address where Stephanie Stafford had received her regular deliveries from Keegan. The place actually belonged to Stephanie's brother-in-law, Darryl James, and her sister, Denise. When Stephanie could no longer look after herself, Denise had taken her in and set her up in their spare bedroom. Pierce had called ahead and received the *Reader's Digest* version while arranging a time for the interview, but Denise had only talked about her sister on the phone, while Pierce intended to dig around for any information she might have on Keegan that would help his investigation.

Darryl was outside, watering the front lawn. He turned off the hose and dropped it on the ground. As Pierce strolled up the driveway, Darryl dried his palms on his jeans.

"Detective Constable Pierce, OPP." They shook hands. "I spoke to your wife on the phone."

"Yeah. This way." Darryl led him through a gate into a fenced backyard. Behind the house was an octagonal gazebo, screened in, with an imitation cupola on top that gave it a pleasant, Victorian look. Inside, a woman sat in a reclining chair, waiting for them.

"Nice," Pierce said as they approached it.

"Built it myself." He opened a screen door and waved Pierce inside.

"Mrs. James? Detective Constable Pierce." He showed her his badge and warrant card. "Thanks for seeing me."

"Glad to," she said, giving his credentials a quick glance. "Such a fine day, for so early in May. Darryl couldn't wait to get out and start on the yard work."

"Sit down," her husband said, pointing to a chair next to Denise. "Lemonade?"

"Uh, sure, thanks." Pierce settled into a patio chair and took out his notebook as Darryl poured him a tall glass from a carafe that jingled with ice cubes. He set it down on the table next to Pierce's chair. "It's unsweetened; all natural. There's sugar if you want it."

Pierce picked it up and sampled it. Tart. Cold. Wet. "It's good," he said, setting it down again. "Like a nice day in August."

Darryl patted Denise's wrist.

Pierce looked at her legs, which were elevated in the recliner and covered with a hand-knitted quilt. The right foot was partially uncovered, and he could see that it was encased in a walking boot.

"Did you injure yourself?"

She gave Darryl a rueful smile. "Carelessness, wasn't it? Foolish."

"Not at all."

"I'm an early-childhood educator at the daycare on Foster Street. I'm supposed to keep the floor clear of clutter to prevent accidents, but I didn't see a sponge ball next to the leg of a chair and I stepped on it."

"She went down hard," Darryl said. "Hit her head. She had concussion symptoms for several days."

"I tore all the ligaments in my ankle. It was what they call a Grade Three injury, the worst kind of sprain. It hurts like you wouldn't believe."

"I'm sorry to hear that," Pierce said.

"They gave me painkillers to manage it. I hope I don't seem spacey to you right now. They really help, I'm telling you. When they're done, I switch to ibuprofen. Hopefully I won't have an addiction to the good stuff."

"You'll be fine," Darryl said.

She looked at Pierce. "You wanted to talk about Stephanie."

"Yes," Pierce said, deciding to take his time.

"It'll be thirteen years, this summer. Hard to believe. Feels like it was only last week."

"She had a long battle with cancer, as I understand it."

"Yes. Liver cancer."

"For which she received weekly shipments of medicinal CBD."

"We have copies of the doctor's prescriptions," Darryl said. "We kept them in case we had to prove that it was all legal. But holy crap, man, that was a long time ago. Is that why you're here? Do you want me to go get them to prove she wasn't doing anything wrong?"

Pierce shook his head. "I'm not interested in that. I'm more interested in the relationship Stephanie formed with the guy who delivered them to her."

Denise nodded. "I thought so."

"Why do you say that, Mrs. James?"

"He wasn't an easy man to get along with. He seemed moody and broody, if you know what I mean. Oh, don't get me wrong. He was great with Stephanie. When he started coming around on his off hours, it was like an extra dose of medicine for her. She fell for him head over heels. Poor girl. But when it was just the three of us, when Steph was in her room getting dressed or something, he was hard to talk to."

"It bothered me that he was such a gun nut," Darryl said. "Not that I've got anything against guns necessarily, but when you tried to have a conversation with him, that was all he wanted to talk about. Guns. Ammunition. His hobby."

"It made us feel uncomfortable," Denise said, her voice low. "You know, that he had such an obsession with them."

"You had to wonder how stable he was, and if it could put Steph in a bad situation," Darryl said. "Even though she was sick, and he paid her such good attention, it was a worry just the same. He'd invite her to go out with him to the shooting range, even though he knew she couldn't leave the house except for treatments and appointments. Said he'd pay for a membership for her. It was like a running joke with them. 'When you get better, I'll teach you how to shoot.' Steph played along. It made her feel like he cared for her and wanted to spend a lot of time with her."

Pierce looked at Denise, about to ask another question, but she'd fallen asleep.

Darryl quietly stood and led him out of the gazebo and across the lawn to the gate. "The pills are a bit strong for her. They knock her right out like that, sometimes. I'll be glad when they're done."

Pierce shook hands with him in the driveway. "I appreciate your time. And hers. I hope she's feeling better soon."

"Thanks." Darryl smiled. "The funny part? The sponge ball she tripped on was supposed to look like a little globe, you know what I mean? The planet. A blue ball with green continents and islands. She said to me, 'Well, there's one thing off my bucket list. Now I've had my trip around the world.'"

Chapter 49

Rehearsal day.

Heather stood in the hotel lobby with all the others as the bus rolled up under the porte-cochère. Sergeant Gibbons led the way out the front entrance. There'd only been time for a quick coffee and a croissant, and she was feeling the caffeine shortage rather acutely. After a few moments, she shuffled out the sliding doors in the middle of the pack and waited her turn to board.

This time she had more of a plan. Since many of the seats were already taken, she could pick and choose whom she sat beside instead of getting stuck next to Sombrero Skelton. She chose a traffic constable named Seabrooke, who obligingly shuffled over to the window seat to allow her to sit down next to him.

Their orders for the rehearsal were to wear normal business attire, which for non-commissioned officers meant their regular uniform, and for plainclothes officers such as herself, a suit. Of course, normal business attire for Heather usually meant a T-shirt featuring Elmer Fudd or the Incredible Hulk along with comfortable, well-worn blue jeans. Not wishing to piss off senior management, she'd brought her best pantsuit, a navy blue thing that her mother had bought for her last year when she'd visited them in Bermuda. It had cost about the same as a high-producing dairy cow would have set them back while they were still operating the farm, and she'd been a little upset at the time. Her mother had told her to shut up and enjoy it. So she did. The shut-up part, anyway.

When she packed, she'd rolled it up and stuffed it into the bottom of her knapsack, the garment bag being reserved for her uniform, her peak cap, her black dress shoes, her gloves, and so on. When she pulled it out this morning while getting dressed, she wondered if she would have to grab the little iron on the hall rack and give it a quick going-over to discourage the wrinkles. She was dismayed to discover both the jacket and the pants were wrinkle-free. Flawless.

I told you so, her mother whispered inside her head. *It'll take everything you can dish out, and then some. That's why it costs so much. It's a Heather Hope Special Edition.*

It took about fifteen minutes to get everyone on the bus, speaking of cattle and the absence of a good herding dog, and the drive from the hotel to the arena was only a ten-minute jaunt, including two sets of traffic lights which both turned red just before they reached them.

The arena itself, although seventy-five years old, had recently undergone a major renovation which left it, in Heather's opinion, with a very nice combination of 1940s-style exterior architecture and a twenty-first century modern interior. She took a quick look around before following the others into the main event space, which was normally the ice surface but was now covered by some sort of space-age insulated flooring topped with carpeting.

They trooped up the aisle between the double banks of temporary seats toward the front, where a stage had been set up complete with podium, lighting, and microphones. The stands were empty, except for a few observers here and there, but the arena could accommodate at least three thousand people, including the seating at ice level, and Heather knew that tomorrow the place would be packed.

Chief Superintendent Malcolmsen was serving as funeral commander for the ceremony. He gave them a quick overview of the upcoming rehearsal and what they should expect, introduced Reverend Mary Rose Morgan, the family pastor, who would perform the duties of chaplain for the service, and then kicked things off by instructing the pallbearers to gather at the main entrance where the casket would be brought in from the hearse after its arrival from the funeral home. Thankfully, Heather had been spared that particular duty.

A stickler for detail, Malcolmsen had persuaded the funeral home to loan them an empty coffin, which was brought over to its place of honour in front of the stage, under the spotlights. The invisible audience was directed to stand, and a uniformed constable Heather didn't know sang the national anthem. After a moment of silence in honour of their fallen brother, the regional commander launched into his opening speech.

When he was done, there was random coughing and shuffling of feet while he conferred with several people behind him on the stage. Finally, he introduced the Lieutenant Governor of Ontario. A young woman, likely her executive assistant, took the microphone and droned her way through a sheaf of notes covering the highlights of the remarks the lieutenant governor planned to deliver tomorrow.

Malcolmsen then introduced the premier, who was represented by a young man who was no doubt another EA. Blah, blah, and then it was the turn of the Solicitor General of Ontario, the politician responsible for the OPP, provincial Corrections, the Centre of Forensic Sciences (to which they all sent their most important lab work), the Office of the Fire Marshall, and other such very important portfolios. It so happened that the SolGen himself had made the trip up to Collingwood from Toronto this morning to attend the rehearsal in person, which was appreciated by the Lanark team as a solid display of loyalty and support.

He skimmed through his remarks and finished up in about five minutes. Another point in his favour.

After that, Heather's attention began to flag. She moved around as directed, stood with the others where she was told to stand, and drifted off into a world of her own. The last funeral she'd attended had been Scott's, ten years ago. She preferred to avoid them like the plague. Desperately, she fought to suppress the memories of that day. After much scrambling around in her head, she decided one more time to run through the pros and cons of creating a database catalogue of her comic book collection. Was it too much work? Would she use it after all that time and effort?

Finally, they were dismissed for an hour-long lunch break, after which they would reconvene and the rehearsal would continue.

Lunch was catered in the arena food court, a selection of sandwiches, salads in green-conscious containers, and beverages. Heather sat at a table by herself, head down, elbows in, hoping that no one else would come along and decide she needed company.

The food was good, and it relaxed her enough that her chin eventually came up and she began to take stock of her surroundings.

The only other females in sight were Colleen Galvin and Deputy Commissioner Leanne Blair, the provincial commander of Investigations and Organized Crime. They sat together over on the far side of the food court with some young civilian guy Heather didn't recognize. He wore an expensive-looking black suit, and his haircut looked as though it had cost more than Heather spent on groceries in a week. He was doing most of the talking, while Galvin and Blair listened politely, their expressions neutral.

As Heather watched, a grey-haired man stopped at their table and bent over to say something to the young guy. Heather recognized the older man from his photograph in the Annual Report—Deputy Commissioner John Goss, provincial commander of Field Operations. The young suit guy listened intently, nodding, and quickly got up so that Goss could take his seat. Then he said something to Galvin and Blair—see you later, or words to that effect most likely—and hurried off, taking out his cellphone and punching in a call.

Heather, reminding herself that she was a detective by trade, wondered if the young guy was yet another executive assistant. Maybe the commissioner's? Who knew?

After a few more minutes, people began to stand up. They gathered their refuse, dropped it in the appropriate waste bins, and wandered back to the rink area. Heather took the hint and followed suit.

Malcolmsen was waiting for her at the garbage bins. "You're on casket watch, Hope."

Her heart sank as she threw out her wadded wrappers and milk carton. "I am?"

"Sergeant Gibbons will be taking the detail over to the hotel for your Number Ones in fifteen minutes. Don't keep him waiting. Visitation starts at sixteen hundred."

"Yes, sir."

Great.

Back in position, she listened to the head of the union deliver his remarks with fiery intensity and was startled when Sergeant Gibbons tapped her on the elbow and gestured with his chin toward the exit. There were three others waiting for her: Provincial Constable Paul Wainwright, the SOCO; Provincial Constable Guindon from Traffic, and Provincial Constable Sakari Burkhart from the drug team. A limousine belonging to the funeral home delivered them to the hotel. In the lobby,

Gibbons tapped his watch and gave them the look.

"Fifteen minutes."

The Bellefeuille and Wilson Funeral Home was the oldest and largest mortuary in the town of Collingwood, having been in continuous operation since 1947. From the outside, it looked much like it had in the old days, with its clean white siding, stately Grecian-style pillars, and canopied front entrance. Inside, however, much care and expense had been dedicated to modernization of the facility to ensure that clients and their families and friends had a comforting, twenty-first century experience.

Inside the main entrance, discreet furniture groupings invited visitors to use the lobby as a break area and meeting place. Electronic displays gave the names and visitation times for both reposing areas, the Carmichael Room and the Huron Room, and how to find them, or the chapel, or the main office.

The Carmichael Room had been set aside for the Terence Maynard party. According to the notice board, visitation would be held between 3:00 PM and 8:00 PM.

Sergeant Gibbons had presided over the movement of the casket from the prep area, or wherever it had been, into the Carmichael Room. It was on a gurney, and the two funeral attendants in black suits and silent black shoes who brought it in were able to move it around with no difficulty until it was situated to Gibbons' liking. They withdrew, and the casket watch party took over.

The casket was closed, of course, due to the grievous head wounds that had taken the life of the deceased. Gibbons covered the coffin with a Red Ensign, the official flag of the province of Ontario. He fussed at bit with its placement, then stepped back and nodded.

"Hope and Wainwright, first watch. Guindon and Burkhart,

second watch. One at the head, one at the foot, facing each other." He looked at Heather.

She moved to the head of the casket, and Wainwright took the other end. Their eyes met, then Heather picked something over his shoulder to stare at instead.

"Hope, where are your gloves?"

She jerked. "Sorry, sir." She pulled them out of her pocket and wrestled them on. They'd always been a fraction too small, and she hated wearing them.

Gibbons consulted his watch. "The family should be here in five minutes. Your shifts are thirty minutes long. Hope and Wainwright, your first shift begins now. You'll be relieved at fifteen thirty."

"Yes, sir," Wainwright murmured. Heather limited herself to a curt nod, already slipping into the role.

The two attendants reappeared, one carrying an easel and the other a large framed photograph of Terry Maynard. Heather sneaked a peek at it as they carried it past her. It was a studio photograph. Maynard was smiling, a crooked, shit-eating grin. He looked neat and professional in his uniform, proud to be a cop and that's all there was to it. Anyone looking at it would be heartbroken at the tragic loss of such a fine, upstanding man.

They set it up behind the casket, at Heather's seven o'clock where she couldn't quite see it in her peripheral vision. When Gibbons was satisfied with their work, the attendants walked around Heather again and were met at the doorway by a party of four women. One of them handed over a large cardboard display board covered with snapshots. A second easel was fetched, and the gallery of photos featuring Maynard in various stages of his life was positioned at the other end of the casket, at Wainwright's five o'clock.

Gibbons stepped forward and introduced himself, offering his sincere condolences. From what was said, Heather understood the elderly woman to be Maynard's mother, Roberta, and the middle-aged woman his sister, Theresa. A third woman, somewhat older than Theresa, proved to be Sylvia Turner, Maynard's ex-wife, while the fourth was the Reverend Mary Rose Morgan, the family pastor.

As they approached the casket, tears began to flow in earnest. Heather tuned out, knowing it was the only way she'd be able to pull off the Buckingham Palace King's Guard thing that was expected of her, the blank and wooden stare, the vigilant watch over a fallen comrade, the stoic endurance of life's slings and arrows. She struggled with it for a moment until, as usual, her thoughts turned to the subject of comic books.

Comics were not only her hobby but her consuming passion. Her collection, which numbered about six thousand books at the moment, could be divided into two groups. The first consisted of what were known as reading copies—comics that graded between Fair and Good condition and were intended to be handled, read, and enjoyed without worrying about what kind of shape they were in and what value they might have. Some kid may have written her name across the front cover (ahem) or cut out the coupons inside to send away for x-ray glasses or a seahorse family, but the interior was complete and the stories could be read from start to finish with a plate of peanut butter sandwiches and a glass of Coke on the side.

The second portion was made up of collectible issues that she'd added not only because she liked them but because of their value. These included a selection of 1950s Dell Four-Colour comics based on TV programs and other licensed properties; Silver Age comics leaning heavily toward Marvel Comics superheroes; and early *Archie* issues that held a surprisingly high value, relatively speaking. Included were a number of so-called keys, issues that featured the first appearance of some important new character or significant work by a particular artist, the value of which was higher than other issues in the series. She kept careful track of keys, and occasionally added one or two when she spotted them.

Some of the books in her collection were slabbed, meaning

that they'd been graded by a professional company and sealed in a plastic container, thereby preserving their condition for eternity. She'd never herself sent any comics off to be graded, not caring to incur an expense that could be devoted instead to another batch of "raws," but she'd bought a few at conventions or other shows and she liked having them. As long as she also had a reading copy of the issue as well, of course. One to look at, and one to read while munching on salt and vinegar potato chips washed down with a large bottle of cream soda.

Vaguely aware that the doors had been opened and the visitation was now under way, her thoughts strayed to her wish list. She liked to review it in her head from time to time and switch up the order in which her wishes were listed, and she did so now. On impulse, she made an executive decision and moved *Magnus, Robot Fighter* up to the top. She had a few issues and liked the stories, and on the spur of the moment she decided to pull out all the stops and try to put together a complete run of volume one of the series.

Created in 1963 by Russ Manning for Gold Key Comics, an imprint of Western Publishing, the original series ran until 1977 with a total of forty-six issues, so it wasn't a completely impossible mission for her to collect the complete run. In fact, she already owned a copy of the first issue, which clocked in at around $2,500 in Very Fine to Near Mint condition, but hers unfortunately was what was jokingly called a "rat chew" copy. She'd bought it at a convention in a mylar sleeve with an acid-free board backing, but it had definitely been gnawed at by vermin, as the top edge was worn away in a serrated crescent. She'd paid thirty bucks for it at the end of the show, the vendor too tired and distracted to care, and she was pleased to have it as a placeholder. But at some point—

"Hope."

Snapping out of it, she shifted her eyes to the right and saw Constable Burkhart staring at her. "I relieve you."

Constable Guindon stood beside Wainwright, who was also

waiting for her to return to the twenty-first century from AD 4000 North Am. She nodded at Burkhart and they went through the ritual of changing the watch.

She and Wainwright then followed an attendant through the crowd, which stared at them with mute respect. Out in the corridor, they were shown to a break-off area where coffee and pastries waited for them. Heather stripped off her gloves and dug in, never so glad to be out of a room in her life.

Chapter 50

"Thanks for coming in," Kevin said, closing the door behind him. "Hopefully we won't have to take up too much more of your time this afternoon."

"It's a Sunday afternoon," Ronald Robert Barlow crossed his legs. "What else is there to do?"

Kevin sat down and opened his file folder. After Patrol had brought Barlow in and he was walked through the basics, Kevin had let him sit for about twenty minutes to see if the suspense would generate a reaction. Watching on the video feed, he hadn't seen any. Barlow had remained calm and unconcerned throughout the wait.

"My name's Detective Constable Walker. You've already had your rights explained to you, you're aware that this interview is being recorded, and you've waived your opportunity to consult with counsel. Is that correct?"

"Yes, it is."

"We're investigating the murders of OPP Provincial Constable Maynard and Drummond resident Dorothy Kerr, and you've been identified as a person of interest in this case. Do you know what that means? To be a person of interest?"

Barlow's forehead creased. "I think so."

"It means we believe you may have information that will lead to an arrest. Not necessarily *your* arrest, although if we get to that point I'll caution you all over again and you'll have another chance to talk to a lawyer. But at the moment I'd really appreciate some answers to my questions. How are we doing so far?"

"I understand what you're saying, if that's what you mean."

"Good."

In his mid-forties, Barlow's voice was soft and low. He spoke carefully and with a faint accent, perhaps picked up from his time in England. He was short and balding, with a pot belly stretching out his blue cardigan sweater. His tan polyester trousers were neatly pressed, and his black slip-on shoes were polished and buffed. He looked like a guy you'd pay to do your taxes at the last minute in April on the advice of a co-worker who'd used him before and thought he'd done a decent job of getting a refund.

"You were seen on Saturday afternoon at Searle Meat and Potatoes," Kevin said. "What were you doing there?"

"Just picking up a few things."

Kevin pulled a photograph out of the file folder and slid it over. "This is your car, right?"

"Yes, sir, it is."

"An Audi Quattro. Nice car. As you can see, it's parked in front of the Searles' store. Correct?"

"Yes. Yes, sir, it is."

"Here's you going into the store. What's that you're carrying, Mr. Barlow?"

"Uh, my bag."

"A duffle bag, right? Not a reusable shopping bag like you take into a grocery store, but a duffle bag. Leather, from the looks of it. Do you usually take a duffle bag with you when you go shopping?"

The furrows on Barlow's forehead deepened as he hesitated. "Uh, no, sir."

"What was in the bag, Mr. Barlow? When you took it into the store?"

"Nothing, really."

Kevin leaned back. "Nothing? Are you sure? The bag was empty?"

"Well, my notebook was in it, and a couple of pens, a few things like that."

"Oh, okay. Not quite empty, but empty for all intents and purposes."

"Yes, sir."

"What was in it when you came out of the store?"

"Nothing. Well, the same things I just mentioned."

"Did you leave anything in the store?"

"No, sir."

"Did you buy anything?"

"No, sir."

"Did you take anything out of the store with you when you left?"

Barlow shook his head. "No, I didn't."

"Okay." Kevin pulled out another picture. "You went from the store into the abattoir. What was your business in there?"

Barlow leaned over and politely examined the photo. "Tommy and I are friends. We've known each other for some time. I was in the area, so I thought I'd stop in to say hello."

"Do you always carry a duffle bag with you when you visit old friends?"

No response.

"Here you are coming back out after your little visit." Kevin dealt another photograph onto the top of the pile. "Is it just me, or does the bag look heavier? The way you're carrying it. And here," he added another shot of Barlow opening the passenger door of his vehicle, "you carefully place the bag on the seat before you get in behind the wheel. I'm thinking to myself, man, if that were me and the bag was empty, I'd just toss it across the seat before I got in. Why bother with the other door first? Unless there was something in the bag that needed careful handling."

Barlow studied the fingernails on his right hand.

Kevin gathered up the photographs and slipped them back into the folder. "I understand your reticence, Mr. Barlow. I really do. For a couple of reasons."

He slid the folder aside, as though it were finished business. "I did my homework on you. You're an educated man, come to find out."

Barlow glanced at him cautiously. "Yes."

"A Master's degree in Jewellery and Silversmithing from the London Metropolitan University. You could have knocked me over with a feather. I wondered at first how you could have possibly afforded it back then, a young man from Smiths Falls with a degree from Carleton University and a modest résumé living and studying in England, but then it seemed pretty obvious once I thought about it. You were already over there, working in the trade and getting valuable experience in the field while you covered off the knowledge base side at school. Wow. Impressive, Mr. Barlow."

"Thank you."

"But you had to come back to Canada because your mother got sick and there was no one here to look after her. Isn't that true?"

"Yes."

"She passed away a couple of years ago, as I understand it. My condolences."

"Thank you."

"Why didn't you go back to England after the funeral?"

Silent for a moment, Barlow eventually shrugged. "My

place had been taken by others. There was no room for me any more."

"Competitive business, eh?"

"Yes. Yes, sir, it is."

"So you built up your business here, instead." Kevin studied him for a moment. "I looked at your website. You make some beautiful stuff. Earrings, necklaces, rings, brooches. High-end merchandise."

"Thank you."

"There's another part of your business that isn't on the website, though, isn't there?"

Barlow said nothing.

"Although you probably cover it on the dark web. Do you have an account there? If we look, will we find it? 'Ronnie the Rock Man-dot-onion' or some such thing?"

"I'm sorry, I don't know what you're referring to."

Kevin stirred. He moved around in his chair and crossed his legs, as though settling in for a more friendly talk. "It's too bad that you got hit with that conviction for possession, back when you were still in London. Only twenty-two. Tch tch. Rookie mistake? Cost you three months. How did you explain it at school? Emergency trip home?"

Barlow was silent, his face expressionless.

"Found it through Interpol. Sometimes it pays to be thorough."

"I suppose it does," Barlow said.

"See, the thing about a record is that it puts you on our radar when break-and-enter season heats up. Not when somebody loses their TV and home entertainment system, or their antique furniture, of course. We know that's not you. That's just some dumbass punks hoping to make a few bucks selling stuff off the back of their truck. You, on the other hand, you deal in the smalls, don't you? Rolexes and expensive brooches, diamond rings, pearl necklaces. Antique clocks. So when that kind of break-in happens, well, we naturally want to talk to you about it.

You see the logic in that, don't you?"

"I suppose I do."

"Okay. So, the other thing I did while I was getting ready for our meeting is check in our system for recent B-and-E cases along that line. Jewelry, coins, what have you. It so happens that there've been several. Two just north of Kingston, one in Westport, one at Sharbot Lake, and one near Pakenham. All expensive properties owned by rich people with lots of precious valuables that disappeared while they weren't at home."

He paused, watching for a reaction. There was none.

"How long did you say you've known the Searles?"

"For some time."

"How long would that be in years?"

"I don't know, really. We met before the pandemic."

"So, more than five years? More than ten?"

"Not more than ten."

"Who'd you meet first? Thomas Searle, or his sons?"

Barlow hesitated for a long time. He scratched his upper lip, tapped his left index finger lightly on the back of his right hand, and shifted uneasily. Apparently weighing his options. Then he met Kevin's eyes with a wan smile.

"Actually, it was Mrs. Searle. Winnie. She's the brains of the outfit."

Kevin hid his surprise. "Winnie?"

"Sure. She's the one who, uh, contacts me if Thomas wants me to visit."

"How did you meet her?"

He made a face. "Through a mutual acquaintance. Someone I thought had better judgment."

"You don't like Mrs. Searle?"

He rolled his eyes.

"Why visit them when you don't like them?"

Barlow said nothing for a moment. "I suppose you could say it's a form of extortion. She's bloody cutthroat, that one. Knows which threats to use, and when to use them."

"She threatens you?"

He picked at an invisible hair on his sleeve. "Let's say she says the right thing to make me want to come round for a visit."

"Do you know anything about the break-and-enters I mentioned?"

No response.

Kevin grunted. "Sorry, I must have misunderstood you just now. I was under the impression you wouldn't mind getting out from under the thumb of Winnie Searle. I'm sure you must have better clients than that."

A tiny shrug.

"I'm going to let you think about it for a few minutes." Kevin uncrossed his legs and crossed them again in the other direction. "How often do you visit the Searles?"

"It varies. Once a month on average, I suppose."

"How do they behave? Are they polite, or do they act like hillbilly good old boys with a chip on their shoulder?"

Barlow smiled, faintly amused. "The latter, mostly."

"When you were there on Saturday, how were they? Any different than at any other time?"

"Hmm." He thought for a moment. "Quieter. I didn't think much of it, but now that you mention it, they were almost subdued. Like something serious was going on."

"Any idea what it might have been?"

"No."

"Are the sons there when you come around to visit?"

"Sometimes yes, sometimes no."

"How do you find them?"

"Surly, for the most part. The eldest, Al, the butcher, goes around with a cleaver shoved in the waistband of his apron. Bert, as I understand it, takes care of the potato side of things and likes to throw his weight around. It's the youngest, Gary, that I truly fear. Showed me a gun once when he thought our, ah, conversation wasn't going in the direction his father wanted.

Made it clear he liked using it. I believed him."

"Was he there on Saturday?"

"No, thank God. Just Al and Bert with their father."

"And they seemed to be upset about something."

"Yes."

"What were they talking about? Among themselves, I mean."

"I don't know. They went quiet as soon as I came in."

Kevin gave him a long look. "Mr. Barlow, three more related questions. Important ones. Do you think the Searles are capable of committing an act of criminal violence?"

"Yes." No hesitation.

"Do you know of any such acts in particular?"

"No. I don't."

"Last one. Do you think one or more of them would be capable of attacking a police officer?"

Barlow's eyes widened. "Not you, I hope."

Kevin waited. He watched the wheels turn inside the man's head as he suddenly remembered the murders of Terry Maynard and Dorothy Kerr.

"Gary, and that damned gun. Christ." He made a face. "You know, I wouldn't put it past him."

Chapter 51

It was Monday morning. Standing in front of the dresser mirror, Kevin tried for the third time to knot his tie at the proper length so that it would reach the top of his belt buckle but not cover it. The tie was charcoal and went well with his black suit, but it was a pain to tie. This time he overcompensated and finished with it almost two inches too short.

A sigh from the bedroom door caught his attention. Pulling out the knot, he glanced over. "Hey, Cait."

"Want some help?"

"Do you know how to tie one of these things?"

"I should. I've watched Mom do it enough times."

Janie was currently unavailable—running late; in the shower; in a bad mood.

Kevin released his death grip on the silk tormenter and held out his arms. "Have at it."

She sawed the tie back and forth around his neck until she

had the ends where she wanted them. "Are you sure I can't come with you?"

"School," he said. "I'll make sure it gets read."

Caitlyn had written a poem in honour of Dorothy Kerr, whose funeral was at eleven o'clock. "It's not just that. It's that I've never been to one before. I didn't even go to Johnny's, and he was my grandfather. I think it's time."

"It's not time. It's never time. How the heck do you do that?"

She'd knotted the tie, snugged it up, and then lowered his collar over it in no time flat. She patted his shoulder. "It's a secret."

"Are you riding your bike?"

She nodded, handing him his suit jacket.

"Be careful."

"I will."

It was a few minutes after nine o'clock when he edged his way into the meeting room, where two television sets on rolling carts were showing the coverage of the funeral in Collingwood. The procession was preparing to leave the funeral home, and the narrators were discussing the risks involved in modern-day policing, not only in the United States but also here in Canada. Kevin found a place along the wall between Sonja Freeling and a drug enforcement officer he knew slightly and watched as the broadcast shifted to a camera covering the side doors, out of which the honour guard was expected to emerge very soon with the casket containing Terence Maynard's remains.

No one in the room spoke. Kevin imagined that some of them were thinking about themselves and the possibility it could be their body lying in that coffin and not Maynard's. Grim, depressing thoughts.

The doors opened. They were large sliding doors that didn't need to be held, but a member of the honour guard took up a position on each side, just in case. One of them was Heather Hope. She stood at attention, back straight, gloved hands at her sides. Kevin's heart went out to her, knowing how much she hated being there. Just the same, she looked great. Professional; serious; a credit to the service.

An attendant emerged first, leading the way to the hearse that waited for them, its back door open. Another attendant followed, stepping aside as he offered words of instruction to the six pallbearers, who guided the gurney along the pavement to the hearse. They were all familiar faces to Kevin. It was strange, watching them on television in this context.

The camera stayed with the casket until it was loaded into the hearse and the back door was closed, then the broadcast shifted to a shot from across the street. The commentator explained that the route was already lined on both sides with first responders, including Lanark colleagues of the deceased, OPP personnel from across the province, members of other law enforcement services such as the Toronto Police Service, Ottawa and Kingston police, the Sûreté du Québec, and firefighters and paramedics. The public had gathered at designated areas along the route as well to pay their respects.

Sonja leaned over. "What time does the Kerr service start?"

"Eleven," Kevin said.

"What time are you leaving?"

"Shortly."

They watched two OPP motorcycle units lead the way out of the parking lot, lights flashing, followed by an OPP SUV with its light bar also turned on. The hearse followed, slowly pulling out into the street. Next were two black limousines carrying the honour guard, Maynard's mother and sister, their minister, and a few other VIPs. Civilian vehicles belonging to neighbours, a few old friends, and others brought up the rear.

All along the route, hands snapped up in salute as the procession came into view. It was an impressive sight.

One of us.

Chapter 52

Safe passage of the late Terence Robert Maynard had been entrusted to the Ontario Provincial Police ceremonial unit, which made its appearance through the protective tenting at the front entrance to the arena. With a funeral home attendant fore and aft, eight pallbearers guided the flag-covered casket forward on its gurney for several metres before stopping. They lifted the casket, allowing the attendants to remove the gurney and clear out of the way. The pallbearers then hoisted the casket onto their shoulders and, as the congregation stood, began the long walk down the red carpet.

The bagpipers began to play a song Heather didn't recognize, but it was something that might be piped for a Scottish hero fallen in battle who was returning home one last time. In front of her was Sergeant Gibbons, resplendent in a scarlet sash over his Dress Ones. On her left was Wainwright, holding a fringed ceremonial board on which sat Maynard's peak cap. She followed Gibbons on his right, carrying the deceased's badge on another board. It took forever to shuffle down to the front of the arena. She and Wainwright held back from the spotlight that followed the pallbearers as they lowered the casket onto the bier, just as they'd done in rehearsal, the Red Ensign facing out toward the congregation. When Gibbons was satisfied, he took Maynard's hat from Wainwright and placed it on top of the coffin, then came back to Heather for the badge.

Then it was time to take her place with the rest of the ceremonial unit in the front row on the side opposite that of the family and VIPs. But not time to sit down quite yet. The uniformed constable whose name she didn't catch once again sang the national anthem. Malcolmsen reclaimed the podium and asked for a moment's silence. Then, finally, they could sit down as the regional commander launched into his opening speech.

Although Malcolmsen wasn't a natural speaker, something he'd have to work on as his career continued upward, Heather thought he did a passable job admitting his constant fear of losing a member in his command, something that haunted everyone with people serving below them. He went on to cover the agenda for the service, after which, thankfully, he gave way to the Lieutenant Governor of Ontario, the Honourable Sally Rubenstein.

Heather had never seen her before, not on television or in person, as her appointment had occurred only recently. She was in her early fifties, tall and slender, elegant in a black skirt suit and conservative black hat, her blond hair only just beginning its transition to white. As the King's representative to the province, she said, she offered his royal condolences to the family, friends, and colleagues of Terry Maynard, and she spoke with feeling about grief, the inadequacy of words, and a shared solidarity among those who mourn.

Heather was fascinated. Not so much by the speech, which was fairly predictable, although very well delivered, as by the woman. She reminded Heather of her mother—refined, poised, cultured. Altogether all together, and all the things Heather had always wanted to be but wasn't. She took after her dad, short and wide-hipped; irreverent and brimming with the milk of human kindness. On the other hand, her mother, the daughter of a long-time mayor of Campbellford and a high school principal, was like this woman behind the podium, elegant and well-spoken. Heather had always idolized her mother, and the Honourable Sally Rubenstein suddenly shot right up to the top of the list of people Heather would like to meet some day. Just to see if she was as wonderful in person, in an informal situation, as she was now, conveying the King's condolences.

Next to take his turn at the podium was the premier of the province of Ontario. Unlike almost everyone else she knew, and despite the fact that she habitually voted for another party at election time, Heather harboured a secret liking for the man. He was constantly embroiled in controversy, and frequently reversing course on policy decisions or potentially corrupt backroom deals with wealthy patrons, but somehow he still managed to project an image of someone trying very hard to do the right thing.

As he spoke, Heather was surprised that his voice was shaky and a little uncertain. She'd watched him on television numerous times, usually when trying to bail himself out of trouble for something or other, and he never appeared hesitant or lacking in self-confidence. Now, however, the emotion he displayed seemed to be genuine. As he looked out across the sea of uniforms, he promised to do everything in his power to protect them as they protected and served all of us.

"I'll have your back," he said.

Heather, despite herself, believed him.

She'd already heard the Solicitor General's speech, so she tuned out until the commissioner took the stage. This was the guy they all worked for, the guy who'd helicoptered down from

Orillia to attend the first press conference in Perth the day after the murders, the guy who stood next to Malcolmsen on that difficult day as the regional commander expressed his grief and anger and his determination to bring the killer to justice. Now, Cecil Dart gripped the podium with both gloved hands and faced the spotlight.

Near retirement now, his hair thinning and white, Dart's face showed the marks of long service, with its stresses and political pressures and difficult choices. He talked about his own experiences as a young provincial constable, foolishly entrusted by his superiors with a cruiser, back then a Crown Victoria police interceptor, and how it felt to be out there on his own, responsible to enforce the law on our highways. It was an experience that thrilled and frightened him at the same time, and he admitted to a guilty sense of relief when he stepped up to the rank of detective constable and turned the Crown Vic over to someone more competent to drive it.

Terence, on the other hand, was a career traffic constable. He spent more than twenty years enforcing the *Highway Traffic Act* and other legislation for which the OPP was responsible, and he did so because it was what he loved to do.

"It takes a special person to put their life on the line every day to protect the citizens of this province and keep them safe," Dart said. "Being a police officer is not just a job. It's who we are."

He spoke about his own son, Craig, who was now in his mid-forties, only a few years younger than Terence. Craig worked as a detective constable in the Northwest Region, he explained.

"There came a time," Dart said, "when I nearly lost him. When his duties brought him to the point of disaster, when his life was suspended by a slender thread. The person who intervened and saved him is here today, helping us grieve the loss of someone else's son, and there isn't a day goes by that I don't thank her in my prayers. I know what it's like to have a child who voluntarily places himself in the line of fire in order to serve and protect others. I know what it's like to lie awake in bed at three in the morning, afraid for his safety. I don't know what it's like to experience a loss as profound as yours, Mrs. Maynard, but you will always have my deepest and most sincere condolences."

Heather, of course, had heard the story of Ellie's heroic plunge into the icy waters of Sparrow Lake to pull Craig Dart to safety ten years ago, and how it had forged a special bond between her and Cecil Dart. It was part of the legend that was Detective Inspector Ellie March.

Heather didn't realize she was in attendance today, but of course it made sense. Everyone of importance was here. She hadn't seen her, but Ellie was likely with her CIB colleagues, part of the GHQ contingent sitting somewhere behind her, the brain trust of criminal investigation in Ontario. The ones expecting her, Heather Hope from Keene, to get off the knob and find Terry Maynard's killer.

"We will always remember Provincial Constable Terence Maynard's commitment to duty," Dart continued, winding up. "His courage and dedication, his constant vigilance in the protection of our communities, and we accept willingly the responsibility to carry on where he left off, to ensure his legacy will never be forgotten. Mrs. Maynard, Theresa; you will always be a part of our family."

Lowering his head, Dart left the stage.

Heather felt a single tear run down her cheek. Her dislike of Terry Maynard momentarily forgotten, she knew she had bought into every word the commissioner had uttered.

Chapter 53

Another Monday funeral.

Kevin sat down in a pew toward the back, unbuttoning his suit jacket. A pleasant-looking man in a clerical outfit stood at the front of the chapel with Patrick Dillon, publisher of the *Sentinel*, and a woman Kevin didn't know. The woman was mid-twenties, smallish, with shoulder-length black hair tied back with a long black ribbon. She wore a black jacket and skirt combination, both leather, and flat-soled pumps. As Kevin watched, her hand stole into Patrick's and gave it a little squeeze.

According to the program Kevin had picked up from the table in the hallway, the minister was the Reverend Peter Selleck, from the local United church. Kevin had spoken to the funeral home manager, who told him that Dorothy Kerr had pre-arranged her funeral and paid it off six years ago. In it, she'd specified that there would be no wake, that she would be cremated, and that

Selleck would deliver her eulogy. Apparently she'd been an occasional member of his congregation.

Dorothy's urn sat on a pedestal designed to look like a Greek column. After the service, which was expected to be brief, the urn would be placed in a niche in the columbarium at the local non-denominational cemetery.

There would be no music.

Dorothy Kerr, Kevin decided, was not someone interested in having a good time, alive or dead.

Three rows back, on the right-hand side, four middle-aged women had settled in and were quietly talking among themselves. They looked like four crows huddled together on a tree branch. Kevin recognized them as members of the quilting group Dorothy had belonged to, and although he hadn't talked to them himself, they'd been interviewed by ERT and had had nothing useful to offer in the way of leads. Their main contribution was a firm opinion that Dorothy wasn't much of a quilter, herself, but was an enthusiastic supporter of the hobby.

Sitting behind them was Sue Pembroke, the owner of the bookstore, According to Type. Next to her was a distinguished-looking elderly couple. The man, Kevin realized with a shock, was Mark Heron, the famous cartoonist. Whose autographed book he'd just bought.

Kevin watched Patrick and his friend take their seats in the front row on the left side, next to Larry Wilson, his staff reporter, and Jane Stewart, his copy editor. They exchanged words, and Wilson patted Patrick on the shoulder.

There was no one else in the chapel.

Unlike Terry Maynard, whose memorial service had filled an entire arena, Dorothy's was much more modest, to say the least. Even Johnny Walker had drawn more of a crowd.

At least Patrick would give it respectable coverage in the next issue of the *Sentinel*.

Reverend Selleck glanced at his watch. Looking at the door, he decided this was it for his audience. He moved to the podium to get things under way.

Kevin was attending for several reasons. For one thing, he wanted to pay his respects to the deceased. Dorothy Kerr had been a solitary and somewhat sad figure, and he thought he should be present to acknowledge her passing. For another, he wanted to see who else would be here, in case someone of interest showed up, someone unexpected, such as the killer, filled with remorse for his evil deeds and seeking redemption. For yet another reason, he'd brought with him Caitlyn's poem.

He studied the people in front of him for a few moments before deciding there was nothing here that would help the case. No one in attendance at this modest little celebration of life would be capable of shooting an OPP officer in the head, let alone chasing Dorothy Kerr out her back door and killing her in cold blood.

Kevin didn't mind spending the time, though. It was why they paid him the big bucks, wasn't it?

The ceremony was brief. A prayer; a Bible reading; another prayer; and Reverend Selleck's eulogy.

"Although I had the privilege of meeting Dorothy in person once or twice after church services, I was never honoured with the opportunity to get to know her," Selleck said. "Like the rest of us, though, I read her stories in the newspaper and had a great respect for her hard work, honesty, and integrity. Her colleagues who are here today can attest to her professionalism as a journalist."

He paused, smiling. "They can also tell you how much they liked her as a person, as can her quilting friends, bookstore friend, and everyone else in attendance today. While it's true that there aren't many here to celebrate her life, perhaps this will help."

He held up a piece of paper. "A local high school student has written a poem—a sonnet, to be precise—that she hoped might be read today in Dorothy's honour. She can't be here to read it herself because, well, she has classes to attend, but I'm more than happy to read it on her behalf. It's called 'Dorothy's

Sonnet,' by Caitlyn Walker."

He slipped on a pair of reading glasses. "It goes:

"Dorothy's Sonnet

When darkness falls and time has disappeared,
Oblivion has taken you to heart;
Your journey's done, there's nothing to be feared,
It's over now; existence pulled apart.
Is no one left behind to mourn your loss?
Not parents, brother, sister, cherished friend?
Not one to say a prayer as you cross?
Not one to wish safe travels at the end?
Not so! for in this room we gather now
To make it known that you were once alive,
To laugh and cry as fortune would allow,
And face each morning as it would arrive.
We'll be your family, neighbours, friends:
We'll be the ones who try to make amends."

He took off his reading glasses. "May Dorothy's spirit rest in everlasting peace."

Kevin closed his eyes, his heart bursting with pride and love for his daughter.

Finally, a funeral he was glad he'd attended.

Chapter 54

Pierce decided that today would be a good day to confront Daniel Keegan with the mounting evidence of his antipathy toward Terry Maynard. If pressed enough, he might admit to having fired the fatal shots. A call to his workplace told him that Keegan had not reported to work, and a second call to Mrs. Parashar, his landlady, confirmed that he was at home, locked in his upstairs rooms. Making a bit of noise, she said. "Can you come over and see if something can be done to settle him down?"

Pierce considered sending a patrol car around to pick him up and bring him in for questioning, but he really wanted a look at Keegan's living quarters, hoping that evidence might be lying around for him to seize under the plain view doctrine. His entry into the house would be legal, thanks to Mrs. Parashar's request for help, and if Keegan would voluntarily open his door and allow him to come into his private rooms, then the other two conditions of plain view seizure might be satisfied—if he saw something specific he wasn't necessarily expecting to see, and if that particular something were immediately apparent to him as possible evidence connected to the murders. It was certainly worth a try.

So off he went.

Mrs. Parashar was very upset. She closed the front door behind him and led him down the hall to the kitchen, where she sat down at the table and folded her hands. "He's drinking. He was drinking last night, and the noise only stopped for an hour or so between three and four o'clock. I didn't get a wink of sleep."

"Did something set him off?"

"I don't know. He gets like this sometimes. He'll start on a binge and doesn't go outside for several days. Just drinks."

Pierce glanced at the ceiling as footsteps crossed above him, heavy and irregular.

"His kitchenette," Mrs. Parashar said. They listened to a thud. "The fridge."

"What all does he have up there?"

"It's a little suite. When you go in, that's the sitting room. On the left is his bedroom; on the right, the bathroom with a tub and shower, sink, and toilet; then you go through the sitting room into the kitchenette. That's it. I charge a reasonable rent; less than other people for not as much square footage as that."

The footsteps receded from overhead. There was a dull crash somewhere and the sound of cursing.

"All right. Please remain here in the kitchen, Mrs. Parashar, and don't come out until I tell you to. Understood?"

"Yes, I understand."

Pierce went down the hall and started up the stairs, which creaked loudly with each step. He didn't really care, though. He wasn't trying to sneak up on the guy; in fact, he wanted him to know that someone was coming up to see him.

At the top of the stairs, the hallway ran right and left to closed doors that led to Mrs. Parashar's rooms, while the door right in front of him was Keegan's. Remembering that Keegan was said to keep firearms in there, Pierce took up a position just to the right of the door before pounding on it with his fist.

"Mr. Keegan? Daniel Keegan? This is Detective Constable Pierce of the OPP. Can you let me in for a minute so we can talk?"

No response.

He heard a tinkling sound. Probably ice cubes in a glass. Which meant that Keegan was drinking hard spirits and not beer.

He rapped again, this time using his knuckles instead of the edge of his fist. "Mr. Keegan? Are you okay in there? Can you let me in?"

"Fuck off and go away."

"People are worried about you, Mr. Keegan. You didn't call in sick, so your coworkers are concerned. Can you text them now to let them know you're okay?"

Silence, then more tinkling. Prolonged; likely refilling his glass.

"Can you let me in so we can talk about what's bothering you?"

"I'm not interested in talking. I'm interested in shooting."

Pierce thought for a split second before making the mental adjustment from potential evidence gathering to possible danger. "Mr. Keegan, is anyone else in there with you?"

"No, asshole. No one here but me."

"Mr. Keegan, do you have a firearm in your possession right now?"

Pierce listened to footsteps approaching the door on the other side. Then he heard the unmistakeable sound of shells being racked in a shotgun.

"That answer your question, dickhead?"

"Please put away the firearm so we can talk this thing over."

The footsteps receded again. Couch springs creaked and something dropped on the floor. The gun?

Pierce went back downstairs. In the kitchen, he got Mrs. Parashar to her feet and guided her out the front door. He took her down the curb and put her in the back seat of his car.

"Stay here until this thing's resolved. All right?"

"Yes," she said, clearly frightened.

He closed the door and went around to the back of the car. He popped the trunk and grabbed his bullet-resistant vest. Pulling it on, he shut the trunk and leaned his haunch on it as he took out his cellphone and called it in. A barricaded-person incident, he explained, requiring Tactical backup, a crisis negotiation team, and EMS. The dispatcher asked whether or not the situation was stable or volatile at the moment. He told her it was the former, but he didn't know how long it would stay that way. After a moment, she gave him an ETA of fourteen minutes on Tactical, twenty-five on CN, and twenty on EMS.

He put the phone away and then hauled it back out again to call Sonja.

Chapter 55

Pierce's mind spun as he waited for them to arrive, replaying the situation over and over in his head, asking himself if he should have handled it differently. Had he been too aggressive? Should he have backed off right away when he heard Keegan was drinking, waiting for a better time to approach the man?

He folded his arms, staring at the front door of the house. Was there even such a thing as too aggressive in a murder investigation? A double murder, where one of the victims was a police officer?

Retracing his steps from witness to witness, adding up the facts gleaned from the statements, he was definitely convinced that Keegan was a viable suspect. Logically, the next step would be to question him—interrogate, that is—to obtain some kind of statement as far as his whereabouts last Monday morning, the obvious motive of his hatred of Maynard, and whether one of the firearms in his possession, specifically an illegal handgun, was the murder weapon.

After that, he could deal with the tire tracks at the scene. Did he have access to a dually truck, maybe from someone at work? And why did he shoot Dorothy Kerr? Had she seen him when he murdered Maynard in his cruiser?

At this point, his thoughts were interrupted by the arrival of the team from the Tactics and Rescue Unit, followed seconds later by a backup patrol unit. Until an incident commander arrived and took charge of the scene, Pierce was still in command. He explained the situation to the team leader, and then directed the patrol constable to remove Mrs. Parashar from his car and put her into the back of his cruiser, where she'd be more secure.

The constable frowned. "Who?"

Pierce hurried over to his car. It was empty.

He looked at the house. The front door was closing.

He sprinted up the sidewalk and took the verandah stairs two at a time. She was already halfway up the staircase, calling out to Keegan to be a nice man and come downstairs to talk.

He reached her at the top of the stairs, where he grabbed her around the waist and pulled her down. Boots thumped behind him.

"I've got her! I've got her!" shouted one of the TRU guys, reaching around him.

Pierce swung her into his hands, and as they thumped back downstairs to safety, Keegan pounded on the door.

"Get the fuck out of here and leave me alone! One cop's already dead! No one's going to give a shit about another one!"

Three more TRU officers came up the stairs. One guy had a battering ram, the second held his tactical carbine in a high-ready position, and the third, handgun out, was the sergeant. Moving up from the top step to crouch on the landing, Pierce kept his eyes on the door as the others edged around him to take up their positions.

"Put down your weapon and open the door slowly," Pierce

called out. "There's no need for this to go any further. We don't want anyone to get hurt, do we?"

The doorknob was on the right side, and the door opened into the room. The guy with the ram eyed it for a moment and then, nodding to his sergeant, took up a position to the right of the doorframe. The sergeant slid in behind him. The officer with the carbine moved toward the left side of the door. The guy who'd taken Mrs. Parasher outside pounded up the stairs to join them.

The sergeant tapped the guy with the ram on the shoulder. The guy gingerly reached out and tried the doorknob, then shook his head. Locked.

Keegan shouted, "What did you say, detective? Come closer, I can't hear you."

At that moment time slowed to a crawl for Pierce. Peripherally, as he took a step forward, he saw the sergeant's hand come up in a *stop* gesture. The officer with him hefted his ram.

There was a deafening explosion, and the door panels flew out in jagged shards as the shotgun blast ripped through them. Something struck Pierce in the vest, followed by a hailstorm of pellets, and then something else deflected off his right cheek.

He dove to his left and landed against the wall, behind the TRU officer.

The ram guy stepped out and smashed the door, splintering the frame and propelling it inward.

Keegan threw his shotgun aside and dropped to his knees, hands on top of his head, a split second ahead of the trigger fingers confronting him, which, through years of training and well-honed reflexes, miraculously eased up, denying Keegan his apparent wish for a death-by-cop end to all his grief and anguish.

Struggling to his feet as the TRU team filled the room and took their man into custody, Pierce felt the adrenaline coursing through his body and knew there was nothing, absolutely nothing, he'd rather be doing with his life than this.

Chapter 56

Ellie had trained herself years ago to be patient. She understood through long experience that most things were part of a process, that it was necessary to allow events to unfold as they would, one after another, following whatever logic had brought them together in the first place, until, finally, inevitably, the end was reached.

Funerals, however, taxed her patience to the absolute maximum.

Commissioner Dart had done a fine job addressing the troops and rallying them to a strong sense of esprit de corps in which Maynard's mother and sister could feel they shared, part of a greater family founded on the noble principles of law enforcement, dedication to duty, and respect for tradition.

For a few moments, at least, it took everyone's mind off the grisly fact that someone had put two bullets through Maynard's head and was still at large.

The head of the union followed with a somewhat less inspiring address, and now it was the turn of the designated family member. Given that Roberta and Theresa were in no shape to stand up in front of an arena filled with uniforms and deliver a speech about their beloved Terry, a cousin from across town had volunteered to do the job. Donny Belcher was Roberta's sister's oldest boy, a stout, longhaired man who worked as a janitor at the local high school.

Donny was proud of his cop cousin, proud that he'd made something of his life and been dedicated to something larger than himself. Donny gave a few examples of things Terry had done as a kid growing up—or, at least, things he'd heard Terry had done—that had made everyone doubt he'd get to where he finally did, but darned if he didn't show everyone after all. What an incredible guy he was.

It was all very embarrassing, even more so because Donny had fortified himself with a pint of Jack Daniel's in the car before coming inside, and hundreds of cops were making a mental note to make sure the boob didn't drive himself home afterward.

He was just winding up when Ellie felt her cellphone vibrate. She took it out, saw that it was Sonja Freeling, and declined the call. She leaned over to her supervisor, Superintendent Gavin Elliott, who was sitting next to her.

"A call I have to take."

She stood up and edged past Detective Inspector Kate Greene, Detective Inspector Tracy Drummond, and Detective Inspector Justin Drake into the aisle, where she faced the casket, gave a small bow as though she were in court, and strode up to the exit.

"What's happening?" Ellie said as soon as Sonja picked up. She moved away from the front doors to a quiet spot a few metres away, craving a cigarette in the worst possible way.

"We've made an arrest. Pierce took down a suspect in town, a former friend of Maynard's who was on the outs with him.

There were several violent run-ins before the shootings. It was messy, though."

Ellie closed her eyes for a moment. *Messy.* "How so?"

"The suspect, Daniel Thomas Keegan, barricaded himself in his rooms on the second floor of the house where he's been boarding. He was intoxicated and armed with a shotgun. He fired through the door a moment before TRU broke it down and took him into custody."

"Casualties?"

"Pierce needed eight stitches for a cut on his face from a flying splinter. Otherwise, nothing."

Ellie calculated the driving time between Collingwood and Perth. It was a distance of about four hundred and thirty kilometres, so it would take her almost five hours.

"I'm on my way."

Chapter 57

Kevin returned to the detachment office after Dorothy Kerr's funeral to find the place in an uproar.

Thomas Searle was in an interview room being questioned by Sharon Giles; Bert Searle was in a holding cell raising almighty Cain about his constitutional rights and illegal arrest and lawsuits right around the corner; some guy who apparently was the Searle family attorney was arguing in the corridor with Sonja Freeling; Tactical officers were milling about, babbling as though they were hopped up on caffeine; some guy in the holding cell next to Bert Searle was busy puking his guts out; and Bob Pierce was walking around with blood spattered on his Kevlar vest, a large white patch on his cheek.

Kevin took a moment to make sure Pierce was all right, getting a condensed version of the Daniel Keegan arrest, and then made his way to the video room, where Alaric and Gray were observing the Thomas Searle interview.

"Quite an attitude," Alaric remarked as Kevin dragged up a chair and sat down. "The usual quasi-American constitutional rights of free speech and protection against unlawful arrest and so on and so forth. He won't admit to calling you, though. There's free speech, and then there's not-so-free speech."

"It was him," Kevin said.

"I'm sure it was." Alaric leaned back and crossed his legs. "They call it voice anonymization. The software alters pitch, replaces sensitive words with more neutral ones, and does other things to hide the person's identity. Of course, there's a perfectly legitimate use for it, since big corporations and bad actors alike are busy making voiceprints of us whenever they can to use for their own nefarious purposes, but nothing's foolproof. We have software that'll reverse engineer some of that anonymization, and I'll bet the app he used is a cheapo one. It's too bad you weren't able to record it, Kev. We'd be able to—"

The door opened and Ellie walked in. There weren't any other chairs in the room at the moment, so Kevin stood up and gave her his.

"How's it going here?" she asked.

"Hasn't admitted to making the call to Kevin." Alaric shrugged. "Just a bunch of rhetoric at this point. I expect he's figured out we don't have a recording and can't pin it on him."

Kevin had already explained his failure with the recording app on his phone and had promised to fix it when he got a moment, but he still felt guilty about the whole thing and wished Alaric would stop bringing it up.

"It was him," he repeated stubbornly.

Alaric turned to Ellie. "How's Keegan coming?"

"I want you sit down with Pierce right away and start putting that case together." She frowned. "There's too much connective tissue still missing. And his blood alcohol is still through the roof, so we're not going to question him until he's sober enough to—"

"Understand the consequences of his statements," Alaric finished. "Understood." He got to his feet. "I'll get started with Pierce right away."

When the door closed behind him, Ellie looked at Kevin and Gray. "Where are we at with this bunch?"

Kevin gave her a brief rundown on the threatening call, the questioning of Ronnie the Rock Man, the distinct possibility that the Searles could be connected to a series of break-and-enter cases in the area, and his belief that they were legitimate suspects in the dual murders.

"Circumstantial at best right now." Ellie watched the monitor for a moment as Sharon Giles continued doggedly to press Thomas Searle. "Keep working on it."

"Will do."

"And tomorrow morning," she added, "we'll get Doug busy on the B-and-E side of it. You concentrate on Dorothy Kerr."

"Will do," Kevin repeated.

Chapter 58

The bus dropped them off in the detachment office parking lot a few minutes after five in the afternoon. Heather stood in line with the others to retrieve her luggage and then trudged over to her car at the back of the parking lot.

She was aware peripherally that there was some kind of media presence buzzing around, vans and trucks and guys messing with cameras and equipment, but she paid it little attention. Maybe they wanted statements from the honour guard about the funeral, and if that was the case, Sergeant Gibbons could do all the talking.

She was leaving. Right now.

She drove across the street first of all and went into the grocery store for a few things. Fresh milk; eggs; a bag of frozen French fries; other comfort food fixings. She didn't have to report for duty until tomorrow morning, so she was going to eat, watch TV, and sleep. Not necessarily in that order.

Tired and unfocused, she nearly turned left onto 43 to make the drive west to Maberly, where she used to live on Bolingbroke Road, but caught herself and turned right instead. Last fall she'd decided to spend some of her savings to buy a condominium in a nearly new building on Dufferin Road, just north of the highway. It was only a ten-minute drive from the detachment office. More importantly, her eighth-floor balcony gave her an unimpeded view of the cemetery where Scott was buried.

She rode up on the elevator, groceries in hand, and let herself in.

Maybe she should get herself a cat. One that would mosey out of the bedroom when she got home and, tail up, would welcome her back to their comfy little pad.

She scrambled some eggs, toasted a waffle, poured a glass of milk, and took it all out onto the balcony where she cried and ate, talked to Scott, cried, and ate some more.

Chapter 59

Once again the media mob had been referred to RHQ in Smiths Falls for an update on happenings in Perth, so the parking lot was quiet when Kevin left the building and walked back to his car.

Someone was leaning on the driver's-side door. He slowed, saw it was a woman, recognized Winnie Searle, and reached inside his jacket pocket for his phone. He started the voice recording app, which he'd duly updated to avoid future embarrassment, and dropped the phone back into his pocket.

"We need to talk," Winnie said, pushing off the door of his car.

"About what, Mrs. Searle?"

She sighed theatrically. "They've been calling you on the phone. They're men; they do dumb things. Playing with their toys, thinking they're smart with their technology crap when they're really pretty damned stupid. I think it's better if we have a face-to-face. You know. Talk things over. You and me."

Kevin folded his arms, waiting.

"You're pushing too hard on them," she said. "There was no need to bust Bert. He was rowdy, but I thought you guys were paid to handle stuff like that."

"I wasn't there, Mrs. Searle, but it's my understanding he struck an officer, which is a criminal offence."

"Oh, bullshit! I saw it. Hell, he's hit me harder than that, and didn't even knock me down. Well, he did once, yeah, but I hit him back hard enough to loosen teeth. Smartened him up, all right. But we're off track. He shouldn't have been brought in just for that. I want him let go, right now."

"I'm afraid that's not possible."

"Jesus, Mary, and Joseph. What about Tommy? You charging him with some bullshit, too?"

"I think they're going to release him shortly."

"So, fine. Release Bert while you're at it."

"Bert committed a crime, Mrs. Searle. He'll have to face the consequences of his actions, I'm afraid."

Winnie's hands curled into fists and her bulldog jaw tightened. "Consequences. A fine word for *you* to use. And another thing. Thanks to your interference, a business contact of ours calls me up and tells me he won't be dealing with us any more. That's not a very considerate thing to do."

"If you're referring to Ronald Barlow, we're already well acquainted with his record. You don't have anything to hold over him, Mrs. Pierce. Might as well just let him walk away."

"I don't appreciate any of this."

"I'm sorry you feel that way." He started to move around her to unlock his car door when she grabbed his forearm.

"You're not listening to me. I'm trying to offer you a deal. Leave us alone, and we'll leave you and yours alone."

"Are you threatening me?"

"I'm saying we should all live and let live. To avoid any bad consequences our actions might have."

Kevin twisted his arm out from under her hand.

"You're sure?" She stared up at him, narrowing her eyes. "More trouble gets fixed by calm negotiations than by butting heads."

"I'm sure." Kevin opened his car door.

"Can't say I didn't try," she muttered, walking away.

Chapter 60

That evening, worn out from the day's events, Kevin dozed
in his recliner, feet up, with the baseball game on mute. The
flickering of the television occasionally penetrated through
his slitted eyelids, attracting his attention, but he wasn't really
following the game, so inevitably he'd lapse back into a semi-
doze, comfortable and warm.

Caitlyn and Brendan were playing cards at the kitchen table,
some sort of two-handed game that Brendan had taught himself
out of a book. Kevin was faintly amused that they were spending
time on an old-school form of entertainment, and a little surprised
when Brendan had dug out a deck of cards from somewhere.
Games of skill and strategy were his newest interest, it seemed
(along with mineralogy), and he'd talked Caitlyn into joining
him by insisting that it was a better way to communicate with
each other than solitary activities on their electronic devices.

Kevin caught snatches of their chatter as they played but paid little attention until Caitlyn launched into a long explanation of something unconnected to cards. When he heard the word "compartmentalization," he came fully awake, although he kept his eyes closed in case they happened to look in at him.

"Psychologists call it a defence mechanism," she was saying, "and although sometimes it can be unhealthy, sometimes it's very helpful when we need to cope with something very heavy."

"Your draw, Cait."

"Mmm hmm. Like I said before, it's like taking upsetting thoughts and feelings and putting them into a box, and putting the box away in the back of your head to deal with at another time. Do you know what deferral means?"

"Yes, Cait, I know what deferral means. Shit."

"Shh. I'm just explaining that compartmentalization is deferral in a general sense. Which can be unhealthy if the traumatic experience is really bad and needs to be dealt with instead of allowing it to fester, but in our case where the trauma connects to something that *may* happen, sometime in the future, instead of something that *did* happen and messed us up, it's not necessarily a bad thing."

"Gin."

"Oh, crap."

"Shh."

Kevin listened to cards being scraped up and shuffled.

"There are a couple of books on the subject," Caitlyn said. "There's one, *The Art of Compartmentalizing Stress*, that I read in the school library. It's very short, not even fifty pages, but it's like a step-by-step self-help book. I could bring it home for you to look at if you're interested."

"Sure. Thanks. You need to pay better attention to my discards."

"Yeah. Deal, Bren."

Kevin missed the rest of it, having drifted off into a deep, dreamless sleep.

Chapter 61

The next morning, Ellie was opening her office door when her cellphone began to vibrate. Sitting down behind her desk, she took it out and looked at the call display.

"Good morning, Dave."

"For some of us, Ellie, but not necessarily for others. Personally, I have a vague recollection of something called sleep, which is supposed to be good for you and a pleasant experience, but I've come to the conclusion it's meant for others and not for me."

"It's not like you to whine like this." She peeled the lid off her coffee cup and took a sip.

"I'm not the only one who's going to be whining." He coughed raggedly. "Sorry, I think I'm getting a cold. Look, this Keegan guy is a flop. No handguns at all, just the damned shotgun and a couple other long guns, along with the requisite permits. His feet are too small to match the footprints at the scene. His fingerprints don't match what we collected at the Kerr house. And I'm willing to bet that Bob Pierce is having zero luck putting him behind the wheel of a dually instead of that shitbox Focus that he drives around town."

"Damn it all to hell."

"Ellie!"

"Well, I'm getting a little tired of finding the guy and then finding out it's not the guy."

Martin blew his nose and coughed a little more. "Don't shoot me, I'm only the piano player."

"I know. Sorry."

Someone knocked on her doorframe. It was Kevin, with a piece of paper in his hand. She waved him in. "Just a moment, Dave." She switched him to speaker so he could listen. "Yes, Kevin?"

He held up the paper. "Search warrant for all vehicles on the Searle property. If the dually's there, we're bringing it in."

"There's a spot in the garage just waiting for it," Martin croaked. "If this is our truck, Kevin, I'm going to kiss you right on the mouth."

"He's got a cold," Ellie warned.

Kevin made a face. "I'll settle for a good firm handshake, Dave."

"Get me that truck. We'll see what happens after that."

Chapter 62

Searle Meat and Potatoes was closed, and so was the abattoir. There were no vehicles around either building, so their little procession headed up the laneway to the house.

Kevin and Gray led the way in the Charger, followed by a Tactical team poised in their van as though spring-loaded, ready to fly out as soon as the doors opened; two OPP cruisers carrying two constables each; and Identification Constable Serge Landry, Dave Martin's tire treads and vehicle specialist, bringing up the rear in his well-stocked van, driven by Scenes of Crime Officer Gabriel Laviolette.

The house was a large frame structure, its wood siding recently painted white and its tin roof in good repair. Off to the right was a large barn with its doors open. Kevin could see an older model tractor inside, a hay mower, and other shapes, one of them black.

Kevin banged on the kitchen door of the house, and after a few moments a young woman in her early twenties opened it and stared out at them. He identified himself, held up the search warrant, and asked if Winnie Searle was present on the property. The young woman shook her head, confused.

"She's not here right now," she said.

"What's your name, ma'am?"

"Frankie. Francine."

"What's your last name, Frankie."

"Searle. What's this all about?"

Kevin handed her the warrant. "As I said, this gives us the power to search the property for any vehicles and seize them if we have reason to believe they were used in the commission of a crime, specifically the murders of Terence Maynard and Dorothy Kerr."

"Yeah, you said all that. I just don't understand why you need to look here."

"Do you live here, Frankie?"

"Yeah. My room's in back, looking out over the forest."

"Anyone else here right now besides you?"

She shook her head. "I'm the only one."

"Where's your mother right now?"

"I'm not sure. Dad neither. They might have gone over to my sister's."

"Have your parents and brothers been talking about the murders I just mentioned?"

She shook her head. "I stay in my room most of the time. Mom doesn't like me to get involved with family business. She says I'm too slow to be of any use."

There were footsteps behind him, and he turned around to look at Serge Landry.

"Got it," Serge said.

"In the barn?"

"Yep. Tires match."

Kevin nodded. He kept a straight face, although inside

he was jumping up and down and pounding his fist in the air. Finally! Serge would have already compared the treads on the dually in the barn to photographs of the tire prints collected at the scene and then run them through the tire tread database on his tablet. If he said they were a match, they were a match, although once they had the truck back in the garage they'd redo the comparison to lock it down with scientific precision. Along with a full processing of every square centimetre of the vehicle, of course.

"You're going to have to come with us," Kevin said to Frankie.

"Me? Why? What did I do?"

"We're going to have to question you more about what you know concerning the murders under investigation. Please go with these officers."

He watched two constables lead her across the dooryard to their cruiser and then followed Serge for a look at their prize.

"I've called the tow truck," Serge said. "We're getting it ready for transport."

"Great!" Kevin's cellphone buzzed. He took it out and saw that it was Janie. It was very unusual for her to call him at work, so he moved aside and answered.

"Kevin, it's Caitlyn. I can't find her. Something's happened."

Chapter 63

"Slow down, Janie. Tell me what's going on."

"Okay, okay. Don't snap at me." Janie took an angry breath. "I got a call from the school. She didn't show up for first period. They were concerned because there was no call from us, and she never misses classes. I called her cellphone. It went straight to voice mail. I called home; it rang and went to voice mail."

Kevin walked down to his car and leaned over the door, elbows on the roof.

"Thankfully, Lauren's covering for me. I drove home, and she wasn't there. I decided to drive to the school. The way she'd go on her bike. Kevin, I found it on the sidewalk. Just lying there."

"You found what? Her bike?"

"Yes, her bike. What the hell did you think I was talking about?"

"Did you check the hospital?"

"Of course I did. And I left about six messages on her phone. Kevin, something's happened to her."

"I'm sure she's fine," Kevin lied, trying to calm her down while his own pulse was threatening to jump right out through the top of his head.

"She's not fine. Something's wrong. Kevin, you've got to find her."

"I will. Where are you at right now?"

"Back home. I don't know what else to do."

"Okay, that's good. Stay there. Call me if she gets there."

"Okay. All right. Should I call anyone else?"

"No, I'll make the calls. Just stay put, and I'll get in touch as soon as I know something."

"Oh, God, Kevin. I'm really worried."

"I know. Just leave it to me. I'll find her."

He ended the call and immediately called the hospital. After an eternity of waiting on hold and being passed around from desk to desk, he was told the same thing Janie had been told, although in more detail—no Caitlyn Walker treated at Emergency; no Caitlyn Walker on their admissions list; and no Jane Doe matching her description.

He called the school and was told that Caitlyn still hadn't reported in.

On a sudden inspiration, he called the public library. He spoke to a librarian who knew him slightly and knew Caitlyn very well. She wasn't there.

He texted Gray that he needed to leave and asking him to stay with the truck until it was transported. Gray replied immediately that he would.

Kevin jumped in the car and headed for Perth, his dash light flashing. He was close to the edge of town when the car's audio system signalled an incoming call on his cellphone. The caller ID on the radio display was "Private Number."

He eased off the accelerator and pulled over onto the shoulder of the road as his thumb hit the button to answer the call.

"Detective Walker," Winnie Searle said, her voice sounding apologetic through the car speakers, "your daughter's having a nice little visit with us, but we need to have another talk to make sure nothing bad happens."

Chapter 64

"Goddamn you—"

"Whoa, whoa, detective. If we're going to talk like two normal adults solving a problem, I can' t have you swearing at me or using abusive language. Do you understand?"

"If you touch a hair on her head—"

"Did I not just say we were having a nice little visit? Right now she's sitting at the kitchen table with my daughter chattering away about something or other. That's my older daughter, you understand. Belinda. I'm told you just arrested Frankie. You're wasting your time with her, but I can't tolerate this sort of thing continuing. We need to get down to brass tacks right now."

Kevin made a supreme effort to swallow what he was going to say next. He had to get a grip on himself. He had to calm down. He had to focus. He had to handle this just right. Caitlyn's safety depended on it. He took a deep breath.

"I want to talk to her."

"Sure. I understand. Proof of life, and so on. I don't see why not."

There was a muffled sound, as though the speaker on the phone were being covered up, then more sounds, and then Caitlyn's voice.

"Kevin? I'm okay. You won't believe this. It's incredible. I—"

"That's enough," Winnie said, pulling the phone away. "Now, here's what I want. Bert needs to be released right away and his charges dropped. Then—"

"I can't do that," Kevin said, "and you know it."

"Don't hand me that. Next, I want you to send Frankie and Thomas home, and I want the truck back. Thomas can drive it."

"You're not being realistic, Mrs. Searle." Kevin took another breath. "You don't want to hurt Caitlyn. Tell me where you are, I'll come and pick her up, and we'll take it from there. Does that sound reasonable?"

Winnie snorted. "You're the one who's not being realistic, Walker. Now get busy. When Thomas calls to tell me it's been taken care of at your end, we'll have the girl taken some place you can pick her up."

The call ended.

Chapter 65

Kevin called Janie right away.

"I just spoke to her," he said. "She's fine. She's at somebody's place right now, and I'm going to go pick her up."

"What in the name of God's she doing at someone's *place*? Without telling us? And leaving her bike on the sidewalk in the middle of town where anyone could steal it?"

"Where's the bike right now?" Kevin broke in.

"In the trunk of the car. I wasn't going to just leave it there. When I get a hold of that girl—"

"Leave it there. I'm sending someone over to pick it up."

"Pick it up. Who? Why? What's going on, Kevin? What the hell are you not telling me?"

"I have to go. Stay there while I go get her. We'll be home soon." He ended the call before she could ask any more questions he wasn't able to answer.

His next call was to Alaric. "Got a situation. I need your help. Could you have a SOCO sent to my place to process my daughter's bicycle? Prints and DNA. There's a possible connection to the case."

"All right. I—"

"Is the dually on the way from the Searles' place?"

"Yeah, I just spoke to Gray. He—"

"One more question. Do you have any information on another Searle daughter, an older one? Probably married? Probably with a different surname?"

"Just a moment." Alaric clacked away on his keyboard, probably happy to have completed a sentence without being interrupted. "Uh, that's a negative, Kevin."

"Damn. Okay. She must be flying under the radar. Well, that's about to change."

"What will you—"

Kevin ended the call. He thought furiously. How could he find out what the daughter's name was and where she currently lived? Maybe Ron Pound? Since he was familiar with the area and with the family, he might know where to find her. He was about to make the call when he paused to check his whereabouts. He'd been so hyped when he pulled over to talk to Winnie that he'd lost track of exactly where he was.

When he checked the GPS on his phone, he realized he was only two concession lines over from Pike Lake Road, where Jock MacDuff the farrier lived. He swung out onto the road, turned his dash light on again, and sped off.

In a matter of minutes he reached MacDuff's place. He swung into the driveway and parked behind the man's truck. He jumped out, leaving the engine running. He trotted over to the barn, but MacDuff was nowhere to be seen. He pounded on the front door of the house and was eventually rewarded with the sound of shuffling feet and a gravelly, "Who the hell is it?"

"Mr. MacDuff, open up. It's Kevin Walker. I need your help."

The door opened and the old man peered out at him. "Walker? What is it? I was taking a nap."

"I need to find the Searle daughter, right away."

"Frankie? She's always at home. Why? What's going on?"

"Not her. There's an older one. What's her name again?" Kevin wracked his brain. "Linda. Belinda."

"Sure, married Donald Harris."

"Okay. Yeah. Where does she live?"

"Hanna Road. On the south shore of Christie Lake."

"What's the civic number?"

"What's going on—"

"Civic number, civic number. I need to find the place right now."

MacDuff screwed up his face. "I don't know the number, but it's two places in from Althorpe Road. An old stone cottage. German-built, I believe. I—"

Kevin was already running for the car.

He called up Google Maps on his cellphone and quickly found Hanna Road. He wasn't far. He called it in and was told that backup had been dispatched.

Spinning his tires, he left MacDuff's place and quickly worked his way up to Christie Lake Road, then drove west until he came to a signpost for Hanna Road, where he turned right. The first property was a beat-up bungalow close to the road. The second was a stone cottage with some acreage around it.

The black mailbox had "HARRIS" stencilled on it in white paint. He turned in. There were three vehicles in the driveway: a subcompact Toyota; a Jeep Cherokee; and a blue pickup truck with Searle Meat and Potatoes on the side. He parked behind the truck and shut off the engine.

It was like his brain suddenly went into hyper-drive. Details flooded into his awareness.

It was a nice house. Well kept; heritage limestone; nice front garden; red tin roof. No doubt acquired by the Searles from some family down on their luck and given to Belinda and her husband as a residence. The front door looked to him like many rural homes: more decorative than used. A stone path led around the side of the house to a single-storey addition on the back.

Kevin locked his firearm in the centre console. *No mistakes*, he told himself. *No unnecessary danger to Cait.*

He removed his ASP baton from its scabbard and got out. He followed the stone path until he came to a side window. The curtains were drawn. He stooped, moved forward to the other side of the window, and straightened up again. He was at an angle now that he could see that the stone path ended at a door leading into the addition. The shadow of a chimney jutted from the shadow of the addition's roof. Wood stove, probably. Kitchen, perhaps.

He edged around the corner of the house and approached the door. Knob on the left; opened in. He took a moment to review his options. Knock and identify himself, respecting the legal reality that "a man's home is his castle"; or, exigent circumstances as outlined in section 529.3, subsection 2 of the *Criminal Code*, justifying entry without a warrant where the peace officer has reasonable grounds to believe that entry is necessary to prevent "imminent bodily harm or death."

Knock and talk? Are you kidding me?

Kevin lifted his leg, pivoted, and used his two hundred and fifty pound mass to drive his boot into the door just above the knob and lock mechanism.

The frame shattered explosively and the door banged open.

Kevin stepped inside and snapped open his baton.

"FREEZE!"

Chapter 66

On his right was a kitchen table. Caitlyn sat at the table with a woman who presumably was Belinda Harris. They were playing cards. Belinda had thrown her cards into the air with the shock of his sudden entry. Caitlyn had dropped hers flat onto the table.

Al Searle burst through a doorway, raising his ubiquitous cleaver. Kevin snapped the baton across Al's wrist. He dropped the cleaver. Kevin clipped him across the side of the head. Al fell to one knee, dazed. Kevin brought the baton up under Al's chin and he fell backwards onto the floor.

Winnie Searle was suddenly in front of him, waving her hands. "Stop! Stop! Stop! You're hurting him!"

Kevin took hold of her wrist, spun her around, put a knee into the back of her knee to drop her down, then pulled a locking strip from his jacket pocket to secure both wrists behind her back.

Al was stirring. Kevin brought his wrists together behind his back with another strip, rolled him onto his side, and forced Winnie down so that she and Al were lying back to back. He linked their bonds together with another strip.

He was suddenly aware of noise.

Belinda was standing behind the table, screaming at the top of her lungs.

Caitlyn was shouting. "Kevin! It's all right! They're not going to hurt me! It's all right!"

Thomas Searle and another man had entered the room.

"Stop!" Searle shouted. "Enough! Detective! Enough!"

Kevin shifted the baton from one hand to the other and back again.

Searle put his hands on his head and dropped to his knees. "Belinda! Be quiet!"

She immediately fell silent.

Kevin's eyes shifted to the other man, who looked like he wanted to try his luck.

"No," Searle said. "It's over, Donald. It's time for the rest of us to stop paying for Gary's stupidity."

"I can take him," Donald Harris said.

Sirens were audible outside, approaching.

"No. It's done. It's over."

Donald stared at him.

Kevin raised his eyebrows.

The sirens were coming up the long driveway to the house.

"Fuck," Donald muttered, dropping to his knees.

Kevin secured his wrists and, ignoring Winnie's renewed blathering, moved around the table to take care of Belinda.

Boots clattered on the stone pathway outside.

Kevin looked at Caitlyn. "Are you all right?"

She beamed at him. "Oh, yes! Absolutely!"

"Absolutely," he muttered, as uniformed officers burst through the shattered door to take charge of his prisoners.

Chapter 67

After Caitlyn had been checked out by paramedics and pronounced none the worse for wear, physically speaking, Kevin took her home.

Janie was waiting for them in the driveway. She pulled Caitlyn to her and held on for a long time. Then, because she was Janie, she began to berate her for having gotten herself into such serious trouble. "Leaving your bike on the sidewalk? Going to someone's house without letting us know first?"

"Not out here," Kevin intervened. "Inside."

They trooped into the house and took their morning breakfast places around the kitchen table. Kevin pulled out his phone.

"I'm going to record this, Caitlyn."

"Sure. My police statement."

"That's right." He opened his recording app and started it up. After stating the date and time and giving a quick description of the interview to follow, he said, "Tell us what happened."

"I was riding to school. A car pulled up alongside me. It was that white Toyota Yaris that you saw in the Harris's driveway. It's Belinda's car. Of course, I didn't know it at the time. The passenger window went down and Winnie was sitting there. She asked me where the hospital was, so I stopped. I was taking a moment to decide how to get there from where we were when she got out of the car. I thought maybe she wanted me to point out the directions or something, but she grabbed me by the arm and yanked me right off my bike."

"Damned bitch," Janie snapped.

Kevin gave her a look, motioning with his chin at his cellphone. "Then what, Cait?"

"Belinda got out and moved my bike up onto the sidewalk and left it there. She opened the door and Winnie shoved me into the back seat. There's not much room in the back because it's such a small car, and Winnie had her seat shoved right back, so I basically rode the whole way in a cramped-up fetal position."

"Did they make any stops along the way, or did they go straight to Belinda's house?"

"Straight to her house. They took me inside and sat me down at the kitchen table. Winnie was going to go find some rope to tie me to the chair, but Belinda said, 'I don't think we'll need that, will we Caitlyn? You'll be good and sit still?'

"I promised I would, so Winnie started making coffee for them. Belinda asked me if I'd like a Coke and I said I would, so Winnie got one from the fridge and gave it to me."

"What did they talk about?" Kevin asked.

"Belinda said she didn't like doing this, that it would get her in a lot of trouble, but Winnie told her to be quiet. She put on the radio on top of the stove and we listened to country music for a while." She made a face.

"Yeah," Kevin agreed.

"Then Mr. Searle came in, Winnie's husband, and Mr. Harris, Donald, Belinda's husband. Winnie was glad to see them but was upset that Bert wasn't with them. Is that one of their sons?"

"Yes."

"She went on and on about Walker not knowing what was best for him, but Mr. Searle explained it wasn't going to be that easy. They had Bert dead to rights on assaulting a police officer, and he wasn't going to get off just like that."

"Did she threaten you in any way?"

Caitlyn shook her head. "No, they ignored me completely. It was fascinating, Kevin. The psychological pressures they were under were making them do and say things a person wouldn't normally do or say."

"You just sat there at the table with Belinda all this time?"

"Yeah. After a while they settled down and got some coffee, and Mr. Searle and Donald went somewhere else. Belinda asked me if I wanted to play cards or something, so I said sure. She got out the cards and we played. She didn't know how to play rummy so we played Crazy Eights instead. Which I thought was appropriate, since it was a pretty crazy situation to begin with."

Kevin could tell that Janie was reaching the end of her patience, so he decided to wrap it up for now.

"Caitlyn, while you were with the Searles, either in the car or Belinda's house, were you at any time threatened with physical harm?"

She thought for a moment. "No. They talked about you, and that you might have to pay the price for meddling in their business. I guess that might have been an indirect threat, since I was their hostage to force you to do what they wanted you to do. But I never really felt like I was in danger."

"You didn't?"

She smiled at him. "No, I knew you'd come get me and it'd be okay. By the way, that was pretty cool what you did with the baton."

"I've been taking extra training," he said, reaching for his phone to turn off the recorder.

"I could tell. They never stood a chance, did they?"

Chapter 68

The following morning, which was Wednesday, Kevin went into the lunch room for some coffee and found Bob Pierce ahead of him at the carafe. They were otherwise alone in the room, so Kevin took his coffee over to a table and Pierce sat down with him.

"How's your girl?" Pierce asked, stirring his coffee with a wooden stick.

"She's fine. Back to school this morning as though nothing had happened." Kevin shook his head. "I keep forgetting how resilient kids can be. The whole thing was a big adventure to her."

"At least she wasn't hurt."

"Yeah. Speaking of which, how's your face?"

"Oh, it's fine." He raised a finger to the white bandage covering his cheek. "I put this on so people won't be grossed out by the stitches, but as soon as I get home it comes off so the air can get at it."

"How many stitches?"

"Eight. Two per centimetre is the formula, I guess. It's going to leave a scar."

"That's too bad," Kevin said, thinking that his nickname might change in the future from "The Face" to something more politically correct.

Pierce shrugged. "It's all good. I thought about other actors who worked with real scars, and figured I could probably do something good with it if I wanted to. Take Harrison Ford, for example. He got that scar on his chin from a car accident, but it didn't keep him from becoming a matinee idol. Joaquin Phoenix has a cleft lip scar; Sean Bean has one above his eyebrow after Harrison Ford hit him with some kind of a hook; Mark Hamill had to deal with scars after a car crash. There are a lot of examples."

Kevin said nothing, sampling his coffee.

"I could play it up as a fencing scar, maybe. Or a gang wound."

Kevin chuckled.

"Truth of the matter is, though, that I won't likely be going in front of the camera again."

"Oh?"

"I talked to Georgette about it. She worries a lot, and would rather that I went back to acting, but we hashed it out and she said she'd support whatever decision I make because it's my life. Honestly, I really can't see myself doing anything other than this."

He leaned forward. "You know what I mean, don't you?"

"I know what you mean. It's like Dart said—this isn't just a job, it's who we are." He paused. "Janie deals with it. She's pretty hardnosed in a lot of ways. It's the kids, though. They're reaching the age now where they're aware of what my job really involves, and they're going to have to find a way to handle it."

"Your girl—sorry, what's her name?"

"Caitlyn."

"Caitlyn. Does she show any interest in getting into law enforcement?"

"A cop?" Kevin chuckled. "No. Although there's been something on her mind lately, something she wanted my advice on, but we haven't been able to have that conversation yet."

Pierce drank his coffee.

"From what I heard," Kevin ventured, "your Keegan guy was looking pretty good for the murders."

"He and Maynard had a real thing going on between them for quite a while. Motive up the ying-yang, but his whereabouts could be accounted for that Monday morning. And nothing else fit, either."

"So you've got him for discharging a firearm."

"With intent, yeah. The Crown attorney charged him with attempted murder, too, which I think might stick. But the Maynard and Kerr shootings are off the table."

"Nice piece of work just the same, Bob."

"Thanks."

Kevin wanted to add that if Skelton hadn't been drawn away by Maynard's funeral, the leads pointing Keegan's way would likely never have been followed up on, but he held his tongue. He didn't like to snipe at fellow officers, particularly behind their back.

And Skelton's comeback would always be that Pierce had been tracking the wrong man, after all. Wasting his time and the taxpayers' money. So there was that.

Taking his coffee back to his workstation, Kevin thought about calling Heather. Maybe she could use some cheering up.

He debated the idea before deciding to leave her alone. Sometimes privacy was the most important thing a person could use at a time like this.

He sat down, put his phone down on his desk, then picked it up again and punched in her number.

Chapter 69

A week later, Ellie and Grayson Kennedy met in her office for a post-mortem on his temporary assignment.

He looked good, Ellie thought. Better than he had in a while. His pale blue eyes were clear and sharp, his short white hair showed signs of a recent trim, and his clothing looked as though he'd picked them out of his closet with deliberate intent rather than grabbing randomly and dressing without looking in the mirror.

"Gary Searle's bail hearing was this morning," Ellie said.

"So I heard."

"Didn't go so well."

Gray laughed. "I heard that, too."

Searle had talked back to the judge without being invited to address the court, which hadn't made a good impression right from the start. His attorney then struggled to demonstrate that the person posting bond, his mother Winnie, possessed the qualifications, character, and ability to supervise her son that the court was looking for in a surety.

The Crown argued that Gary was a flight risk, which made sense when the court was informed that a Canada-wide lookout had been posted for him after Kevin's rescue of Caitlyn. Warned by his mother to stay away from the house, he'd stolen a car from a nearby farm and headed for the hills without looking back. He remained at large for two days, trying to hide out with friends who wanted nothing to do with him, until U.S. Customs stopped him while attempting to cross the border at Cornwall.

The Crown also asserted that, if released, Gary posed a threat to commit further criminal offences, given his level of violent behaviour, and a threat to potential witnesses.

Of particular concern were his feelings of ill will toward his sister Frankie. After being brought in for questioning along with the dually, she'd admitted having lied to Kevin and Gray about not having overheard her family talking about the murders. She recounted in chilling detail an argument between Gary and his parents in which the events of Sunday night and Monday morning were hashed out in detail.

Gary had been driving the dually on Sunday evening when he and Thomas had hung around the mall parking lot, looking in on the bus run from Toronto to Ottawa. They did so, Searle asserted to his wife, as a favour to their good friend Peter Humbert, the Kingston businessman who was the front man for the Freedom Defenders, a libertarian group with close ties to the white supremacy movement that had played a large role in the illegal 2022 Freedom Convoy occupation of Parliament Hill.

Humbert controlled a company called Cape Investments that ran chains of laundromats and pizzerias along the St. Lawrence corridor, and he'd often longed for a piece of the human trafficking action that he saw constantly running its buses and passenger vans along Highway 401. He reached out to a few contacts and put together his own run along the back route from Toronto to

Ottawa along Highway 7, figuring that the less-beaten track might prove to be the more profitable one over the long haul.

As Frankie listened in horror, Searle argued with Winnie that it could prove to be a very good business connection for them. It was proof of their good standing in the white supremacy movement that Humbert would tap them for security along the way, and if Humbert bankrolled them to accompany the buses along the entire route, their cut of the action would turn out to be quite lucrative.

Winnie replied angrily that she wanted nothing to do with slavery.

Gary, of course, was all for it.

They'd seen Dorothy Kerr drive away with the escaped woman that night, and had indeed followed her. Frankie told the detectives that her father and Gary had trailed Dorothy to the bus station on Dufferin Street, where they watched her buy the woman a ticket and put her on the coach that would take her back to Peterborough, and presumably on from there to Toronto.

Dorothy watched the bus leave and then drove home, with the Searles tagging behind to see where she lived.

Then it was Gary's turn to bicker with his father, Frankie said. Searle told him not to bother with her, that he'd pass the word on to Humbert and let him deal with it however he wanted, and that's what Gary should have done. Stayed out of it.

Gary was the one most involved with the white supremacy movement—Belinda called him a True Believer, Frankie said—and he saw it as a perfect opportunity to curry favour with Humbert and his bunch. He walked out on the argument and spent the night at his girlfriend's place. In the morning he drove back out to Dorothy Kerr's home, got inside, chased her out the back door and shot her down.

But it was the shooting of the police officer, Frankie admitted, that had upset her parents so much the next time they argued. Gary shouted and screamed that he had no choice, that the cop would place him there and identify him and he'd be screwed, so they both had to go. Besides, Humbert and some of his anarchist associates saw a cop killing as a badge of honour, something to prove his worth to the movement.

"It makes no sense," Frankie had said. "Belinda told me even the Mafia has rules about not hurting police officers. She said it brings a lot more trouble than it's worth."

Her worst sin against family loyalty, however, had been when she confided to detectives that she knew where Gary kept his guns.

"In the barn, in one of the horse stalls," she said. "We don't have horses, so there's a lot of junk piled in there, but Gary has a foot locker hidden under an old blanket. He keeps them all in there."

Warrant in hand, they seized a formidable collection of handguns, one of which, when tested, was a match for the murder weapon they'd spent so much time and effort looking for.

Given that he was a flight risk and there was a high possibility he'd commit further crimes, including intimidation of witnesses, the judge had little difficulty ruling that bail was denied.

At which point Gary attacked his lawyer, breaking his nose and cracking his jaw before he could be wrestled to the floor and hauled off to a cell.

"Interesting item in the news this morning," Gray said.

Ellie waited.

"The Humbert shooting. In the parking lot of one of his pizzerias."

"Cobourg, wasn't it?"

Gray nodded. "I expect the town police service will be reaching out to us for assistance."

"Looks like it's OC?"

He nodded again. "Your friends in Toronto, maybe."

"They're not my friends. By the way, how does it feel to be moving up in the world again?"

He grinned. "It feels great. Thanks for your help."

"I didn't do anything. Just wrote a letter."

"I appreciate it."

"I think Mal got other letters, too."

"I still have a few friends in high places." The grin faded. "Now all I have to do is prove I can still measure up when the situation calls for it."

"You'll be fine."

Staff Sergeant Wilna Hertig had recently been promoted to the rank of inspector and transferred into the vacant position of unit commander at the provincial communications centre in North Bay. Jordan Malcolmsen had tapped Gray to replace her as unit commander of the East Region's Traffic and Marine Unit. It moved him back from a staff position into line command once again. A part of the action, as he saw it.

"Speaking of moving up, I wonder if Walker's been in the same job a little too long."

"He's a fine detective," Ellie said.

"He's an excellent detective. Solid investigative techniques and good instincts. Has a way with people. He'd make a hell of a sergeant."

"I'm not sure he wants to."

"You might be right."

Chapter 70

Her interviews at the Lanark County detachment office essentially completed, Dr. Narayan had arranged to stay a week longer in Perth in case anyone who had avoided meeting with her the first time around changed their mind, or someone wanted a follow-up session. The hospital provided her with a small office to use for her appointments, and while she spent much of her time catching up on her reading, she did see a few people here and there during the week.

Kevin had managed to book an appointment on her last day of availability. Calls went directly to her cellphone, since she didn't have a receptionist to screen them, so he left a message asking if she would call him back to arrange a time to meet.

He was a little nervous when she returned his call, because what he was asking for was outside her current assignment, but his trust in her basic kindness as a person proved to be well founded. She agreed to meet with Caitlyn as requested; she would make arrangements so that he could pay for her time personally, to avoid it being included in the OPP's final bill; and she would speak with Kevin afterward, with Caitlyn's permission, in case there were any recommendations to pass on to him as the girl's father.

Dr. Narayan's temporary office was inside a large set of swinging doors at the end of a basement corridor. Chairs were set up along the wall outside these doors, and Kevin and Caitlyn waited patiently until the psychologist finally came out to greet them.

"I'll speak with you first, Caitlyn," she said, "and then I'll speak to Kevin. I won't discuss with him any of the specifics of our conversation without your permission."

"Oh, you can tell him everything," Caitlyn replied, standing up. "I'll tell him afterward anyway, so."

Dr. Narayan glanced at Kevin, the corners of her mouth turned up ever so slightly, and then she led the way through the doors to her office with Caitlyn in tow.

Although he already knew what Caitlyn wanted to talk about, Kevin had been warned by Dr. Narayan that her first order of business would be to question the girl about her recent kidnapping. Suppression of emotion connected to such a traumatic event could be harmful, and the psychologist wanted to give Caitlyn an opportunity to talk about what happened and how she felt about it, first of all.

After that, they could talk about this other thing that was on her mind.

Thirty minutes crawled by, feeling like thirty hours. Kevin tried putting in the time on his cellphone, but he couldn't concentrate on what he was trying to read. He finally gave up and put the device away. He counted the ceiling tiles. He looked for accidental patterns in the swirling colours of the flooring. He cracked his knuckles, a bad habit he thought he'd given up in adolescence.

Thirty minutes became forty-five. He stood up and mooched down to the end of the hall, looking around the corner at more empty corridor. He wandered back and sat down again.

When forty-five minutes had become an hour, the doors opened and Caitlyn emerged, a spring in her step. She sat down beside him.

"Your turn."

Dr. Narayan was holding open one of the swinging doors.

"I appreciate your taking the time for us," Kevin said as he sat down in her visitor's chair. "We really need your advice on this."

"She's a remarkable young lady. Just as you described her. But first things first."

"The kidnapping."

Dr. Narayan nodded. "There are repressed emotions, no question. She was a bit more frightened than she lets on, and it may result in brief periods of insecurity until she fully resolves all her feelings about what happened. But I have little doubt she'll succeed. She's very resourceful and, yes—very, very intelligent."

"She kept acting like it was a game. Or a case study in a book. I've been worried she wasn't taking it seriously enough. Wasn't acknowledging the danger she was in."

"It was a coping mechanism. One she was using consciously, believe it or not. From something she'd read. She was converting the situation into a learning experience. Observe; analyze; draw conclusions. You've put your finger on it. She saw the people kidnapping her as part of a real, live case study she could write up afterwards as a paper, possibly for publication. She tells me she's made notes but hasn't written anything yet." She steepled her fingers. "I'm really quite impressed."

"Do you think she's being realistic about her future plans?"

"To become a psychologist? Oh yes, quite realistic. She might change her mind—young people often do—but it wouldn't surprise me in the slightest if she follows through and becomes a credit to our profession."

"I'm out of my depth here," Kevin said. "I only went to community college. She's looking at a bachelor's degree, graduate degrees, internships, the whole nine yards. For one thing, I'm not sure how we'll afford it, and second of all, I don't know how I could help her with any of it along the way. It'd be like looking for help from a well-meaning beagle."

Dr. Narayan laughed. "You grossly underestimate yourself. She tells me that her grades are all As."

"A-plusses. High nineties. Even Physical Education."

"Then make sure she applies for every possible scholarship to pay her way through. Let me add before we conclude that I offered to refer her to someone who's completing her internship as a psychologist at the University of Ottawa hospital."

"Oh?"

"Actually, it's my niece. Dr. Saraswati Narayan. Sara and I have talked before about how interested she is in mentoring young women to follow in our footsteps, and I think Caitlyn would benefit from meeting her.

"Sara will want to administer some tests first for intelligence and personality and so on, and you should expect to pay her for those sessions. Perhaps only one will do. After that we shall see, but she may decide to mentor your daughter on her own time if she feels she has a promising future in our field. She can guide her through the scholarship and bursary process as well."

"What did Cait say to all this?"

"Enough to know she's thrilled at the opportunity."

Kevin felt overwhelmed. "This is more than I expected. Much more. I don't know how I could possibly thank you. And your niece."

Dr. Narayan gave him a look. "Just continue to be the kind of father you are right now. Someone Caitlyn can trust to be there whenever she needs you. *Whenever*."

"That sure won't be a problem," Kevin said.

Chapter 71

That evening, after the kids had disappeared into their rooms and Janie was slouched in front of the television, watching a documentary about Johnny Cash, Kevin went outside and wandered through the darkness down to the big rock at the back.

Clouds had moved in overhead, a forewarning of the rain storm that was expected to begin overnight and last all the next day, and so there was very little light to see by as he hoisted himself up on the rock and settled down, cross-legged.

He dug a cigar out of his shirt pocket, stripped off the cellophane, and bit off the end. Firing it up, he exhaled slowly, listening to the sound of the river beyond his property.

The cigar had been handed out this morning by one of the traffic constables whose wife had just delivered their first child, a baby girl. Delighted, he'd decided to go old-school with coronas that had pink printing on the cellophane: "It's a girl!"

Kevin didn't know him. He thought his name was Zack, but he wasn't sure. Seemed like a decent guy, though. He was pleased for him, and he shook his hand warmly, thinking of his own child to come.

Janie had been a little bent out of shape because her doctor had referred to it as a geriatric pregnancy, a term sometimes used when an expectant mother is thirty-five or older. She would be thirty-seven on her due date, but she didn't see that it was such a big deal. Women all over the place who were much older than that were having babies without any problem, weren't they? It wasn't like she was ready for a cane and a rocking chair on the verandah.

Kevin puffed on the cigar. He loved being a father. He loved the responsibility. He loved watching the kids navigate their way through the day, each of them completely different people with completely different habits, outlook, and interests. He loved being there to provide encouragement, advice, and occasionally, yes, a little correction when necessary. He loved it all.

He couldn't understand why his own father had been the way he was. Kevin could only remember the drinking, the bad temper, the periodic fits of violence. He had no good memories connected to him. It was his belief that Johnny hadn't wanted children, that he'd seen young Kevin as a threat to tie him down, to cramp his style as a swaggering man about town. He never paid a lot of attention to his son, and when he did it was usually bad attention.

Kevin had celebrated his birthdays with his mother. She'd bought his presents, baked his cake, and held a little ceremony for him at the kitchen table after supper was finished and Johnny had wandered off into the living room to watch TV. Christmases were the same—they waited until he'd gone out to meet up with his drinking buddies before opening their presents and enjoying a little Christmas brunch.

Johnny had never really ever been a part of his life. And after Estelle had died, his father's disdain had turned to anger and outright hatred. Kevin never completely understood why, but he eventually came to accept it.

One thing Kevin had wanted, one thing that had always been his heart's desire that life had denied him, was to have had a father.

Exhaling smoke from a cigar celebrating fatherhood, staring into the darkness with sorrow and regret for the man who'd gone to his grave despising his child for no fathomable reason, Kevin felt the tears of grief finally begin to run down his cheeks.

Oxford Station, Ontario
April, 2024

Acknowledgments

As always, it's important to point out that this novel is a work of fiction, and while the Ontario Provincial Police is an actual police service, all characters are entirely the product of my imagination, as are the situations in which they find themselves and the things they do as a result. Any variations from OPP policies, procedures, or legislative authorities are the product of my active imagination or are errors or misinterpretations for which I apologize.

The tragic death of OPP Provincial Constable Grzegorz (Greg) Pierzchala, who died on Dec. 27, 2022, after he was fatally shot at Hagersville, Ontario, served as the impetus for this novel. After I'd begun to write the first draft of the manuscript, a second murder occurred on May 11, 2023 when OPP Sergeant Eric Mueller was killed while on duty at Bourget, Ontario, near Ottawa.

After the death of Sgt. Mueller, I decided to put the story on hold out of respect for those affected by his senseless shooting. It didn't seem appropriate to produce a novel on the subject so soon after yet another tragedy, particularly one in eastern Ontario not all that far from my home. Now that time has passed, I hope this story will be received as the thoughtful examination of how law enforcement officers are affected by the murder of one of their own.

"Law Enforcement(Police) Funeral Service Rituals," by Jenny Mertes, posted at www.funeralwise.com/funeral-customs/police/ viewed Jan. 7, 2024, was helpful in structuring the funeral of Terence Maynard, as was the service for PC Pierzchala, which may be viewed at www.youtube.com/live/ZLgzNL_lwPQ?si=SoE4U8yQGhx6hpuA.

Information on the ALPRS may be found in the document *Guidance on the Use of Automated Licence Plate Recognition Systems by Police Services*, a publication by the Information and Privacy Commissioner of Ontario (Toronto: July 2017).

Heather's T-shirt featuring a tuxedo cat riding a chicken is designed and produced by KilkennyCat Art and sold through teepublic.com.

Information on the scrap metal industry may be found on the website of the Canadian Association of Recycling Industries, https://cari-acir.org/.

Thanks go out to Reg Coffey, Kathy Coffey, Gwenda LeMoine, Scott Davidson, Kim Sheldrick, Pam Heney and many others for their constant support. You can only imagine how much it means to me.

Finally, my undying gratitude to Lynn L. Clark, my editor, best friend, and life partner.

About the Author

Michael J. McCann lives and writes in Oxford Station, Ontario, Canada. A graduate of Trent University (Peterborough, ON) and Queen's University (Kingston, ON), he served as Production Editor of *Criminal Reports (Third Series)* and Law Reports Co-ordinator for Carswell Legal Publications (Western) before spending fifteen years at the Canada Border Services Agency as a project officer and national program manager. He's married to author Lynn L. Clark. They have one son.

Finalist for the
HAMMETT PRIZE
for
Best Crime Novel in North America

BY THE AUTHOR OF THE DONAGHUE AND STAINER CRIME NOVEL SERIES

MICHAEL J. McCANN

SORROW
LAKE

"McCann has a convincing
way with character and plot."
—Toronto Star

A MARCH AND WALKER CRIME NOVEL

Sorrow Lake
March and Walker #1

Michael J. McCann
ISBN: 978-1-927884-02-7

Ask your local independent bookstore
to order it today!